Advance Praise for *Trump Sky Alpha*

"In *Trump Sky Alpha*, satirist and cultural commentator Mark Doten writes of a future so near—that it is today. What I used to think of as the absurdity of the everyday has progressed to the dementia of the everyday—the fractured, broken, idea of America, of reality, of truth. Doten has located himself at the center of the time warp in which we lose track of what was terra firma just yesterday, the rubble of the American social, political system, and he has writ it as dramedy. *Trump Sky Alpha* delivers a world where Doten has read the culture, the warning signs and is delivering us fiction as original as it is provocative, and as plausible and illustrative of what is happening around us as any breaking news report. Read this book and then duck and cover."　　　　　　　　　　—A.M. Homes

"With resplendent, even lurid detail, *Trump Sky Alpha* unpacks every contemporary source of American anxiety—the weaponization of data, maximized nationalism, trolls, memes, wars, and most of all the unflagging human desire for love and sincerity and truth when it seems every kind of language has been a blunted into a joke. Mark Doten is a brave and audacious spelunker of the most putrid caves of internet-addled capitalism—he's a marvel and a freak of the highest order."　　　　　　　　　　—Catherine Lacey

"It's a commonplace that no one could satirize Trump. But Mark Doten has done it in this scathing, hectic portrayal of the end of the world."　　　　　　　　　　—Edmund White

"To enshrine in such beauty and intelligence a country that so despises beauty and intelligence is an act of rogue hope and antic compassion. In *Trump Sky Alpha*, Mark Doten emerges as the shadow president of our benighted generation of American literature."　　　　　　　　　　—Joshua Cohen

TRUMP SKY ALPHA

Also by Mark Doten
The Infernal

Graywolf Press

TRUMP

SKY

a novel

ALPHA

MARK DOTEN

This publication is made possible, in part, by the voters of Minnesota through a Minnesota State Arts Board Operating Support grant, thanks to a legislative appropriation from the arts and cultural heritage fund, and a grant from the Wells Fargo Foundation. Significant support has also been provided by the McKnight Foundation, the Lannan Foundation, the Amazon Literary Partnership, and other generous contributions from foundations, corporations, and individuals. To these organizations and individuals we offer our heartfelt thanks.

This is a work of fiction. Names, characters, businesses, places, events, locales, and incidents are either products of the author's imagination or used in a fictitious manner.

Published by Graywolf Press
250 Third Avenue North, Suite 600
Minneapolis, Minnesota 55401

www.graywolfpress.org

Published in the United States of America

ISBN 978-1-55597-828-0

2 4 6 8 9 7 5 3 1
First Graywolf Printing, 2019

Library of Congress Control Number: 2018947091

Cover design: Walter Green

Cover image: US Navy, The Hindenburg shortly after catching fire on May 6, 1937

This book is for Paul Nadal

I was horrified by the past, and I wanted to alter the present by changing the system.

—José Rizal, *Noli Me Tangere*,
translated by Harold Augenbraum

Consider the situation in which several different centers are netted together, each center being highly individualistic and having its own special language and its own special way of doing things. Is it not desirable, or even necessary, for all the centers to agree upon some language or, at least, upon some conventions for asking such questions as "What language do you speak?"

—J. C. R. Licklider, United States Department of Defense
Advanced Research Projects Agency

We will unleash something that's going to be terrific.

—President Donald Trump,
interview with ABC News,
the White House

```
root@kali-rolling:~birdcrash# ls trump_sky_alpha/*
```

TRUMP SKY ALPHA

trump_sky_alpha/1_the_authoritative_horizon

Trump Sky Alpha, the rigid airship that docked on the roof of the White House and the roof of Trump Tower, a thousand-foot vessel from the bridge of which Trump delivered streaming YouTube addresses every Wednesday, DC to New York, and every Sunday, New York to DC, Trump's ultraluxury zeppelin—"Crystal Palace of the Sky"—on which the 224 seats ("Luxury Berths in an Open Loge Style") went for a starting price of $50,000, a figure that jumped with the addition of various ultradeluxe packages and enhancements, "The Golden Encrustment" and "Diamond Troika Elite" tiers, four figures for the "Ten-Star Double Platinum Seafood," "certified eight-pound" lobsters with **TRUMP** embossed on tail fin and right claw, wine pairings offered by animated "Founding Foodie" Ben Franklin on touchscreen, Franklin adjusting spectacles and cataloging flights of Trump Wine ("An Exquisite Taste of Trump"), the *Feu de Cheminée* and the *Blanc de Blanc de la plus Blanc*, the final bill after disembarkment running to twenty pages or more of often obscure fees and surcharges, bag fees and negative weather clemency credits and per-use charges on the ergonomic loge controls— every seat adjustment noted by the system and itemized—the seats arranged in an oblong spiral that looped the transparent floor six times, the entire body of the aircraft constructed from a revolutionary transparent membrane stretched over a skeleton of moth-white aluminum, white ribs inlaid with gold and platinum and "a firmament of crystal jewels," seats facing inward, amphitheater-style, and at center a circular bridge of bulletproof glass, the views from all 224 seats opening vertiginously onto the

National Mall or Central Park and Midtown as the craft lifted off, offering a "pristine God's-eye view of our Great Nation," seats sliding backward on mobile tracks, while a system of giant claws and pulleys yanked other seats up overhead and moved them forward, closer to Trump, the price of your enhancement package determining how far up you went, a leapfrog of one or ten seats, "La Vie In Gold" or "Ruby Resplendency" or "Deca-Diamond Troika Extreme," the last of which, for a modulating cost somewhere in the seven figures, determined by a proprietary pricing algorithm, placed you at Position #1, which you would then enjoy for a minute or an hour until someone else ordered it, everyone knocked back one position, chairs almost continuously moving backward on a track on the floor, clacking and stuttering against each other, Trump's words overlaid with big echoing vibrations like huge Skee-Balls loading, also sharp but stifled human gasps as giant claws snatched the next upgrader, seat after seat whooshing overhead, at any given moment eight or ten or twelve seats zipping around unpredictably above, the transparent floor provoking a certain amount of nervous loge adjustment as Trump spoke (each adjustment itemized), big spenders—corporations and governments—taking their turn up front as Trump gave his twice-weekly address at the helm of the zeppelin, if not the CEOs and governmental ministers, then stand-ins hired by their countries or organizations, attractive actors filling in for executives after earlier accidents and threats and attacks, Monsanto or McKesson or Chevron stitched or stamped prominently on their suits or dresses, Trump's hands on and then off the wheel as he gestured during his livestreamed address, seeming to float at the center of the craft, unleashing all the old familiar gestures, the little pointy duck bill, the poke, the palms-out "stop" that would flow into a second gesture, fingers still fanned but palms turning in to face each other and then squeezing in and out as though meeting a resistant force, a crazy horizontal spring, Trump grimacing with the effort, elbows pinching into his waist, whole body contorting at the sheer ridiculousness of whatever enemy he was describing, Trump putting his rubberized face—by turns frog-lipped and hemorrhoidal, pig- and pop-eyed—through its paces, an array of comical disapprovals, hands resting now and then on the big gold-spoked wheel that at times seemed in his power and at others appeared to turn of its own accord, Trump almost floating there in the sky, drawing no salary, wholly removed from the business side of the Trump Organization and Trump Sky Alpha for the duration of his presidency—but he could still *fly* in it, couldn't he? you're not saying *that's* illegal?—the whole bridge rotating behind its circular glass wall, 360-degree rotations every four minutes, Trump turning and turning as Trump Sky Alpha twice a week made stately progress between New York and DC, rerouting itself without notice every month or so, a midflight impromptu change to Mar-a-Lago—you couldn't let them know in advance, alert them to your plans—the aircraft warping the clouds and sky behind, sailing for Florida or New York or Washington, DC, above it a massive American flag with Trump's face superimposed, squinting and grinning, the flag itself animated LED-enabled fabric, mirroring Trump's expressions via real-time video capture, the highways and port cities of the Eastern Seaboard spread out below, cars pulling over, families stepping out of vehicles to take in the aircraft, the people of America pointing up, saying things like *Wow* and *Look, Dad*, kids and parents and grandparents, these gathered generations, thanking him right there for his extraordinary, truly unprecedented achievements in the White House, more done in these months than in all the decades of all the other guys before, so it was ten out of ten, A+, that they'd have to be giving him as a grade, Trump not only *loved* but widely and almost universally *beloved*, the *most beloved* president in history, just as the Americans below were the best Americans, the most beautiful, saluting or whooping and hollering or standing looking skyward in stunned and adoring silence, Trump rotating and raising a fist, his voice filling the craft, Trump interrupting his own extemporaneous thoughts on the events of the past week to point or wink at a chair that had moved to the front ("We've got Walmart coming up, looks like Ford right behind, try the surf and turf, it's really fabulous!") while several copilots and a whole team of staffers and security personnel and military folks worked in a concealed bay in the aft, a white opaque bay that was markedly empty tonight, no copilot, no staff, no passengers, Trump Sky Alpha tearing itself free of the moorings on the White House roof, shocking the military and Secret Service and the White House staffers who milled about on the ground (even Trump's private security caught flatfooted), staffers and military and members of the deep state who had told the president again and again, all day long, that under the extraordinary circumstances unfolding around the world, the nuclear attacks, the hundreds or thousands of ongoing conflicts, the millions or perhaps tens of millions or more already dead, Trump would absolutely not be permitted to fly Trump Sky Alpha, *Mr. President, we can get you into a bunker with full communication equipment and you can give your address there, you just can't do it in a goddamn plastic blimp at the start of World War III.*

In the afternoon Trump stopped arguing with them, got quiet, it was after Ivanka went on TV, after she said *No*, after she said *no no no*, after the first small and very restrained US nuclear launch, and Trump wouldn't say a word, the screens all showed her kneeling or crouching there, vomit running down her blouse, and he was silent, which they realized later was a warning, a sign of things to come, though it wasn't clear what Ivanka had meant, or if she had even been the one speaking, the mikes were picking up swarms of voices, there had been the movement of her lips more or less in time with the words, and earlier that day there had been all the casualties among which a portion of her family was reportedly numbered, but the video was unsteady, and the voice didn't *quite* seem to track with the lips, and who knows what she meant by it if she'd even said it, it could have been shock, dehydration, anything, if it was even her that had said the *no no no*, but there was Trump sitting catatonic in his big chair in the White House situation room for hours afterward, papers piling up before him, his body slouched and overflowing the chair, he had authorized a plan

8

in the early hours of the morning, a limited nuclear option, and Ivanka had appeared on TV, somehow slipped her minders, just walked out past the security perimeters of Trump Tower, somehow she'd just wandered out dazed into the street and the chaos of protesters and vomited down the front of the cream-colored blouse with the big bow and lowered herself to the sidewalk there at the north side of Columbus Circle, a mass of security all at once pushing back against the chanting and weeping and howling protesters, and even as the camera crews rushed toward Ivanka there was a storm of Secret Service and police in riot gear, batons sweeping the faces of protesters and journalists, cameras all going nuts with movement, Ivanka down on one foot and one knee, palms braced on the cement, and her voice—if it was her voice, and not that of someone else picked up by the camera, saying *no, no no no* (her shoulders seeming to heave in time with the noise and moans of the voice, shaking her whole body crouched there)—and then she was lost to sight, and since then he had just sat there, Trump in the situation room with the joint chiefs and cabinet secretaries, options set down in black binders in front of him, options whose windows were passing rapidly, gone and replaced with new binders, Trump's only real movement when Pence mentioned a possible transfer of power, just for the day, for a few minutes, really, so a couple key decisions could be made, and Trump turned and half stood, slow and bearlike and implacable, and open-palm smacked Pence's face, knocked him down with a crack that silenced the dozen murmured conversations happening on the other side of the room, and there was a tense moment among the Secret Service and Trump's private security, but Pence sat up and rubbed his head and said, *I'm fine, it's fine*, and then all at once people were speaking, *Mr. President there are a range of options, here's the big one, these are more measured, we advise an immediate response, it's a dynamic and unfolding situation, we advise something limited but decisive, it's an ongoing situation, here are the major conflicts, let me walk you through the details . . .* Trump again silent, slouched in his chair, vacantly staring through a deep squint, for long periods his eyes the narrowest slits, possibly closed altogether, it was his favorite day, the day he got to fly Trump Sky Alpha and do his livestreaming, twice a week it was his favorite day, but today something had happened to his favorite day, and there was Pence, hovering again like a maître d', moving between Trump and the other end of the room, where a certain humming awareness was coming into being, a panic that they, the generals and cabinet secretaries, were watching—just watching—the world end, and wasn't there something they could do, weren't there plans, hadn't preparations for certain contingencies been made very early, even before the inauguration, plans drawn up for the Twenty-Fifth Amendment, his mental state, his—it had been decided—his dementia, these whispers going back and forth at the end of the room, yes, clear signs of age-related dementia, changes of mood, confusion, difficulty following conversations, so now was the moment to deploy it, the Twenty-Fifth Amendment, dementia plus the shock of what had happened to his family, it all added up to *incapacitation* and so it was Lewy body dementia, that was the emerging consensus, somehow they had landed on Lewy body dementia, it seemed better than plain old dementia, and they couldn't just watch the world end, not when there was something they could do, Trump's private security at the other end of the room sensing the threat taking shape, casually falling into positions around and behind the president, male figures in dark suits assembling around the listless body, an outsized human form asymmetrically overflowing a big wingback swivel chair, a *squeee squeee* in the chair bottom as Trump shifted his weight almost imperceptibly, eyes heavy-lidded or closed, the generals and advisers and cabinet members and deep state falling into position, feeling increasingly certain that they had to do something, two teams coalescing in the room, those loyal to Trump and those ready to force some kind of change, and so at last Pence gave the nod, and the chairman of the joint chiefs cleared his throat, and the cabinet secretaries rose to their feet, there was an almost slow-motion interplay of dozens of gazes and hands, hands on all sides of the room moving to the guns holstered under fine-tailored suits, it was all about to be resolved, one way or another, when suddenly Trump was lumbering quickly through the White House and up the stairs, in every hallway and stairwell strong-arming Secret Service out of his way, all the way to the roof access, Secret Service and military personnel asking each other at first jokingly and then not so much if they should just tackle him, but it happened so fast, he was already on the roof and half running up the gangway—it was time, the scheduled takeoff time for Trump Sky Alpha, though Trump had been told there would be no takeoff today, not at the start of World War III, *didn't he understand?*—Trump's feet landing with concussive thuds, two Secret Service agents trying to take him by the arm (it's *very dangerous* to grab people on stairs, *everyone* knows that, especially on these flimsy gangway stairs) and with shocking strength for an elderly overweight man, Trump hurled both agents off the gangway and pressed the button that closed it up behind him, three more agents actually grabbing onto mooring cables as the zeppelin lifted off, struggling up their respective cables for a few seconds before plummeting to their deaths like losers—and that's what they were, *total losers*—Trump in his glassed-in enclosure firing off a few quick tweets ("Happy to be flying back to NYC! Beautiful night! Fake News Media WRONG as usual!!!") as the bridge began to rotate, Trump Sky Alpha rising above the National Mall, which was wholly given over now to military operations, dozens of helicopters and tanks and armored personnel carriers on the green ("Generals doing great job! Say they're glad it's me, not Hillary! Don't listen to lying media. We Keep America SAFE!!!"), Trump activating the livestream, an array of cameras that cut automatically between Trump and the amphitheater-style white seating with golden leatherette accents, the seats—the loges—all vacant on what had been until this day a sold-out flight, Trump Sky Alpha heading north, Trump beginning his YouTube address, the latest in his series of twice-weekly streaming monologues, while behind him across the Potomac the Pentagon still smoldered, huge clouds of black smoke visible from several of the camera angles the livestream was cycling through, the sunset a lavender and black-and-orange mélange that added painterly highlights to Trump's coiffure, Trump turning the gold-plated wheel and touching levers and buttons that controlled the stabilizers and the rotor speed, and across the world the other zeppelins in the fleet rose from their moorings, all of them linked together, all of them "Piloted by Trump™," it wasn't a single aircraft he was flying, after all, it was several dozen Trump zeppelins across the globe, a sort of global interconnected organism, so that when Trump Sky Alpha turned right, the zeppelins all turned right, when he turned left, they turned left, and when he accelerated, they did the same, Trump's hologram projected in real time onto the glass bridges of several dozen other zeppelins, all of them linked to his as in a pantograph, as in connected pens that reproduce a single image at various scales ("Based on Benjamin Franklin's 'Pantograph' Invention, the Ultimate in Luxury Travel"), Trump Sky zeppelins in Taiwan, the UAE, Kuwait, the Netherlands, South Korea, Russia, Malaysia, the Philippines, and dozens of other locales, they would take off and follow the same paths, or they had, until this night, when worldwide devastation had already rendered half the fleet inoperable, but against the backdrop of blackouts or massive fires the crafts that remained lifted off with Trump, all at once, though within seconds in Kazakhstan tracer bullets sliced up the Trump Sky craft's cabin, sliced up the people in the cabin, it took off as its floor broke free and all inside tumbled down except those already in the claws, a pair of Kazakh oil executives suspended midair, watching a Trump hologram chatter and gesticulate ("You wouldn't know it from the press, just how beautifully it's going, what we had was a botnet in the cyber—no president has ever had to deal with a botnet in the cyber like this, and the destruction was terrible, but we responded so beautifully, you can't imagine"), and Trump passed over the Patapsco River and hit the button to click off the really tasteless just *nasty* Kazakh live feed, two guys in claws by now shrieking and engulfed in flames, but the button he pressed turned out to be the rear rotor reverse switch, and the nose of the craft went up sharply—noses all across the fleet did—and the 2,000-gallon wheeled lobster habitats crashed against the Mount Rushmore–style sculptures that separated the galley from the main cabin, and 2,000-gallon plate-glass tanks all around the world shattered against sculptures of Trump and Eric and Trump Jr. and Ivanka, sending huge crustaceans flying everywhere as passengers worldwide screamed in one voice.

The initial plans had been to replicate the flight path of Trump Sky Alpha at a 1:1 scale, and in the same compass bearings, though ultimately Trump had been convinced that the zeppelins could be oriented in various directions depending on local need, but since the local need was in many cases nil, it still resulted in zeppelin landing stations in the middle of the desert, or way out in some Hebei province backwater where there were mountains and big ancient pagodas and other obstructions, so at last a further compromise was made, the 207 miles from the White House to Trump Tower could be scaled up or down, and in Yemen, for reasons of security, after the first two were downed midflight by shoulder-fired missiles, the zeppelin now lifted up and went "in place," whereas the route from Brussels to Frankfurt was a near match, and the longest route in the fleet, from Moscow to Minsk, 446.7 miles, required the zeppelin to travel at nearly double the speed of Trump Sky Alpha, which had led to the April disaster, but the craft had quickly been replaced and the route recertified, and if passengers all over the place were a bit leery after all the miscellaneous attacks and accidents throughout the global Trump Sky system, it had nonetheless been made clear that Trump wanted full flights, all of them full, it would not do to simply buy them out and send them up empty, Trump watched the crafts from video screens on the bridge of Trump Sky Alpha, and though there weren't enough commercial passengers to fill them (and indeed, given the routes they took, and the differences in time zones, there was very little utility to the flights, the flights from Brussels for instance left at three in the morning, and on Mar-a-Lago days the crafts across the fleet were permitted to abandon the pantograph notion altogether, they were simply made to turn in circles and then go back to their launch points), but nevertheless, the flights were almost always full, booked far in advance, bought out by the sovereign wealth funds of Kuwait, Saudi Arabia, and Hong Kong, as well as by corporate partners, the latter tricky at first, many corporations at first resisted—they had stockholders they were accountable to, they couldn't be spending tens of millions on luxury travel—but soon it became clear that certain favors were being granted, playing fields tipped, sabers rattled more or less vigorously, regulations loosened or just gone, so that in numerous ways, plausibly deniable and otherwise, those in the zeppelins were accruing certain advantages: money that had previously been allocated to study peatland fires in Indonesia, fires that some alarmists had claimed were major sources of carbon emission and global pollution, had been zeroed out; and State reversed its opposition to certain uses of lèse-majesté in Thailand, after all these people had their own ways and traditions and who were we to interfere; and Trump himself gave a big thumbs-up in a Fox News interview to Azerbaijan's overrun of Nagorno-Karabakh, as part of a larger package of policy initiatives geared to combat terrorism in the region; and in Zimbabwe, human rights restrictions were lifted and the Zim diamond mines were in full swing, despite the fact that in the first months of the new president's term more than two hundred students had been killed by police; and in Taiwan, we temporarily halted follow-on support to certain Tactical Information Distribution Systems that we had sold them; and sanctions were lifted in Yemen and Burundi and Belarus; and the Magnitsky sanctions were quietly scrapped; and those who were not buying into the fleet watched all this from the sidelines until at last they did not, it was the new world-system and it seemed more and more that to deny the way it was, *to refuse to play*, was to lose, but the money that got you advantages a month ago was no longer enough, it was more, always more to feed the global Trump apparatus, and so corporations made extraordinary efforts, each according to its means, some buying out whole ships, and some, in the case of the globally promoted *International British Petroleum Trump Sky Day*, buying out the entire fleet, which was temporarily rebranded, a BP logo added to the rear stabilizers and onto the US flag itself, BP's logo resting tastefully on the canton, while Trump's face mugged and grimaced and gaped (within three months, offshore drilling rights granted to BP all up and down the coast of California), and it all seemed to work, for a time—for a time everyone was still making money, or most everyone, and the money that the global economy generated just seemed to be more and more, and yet the markets were anxious, they'd be burgeoning for days or weeks, and then they'd stumble, the markets would shake for a day or two, there were afternoons they'd lose a trillion, two trillion in value, but soon enough, before a full panic could set in, they were surging again, and the whole time the Trump Sky fleet was going out fully loaded with passengers, the markets in some sense seemed carried on the back of this global network of aircrafts, by Trump Sky itself, Trump joked more than once, that his fleet was recession proof, that that was one sector that would never take a hit, he'd joke with a wild insistent grin that no matter what, they'd fill the zeppelins, and of course there was no recession, he'd add, only unprecedented growth, a galloping, record-breaking market, even if the process was leaving the players shook, even if there was a feeling among the elite getting richer and richer that they still never knew quite where they were, quite what to give, quite what *future* this was all galloping toward, and those who purchased seats but didn't keep up with the rising prices of the ultraluxe enhancements found their interests actively impeded, a less profitable week for a given aircraft could send mysterious vibrations throughout a whole country, a rash of bad fortune and destabilizing influences, said country scrambling to increase its purchases, to spend more, and where would it end, many wondered, where could it all end? so that when the first European zeppelin was taken down by terrorists there were those who sighed a bit in relief—an excuse at last to bail—only to find the Trump Organization suing the European Union, threatening sanctions if the EU didn't assume responsibility for rebuilding the zeppelin and settling the lawsuits of the dead and massively compensating for pain and suffering, not only the families of the dead, but the Trump Organization itself, and in the final settlement there were two crafts built in place of the one that had been lost, twice the demands from the Trump Organization, and across the whole system flights had to be full all of the time, and not only full, the passengers had to play perfectly the roles of enthusiastic supporters, smiling as they listened, applauding and cheering, a pair of protesters once got on board the Trump Sky aircraft in Saudi, a cloth sign was unfurled, TRUMP IS BAD FOR THE WORLD, and when they were executed later that year, Trump tweeted, "LYING CNN MAKE IT SOUND LIKE I WANTED THEM KILLED!!! NOT MY LAWS, DIFFERENT COUNTRY!" though later that night he tweeted that he respected dissent as a bedrock principle of America, even where he disagreed, and on board the flights the cheering got louder and more sustained so that there were mini-instructionals on how to preserve your voice for maximal cheering throughout the course of the flight, and extra hot teas were added gratis, or at a low price— they certainly could have charged *more*—and the clamorous passengers who filled the flights were increasingly good-looking, they were attentive and well groomed, *Look at these crowds*, Trump would say, beaming, *just look at all of you beautiful people, could you ever imagine anything more beautiful than this*, and the passengers were indeed becoming more and more beautiful, it was often models now, and out-of-work actors, and then came another dynamic shift, the move to mix passengers with "modern dress" and "traditional garb," this custom had started the day Trump cheerfully complimented the mix of modern dress and traditional garb in a flight in the Middle East, the thawbs and agals of the men, then wondered out loud the next week why more countries didn't do that, both modern dress and traditional garb, it really gave him a kick, he loved a good traditional garb, and he pointed out a pair of Indian women in saris, and so it happened that the flight after that there were kimonos and kilts and dashikis and Brazilian carnival costumes and Maasai beadwork and Balinese temple dress and Filipino Barong Tagalogs in zeppelins lifting off around the world, audiences serving up rapt and approving expressions, then ovation after ovation, as Trump played on their screens, all those beautiful people all across the globe, the greatest corporations and countries, all the best people in all the world feting Trump twice a week, roaring and rising to their feet, and Trump basking in it, facial features registering *a look of surprise*, exaggerated faux shock and gleeful irony twisting his face, the mock disbelief you show at a surprise party you know is coming, and he stepped on into the planned surprise of it like you'd step into a love you knew you had coming, an unconditional love, a party with everyone you ever wanted in attendance, your friends and even better your enemies, all on their feet radiating the love you'd always known you deserved, the love of the whole world, and it was enough, at last it was enough, this love, or it almost always was, though there were moments when something else crept in. Even though you could see a uniform field of love, a field radiating in a continuous stream from all the monitors tracking all the dozens of flights, Trump's body cast out into each aircraft in 3-D hologram, gifting each zeppelin with his presence, the noise of the passengers' acclaim in his bulletproof central chamber no longer a noise but a *condition*, the air that surrounded him a thunderous buzz of endless and enveloping love, but still, disappointment crept in, because there were the *faces*, and the faces revealed things if you looked too close, if you lost the crowd for a moment and checked the faces you'd see that they weren't communicating the full love, not all of them, not in the first moment the camera fell across them, and sometimes they'd realize they were on screen (monitors facing the passengers had been added for this reason, so that they could check their own reactions and be mindful of how much enthusiasm they were communicating) and eyebrows would shoot up and mouths go wide with a performance of pleasure and acclaim, but still, but there was that gap, that breath of disappointment, and it made him quietly furious, it should have been pure love he was feeling, and they were *ruining* it with their distraction, even at moments something like a smug and ironic superiority, though of course today it was quite different, it was not the usual faces he was looking into, the fleet was half-empty, or the half of the half that had not already been annihilated was half-empty, and on the flights that weren't ghost ships there was an air of disassociated panic, clenched hands, silent tears, occasional screams, headdresses askew or clutched nervously in laps, two women on the Italian zeppelin in dresses and hats out of *La Dolce Vita* rose in hysterical panic as huge lobsters caught in the gearworks above popped and sprayed them with viscera, the women quickly gunned down by twitchy Italian security, blood spraying the white loges as the Leaning Tower of Pisa silently slid by beneath, lobsters elsewhere causing big problems as they were ground into the pulley and claw systems, gumming up the works, so that chairs were dropped in the wrong places, cracking the transparent floor, and in Rio actually shattering it, the passengers plunging into Guanabara Bay, giant lobsters with branded **TRUMP** claws and tails crashing down with them and drifting contentedly to the seabed, Trump still talking, still calm ("People have called me up crying and thanked me for saving their families, so many calls, now we wanted to keep that private, because I don't think it's anybody's business if people are crying and saying *Thank you, Thank you, Mr. President*, but you look at the people and families I've saved, we are talking about millions and millions"), and then, there at the wheel, Trump clicked off the Italian and Brazilian feeds, and soon all the feeds, because what he was seeing was so weak, all the dying, and the roasting humans, and who would the fake news media blame? when it wasn't his choice, wasn't his fault that any of this was happening, when the economy was the best in fifty years and if they wanted to know whose fault it was try the FBI and the people who had wasted their time and the country's time being distracted by phony investigations when there were big dangers they could have been going after including the massive abuses and criminality of Obama and Crooked Hillary that had left us wide open to a truly devastating attack.

But now Trump Sky Alpha was being targeted, they had been tracking him, apparently, through his livestream, foreign fighter jets screaming in from God knows where, Trump couldn't get the nose up, and he crashed in a cascade of sparks into some high-tension power lines that bounced him, sent him sailing starboard, for a few plunging, wobbling seconds, until the next set of lines bounced him back portwise, it appeared that the zeppelin's velocity, and the tensile strength and elasticity of the lines, and the distance between the towers, were all so perfectly calibrated that even though twenty or thirty lines were dangling from the zeppelin's snout, Trump Sky Alpha was staying up in the air, its zigzag path actually helping Trump evade the enemy fighters, giving US planes the chance to shoot them down, Trump still talking, gestures more and more emphatic, conveying, even in their hyper and erratic and *disgusted* affect, a look of confidence and ease, Trump speaking the whole time (even as he glanced at his phone and fired off a retweet of a map that showed how much of America would have been destroyed if Hillary had been in charge, which was much, much more than had been destroyed) while all across the world the linked zeppelins were following his movements without the power lines to bounce them back, and it was a global slaughter, Abuja down, Abu Dhabi down, and in capitals and military encampments and shantytowns and suburbs throughout the world it was being reckoned, how this might affect the future, what it would mean in the coming minutes and hours, how Trump's reaction to the failure of his fleet might affect the future of the world, as Trump lost control, as enemy planes flew at him and a fleet of US fighter jets and helicopters swarmed Trump Sky Alpha, slicing through power lines, jets and helicopters shot down defending the president, and then Trump Sky Alpha finally found its balance, rose up above the lines to a safer altitude, there in North Jersey, and it seemed that the danger had passed, at least for the moment, but then *it* appeared, a dozen enemy fighters had already been shot down or *crashed down* in suicide runs by US aircraft, but this new and massive enemy fighter came roaring in, hugging the ground and then pulling up sharply, huge suddenly at Trump's feet, missiles firing, and there was no one who could stop it, no one to intercept, they could all only watch as a foreign fighter jet turned its nose up and rushed up screaming and unloading all it had into the pale underbelly of Trump Sky Alpha, and it all blew up, Trump's zeppelin, with Trump on board, it massively exploded, taking out a half-dozen helicopters in its escort, the livestream now nothing but noise and fire, and around the world millions held their breath, everyone was watching an instant that seemed to float, the whole world floating in that suspended moment, the death of Trump, the end of the Trump era, *finally*, and would we be able to recover, and what was to become of us, of the whole world, but as the fireball dissipated, as the smoke cleared, it was still chugging along, the aircraft, and there he was, Trump, he was still there, still going, no longer piloting a full zeppelin, envelope and metal frame burned and fallen away, it was just the glass amphitheater, all the empty seats in their oblong spiral coiling around the bulletproof glass bridge, emergency safety rotors extending out over what was now a much smaller oblong shape with Trump at the center, a dozen stuttering rotors of various sizes keeping the craft afloat and working double duty to pump out the smoke of the burn, the now blackened contraption festooned with a multiplicity of spinning rotors, Trump Sky Alpha looking now like an exploded cigar sprouting dozens of propellers keeping it jerkily in the air, the thing chugged and puffed along like an old coal-fired, steam-powered boat, the moth-white rotors blackened and rattling, but still holding the aircraft up, the flag still flying, the flag now a burned gray collection of tendrils writhing like a tub of snakes, and a pale gaping skull-like thing where Trump's face had been stamped, the rest of the fleet unlinked now and crashing, Trump seeming to float, hands at the gold wheel, still speaking, still smiling, his eyes puffy and steadfast, chin set, whole face smeared with soot, his face like a Creamsicle dropped in the dirt, hair up on end in footlong follicles and twirling in the craft's slowly rushing air like some undersea organism, hair rotating and swaying like primitive life seen at great magnification, "It's New York now, it's Midtown, there's Trump Tower, Central Park, the best views, the best apartments. I have talked to the generals and the generals who are with us have given me some really, really wonderful codes to work with, and the codes are beautiful, just beautiful . . ." he said, and he was alive, he really was, there was simply no way of stopping him, no way that the people in the situation room could see to make it end, and right there he authorized it, aboard Trump Sky Alpha, on the YouTube livestream, he authorized the big one, a massive response, lobsters in Bermuda and Turkey and Paris raising branded claws in silent salute as the flames engulfed them, the last remaining cameras going dark, helicopters and fighter jets crisscrossing the airspace around and in front of the big smoky capsule surrounded by whirling rotors, US President Donald J. Trump floating at the center of it all, and he pressed the automated descent button, his face smudged like a chimney sweep's, and the livestream cut out for a final pitch for boutique shopping experiences (Ivanka on video offering bangles and Donald J. Trump signature neckwear and vacation ownership opportunities) and then back to Trump, full frame, at the wheel of Trump Sky Alpha, another thumbs-up to the YouTube livestream audience, to all those watching, those who still had internet, those still alive, and in the situation room, Trump was almost hypnotic, hair a gentle swirl seeming to coalesce on his head before swimming apart, hair alive, undulating and thin and on the verge of collapse, scalp fully visible, pale and fat as a peeled hard-boiled egg, and among and between all the generals and the members of the deep state and now even Trump's private security apparatus, there was a humming awareness, a panic that they were watching, just watching, the world end, and wasn't there something they could do, but it was too many, there were too many different strategies, there were too many shouts, and too many sudden silences, there were murmurs and side conversations and cries for consensus, but they were all locked into their own roles, each of the individual human animals that had been brought into that room by life and chance and skill and theft, they were in the room, just there, a small mass of people had no idea what to do, individually or collectively, and Trump had already announced it, the big option, right there on the livestream, to the whole world, to all our allies and enemies, and around the world protocols and contingency plans were going into effect, there just wasn't any time, just no way to wiggle out of the moment, to say *sorry*, to say *stop*, to say *we fucked up*, nothing to be done, there might have been a chance, once, to resist, there must have been, but that moment was lost somewhere, it had slipped away—where had all the little moments been? there must have been so many chances to not be where we were—but this is where we were, these American human animals were just right there, and there was nothing to be done, they could do the big one, or just nothing, sit passively, hemmed in by life and by all the possibilities they couldn't quite dream into the real, and they understood that to play was to lose, but to bow out, to step away from the table, to renounce play altogether, was no longer an option, if it ever had been, and so it was the football, the gold codes, it was all initiated, it would start very soon, all that just minutes away, the big event, the one we'd been waiting for for the better part of a century, the button got pushed, it was easy, sure, it really was, now that it was done, and across the Midwest and elsewhere the missiles took to the sky as President Trump landed softly on the roof of Trump Tower, not listening for but hearing nonetheless, somewhere far below, faint and inescapable as his own heartbeat, the oceanic roar of protesters flooding the streets of Manhattan, crashing through the doors of Trump Tower and up every stairwell.

trump_sky_alpha/2_the_recursive_horizon

trump_sky_alpha/2_the_recursive_horizon

2_1_information_modules

the sheriff of sucking u off is made of fire

The sentence is handwritten and circled.

Key line, I wrote.

The sheriff of sucking u off is made of fire.

I no longer know if those words were my own, or a piece of found text, a quote that caught my eye the day they brought me to the room where the internet sits on ice, the archive of what's left of the old internet. A massive batch of data waiting for the moment our system will be judged secure enough, robust enough, to reaccommodate it, or some portion of it, post 1/28, in our world of ruin.

howdy. i'm the sheriff of we gom die. We gom die.

1,113 retweets, 3,394 likes.

A man drilled three holes in my skull. He kept things within certain limits. He wanted me to survive. But he was imprecise—brain-damaged himself—and the drill was not a medical tool. Coma followed, and memory loss.

It was a Craftsman cordless—I remember the white-on-red logo, the *S* thick and sharp-edged, a backward *Z*.

The drill came a year after most of the world's population (estimates vary, let's say 90 percent) died during the chain of events that came to be known as 1/28.

A quote: *The internet interprets censorship as damage and routes around it.*

I don't remember who said it. One of the men who set up the conditions for so much of what we would go on to experience as the internet, maybe. He isn't a part of the story I want to tell, not individually. I get stuck on the quote, though. I wonder if he's still alive. I wonder if it's wrong to say: He was one of them, the men who saw the internet as a new utopian space that would dissolve the old industrial giants, the obsolete monsters, those countries and corporations of unfreedom, and usher in new forms of being, or restore the old ways we'd lost.

Another quote: *All those smart men working on something, knowing not to what end. They had their tasks, connect this to that. Connect all you can, multiply the connections, increase the bandwidth, if you build it they will come.*

A third quote, one that became a catchphrase in the old world: *A million dollars isn't cool—you know what's cool?*

Once I wrote about tech and the internet for various publications. I was in that world, even as the whole world was transformed by it. I wrote about start-ups, disruptors, IPOs, surveillance by governments and corporations. We remember these words vaguely, a shadow of what they once were, a fading mythology: the internet of things, in-app purchases, Siri and Alexa, Dishfire and Cambridge Analytica and the SpaceX Facebook satellite.

We have witnessed abuse, harassment, troll armies, manipulation through bots and human-coordination, misinformation campaigns, and increasingly divisive echo chambers.

That from the cofounder of Twitter, on Twitter, announcing an investigation into ways to improve Twitter as a platform, suggesting new ways of measuring *conversational health.*

He said, *We don't yet know if those are the right indicators of conversation health for Twitter. And we don't yet know how best to measure them, or the best ways to help people increase individual, community, and ultimately, global public health.*

From Watergate to Gamergate, from Pizzagate to Trump. A line, perhaps, or lines.

Those shades, those reptiles of the lost world.

Then 1/28.

I'm trying to route around the damage, trying to remember. How the internet worked, how we used it.

What was cool.

01:54:20 And when we come to die . . .
01:54:24 we'll die submissively.
01:54:32 Beyond the grave, we will testify that we've suffered . . .
01:54:38 that we've wept . . .
01:54:42 that we've known bitterness.
01:54:52 you and I, Uncle.
01:54:55 God will take pity on us, and we will live . . .
01:54:58 a life of radiant joy . . .
01:55:02 and beauty.

My first memory of the sheriff (the first after the ones I've lost): a small building beside an airstrip in a southwestern state, waiting for my editor, Tom Galloway. I sat alone in one of several banks of low-slung chrome and blue vinyl chairs. A clear bag of zip ties sat in the facing row, torn open and half-empty. Snow fell onto the tarmac and onto the snowcapped saguaros beyond, large slender figures in various stages of collapse.

I was making notes for the piece Galloway had assigned me on internet humor. This was a few days after my visit to the room where the archive of the internet was kept, and today at the airport I'd been handed a thick stack of printed screenshots—some portion of the screenshots I'd taken back in the room, after they had been vetted and redacted by the Office of Communication Oversight.

The bag was a distraction. The bag *warned*, or seemed to. I wondered: Why had it been ripped open, why had it been left there?

Things in the world over which I had no control were taking on too much meaning, while the screenshots that were supposed to be the basis for my piece remained opaque. I thought back to undergrad lectures on the symbolism of Renaissance paintings, the cat that stands for treachery, the caged robin that means separation from God's grace—why did they mean that? Is that really what they meant?

These screenshots, these pieces of the internet, they did mean something, once. Something I couldn't quite remember.

On 1/28, a locomotive passing though the Panamanian jungle links the Atlantic and Pacific Oceans.

On 1/28, a fifteen-inch snowflake falls on Fort Keogh, Montana.

wow, amaze.

very fire. much scream.

I flipped from those pages to the dialogue I'd grabbed from a pirate subtitle site, a few lines of *Vanya on 42nd Street*.

I was trying to feel something. I had grabbed the lines for a moment like this, when I was alone—when I might see them and allow myself to feel certain things. The language here wasn't encoded, it was perfectly clear. But I was thinking of the bag. The zip ties—three had spilled out onto the seat. I couldn't squeeze the emotional juice I wanted—sadness, something—from the *Vanya* subtitles. So I went back to the sheriff. Then the subtitles again.

I said: *We shall rest. We shall rest.*

I said: *We've known bitterness.*

I said: *We gom die.*

My body sat in the chair and I felt some small things inside me collapsing, but that gave me no relief, it was like a small GIF of collapse on loop, no catharsis, nothing final, and so I made notes for the piece almost on autopilot, barely thinking of what my hand was setting down. Which is perhaps why I can't remember if it's mine or someone else's: *The sheriff of sucking you off is made of fire.*

01:55:06 And we'll look back on this life of our unhappiness with tenderness.
01:55:11 [Chuckles]
01:55:13 And we'll smile.
01:55:17 [Laughing]
01:55:21 And in that new life, we shall rest.

Here's where I am now: a room with a bed and desk. There is a bath-room with a shower. If you squint, you might see it less as a locked cell than as a room in a hospital, or a nice rehab center. There are no windows, though, just a thick reinforced square of glass on the door.

They brought a banker's box of old notes and screenshots and documents to my room. The box holds double-sided color copies of 327 sheets of screenshots, many with my handwritten notes.

There are pages from *The Subversive*.

There are song lyrics from a cassette that was never intended for the future.

There's a fifty-page transcript of what the man with the drill said to me.

I know that material is missing, but I am taking it on faith that of what remains these are all *my* screenshots—that screenshots haven't been inserted by the Office of Communication Oversight, or others.

But I'm not sure.

I want to establish upfront how little I really know.

There are references in the notes to screenshots that don't exist, there are pages that you can see even in the copies have been cut (not torn, but cut with a scissors, without taking care to conceal the cut) from my notebook, and it is not impossible that information has been manipulated or inserted here among my pages.

The scans have picked up some of the dog-earedness of the originals. The page with the screenshot of the Sheriff of Sucking You Off made of fire is discolored in one corner with a brownish spatter, which may be a spilled beverage—my own or that of someone who later handled the pages—or perhaps my blood, or perhaps the man with the drill's.

The screenshot of the sheriff itself takes up a quarter of one side; my own unsteady, slashing scrawl wraps both sides of the page, squirreling up the margins when space becomes scarce.

How specifically did emojis vary between platforms? Did Twitter look different on Android vs. iPhone vs. a browser? Or were they uniform within Twitter app regardless?

Emojis are Unicode (?). How does Unicode work? Where does it sit in layers of internet? Use sheriff meme to show how information traveled. From the 1s and 0s, the pulses of light at the bottom layer to modern ultramassive gatekeepers, Apple, Twitter, Google, FB, etc.

Link layer, internet layer, transport layer, application layer.

Meme originally created by @brandonwardell, later appropriated by Coke "howdy. I'm

The face with cowboy hat, white down-pointing backhands, woman's boots. Arms, legs, and torso built from stacked fire emojis. It would have displayed differently, depending on your device, at least in certain apps, certain contexts.

Evolution of the sheriff meme: sheriff of refreshment (Coca-Cola), sheriff of "cold ones. Crack open a cold one with the boys" "howdy. i'm the bee sheriff. we saving these mf bees" "howdy. im the sheriff of dead memes." (@50_MissionCap @eggsbruh, @dvoeverie, aggregated by @4evrmalone.)

What did the internet feel like? How to describe its loss?

I am a smol burb.

When I've written a full account of all I know, all I remember, and given them the last piece of data, the password I'm hanging onto, they say they'll take me to my wife and daughter, to the particular mass grave where their bodies might be.

From the transcript of the man with the drill:

So you found us.

Through all the stuff of life, and control of life, through all the nodes that had assumed the power to give life and end it: you are here.

It's your life we have and we have it here and we won't end it, no not now.

They say we live in a universe fine-tuned for life. We say: for death.

The universe was fine-tuned for you to find us, just as it was fine-tuned for us to do all that we have done.

It's our hope that you see. To be bound up like this. It's not special. It's all of us.

Nod if you agree, Rachel.

The universe has been fine-tuned for the internet in its forty years to set the conditions of totalization to make the world's end possible. To circumvent the controls of the bilateral mutually assured destruction through distribution, through the insertion of the network into everything.

It spread through the benevolent technocratic California hippies, through hobbyists and web commerce and great military powers.

It gamified microloans and monitored dreams, and every night it cleared fifty trillion dollars in transactions.

In telling this, I might begin on 1/28, when Trump ordered the strike.

I might begin on 1/23, when an attack on the internet larger than any before paralyzed global communications.

I might begin with the Aviary's Pastebin postings.

I might begin with *The Subversive*.

I might begin with Birdcrash.

Here's where I'll start: six weeks before the one-year anniversary of 1/28, with a phone call.

Galloway reached me in Minneapolis and told me he wanted me back on the job.

Galloway wanted an article for the first issue of the newly reconstituted *New York Times Magazine*, to be released on the first anniversary of 1/28.

He wanted a piece on internet humor at the end of the world.

Yeah I'm into ICBMs:
I
Can't
Believe
My life is ending because her email
s

Yeah I'm into ICBMs:
I
Cocks, stick them in my
Butt quick
M
s

Yeah I'm into ICBMs:
I
Can't
Believe
My life is ending because she didn't campaign in the upper midwe
st

Yeah I'm into ICBMs:
I wasted my life on memes
C
B
M
sorry mom

Yeah I'm into ICBMs
I
C
Being dead
M
s

Minneapolis had been known for months off and on in official communications as the Twin Cities Metro Containment Zone.

That it was still more containment zone than Minneapolis was apparent from the fact that in the building in which I was confined (a tapering deco building, completed in 1929 by public utilities magnate Wilbur B. Foshay, just weeks before the stock market crash that would wipe out his fortune) men with AR-15s and bulletproof vests patroled the floors.

It was made clear by the fact that we were in assigned rooms that could be locked from the outside "for resident safety," and by the fact that Xeroxed blue papers, slid under our doorways weekly, provided schedules of when we could "circulate in the building," though we were not to "roam the halls."

It was made clear by the fact that "circulation" and "roaming" were left undefined, thus no need for pretext to escort you back to your room.

Not that they needed a pretext to escort you back to your room.

AR-15s were pretext enough.

It was made clear by the fact that the windows were covered by heavy black curtains backed by a sheet of radiation cloth, and that we were permitted to draw back the curtains for only one hour a day, between noon and one.

Does it sound right, I asked Galloway, that this is the precise acceptable amount of exposure, a year after the event? One hour, no more, no less.

Rachel, Galloway said, everything is arranged. And this is the only way you're getting out of there.

There is a certain wise old Mr. Lewandowski here, I said. Retired military, then a stint at Rand, then some tellingly hazy international consulting work. He went blind in the Fargo blast, but we take it in turns to keep him updated. He actually doesn't believe it, that our eyes have all turned gold. He thinks it some prank we're playing. It's actually funny: we see his blind golden eyes rolling around, and he's saying no, no one's eyes are gold.

Galloway let out a breath. And what else does old Mr. Lewandowski have to say? he asked.

He said if our eyes were really gold it sounded like security theater bullshit, something in the water, and bellowed at length for a Dewar's. After someone brought him some kind of pruno, he crowed for twenty minutes about it being nukes, not climate change, that got us. He was very pleased. Everyone had been saying climate change, oh yes, climate change, it was very fashionable for a lot of years how climate change was going to be our end and apocalypse, but all down the line, he'd kept saying: nukes. And nukes it was! Nukes to beat the band.

Well perhaps you can include him in your piece. Old Mr. Lewandowski. That's fun.

I told Galloway that I was sorry, the piece wasn't for me.

Bullshit it's not for you. Internet humor at the end of the world. A discussion of technology and internet culture that opens up and illuminates the larger system. Says things about who we are as a culture. This is what you do. You can do this in your sleep.

Not anymore. I'm an information worker. They take us to terminals and we sort information. It's necessary work. You have no idea how much. As a matter of fact, it's time for my shift.

I lifted my curtain back an inch. A pigeon on the windowsill looked at me, black eyes shot through with panhandler's gold. With a dulled flick of its head, a half hop, it took off across Marquette Avenue and over the ruins of the IDS Center where it joined an immense flock of various species and sizes, wrens and crows and herons impossibly mixed and turning, a small dark bit of information among thousands of others.

If they truly believed in the curtains, I said, they could have built some control device, automated the process, instead of having us do it by hand.

You're saying they should build you an automatic curtain opener?

My point is they prefer us to think about the curtains and how we're managing them and what they mean instead of bigger questions.

The birds were swooping in crosscutting patterns, forming for a moment into an oblate spheroid that began to distend, taking the shape of primitive life vastly magnified, a unicellular organism reaching out with pseudopods, one to the sky, one toward the Mississippi, it reached and reached, until at some critical point it was no longer a single shifting shape, it was just a seething bunch of birds that flew apart.

Rachel, no one needs you right now but me. And I don't even need you, I can get someone else.

Get someone else. There's a charming young triple amputee here, Nate something. A network engineer. Stanford degree. He told me one. He holds up his last limb, this really gnarly hand, he says, his girlfriend in Duluth, it doesn't bother him that one of her tits is bigger than the other five. And he makes that sort of classic tit-squeezy gesture with his blackened claw.

Don't you want this? You'll be able to travel. You can *circulate and roam*, totally at your own discretion. See the little black room where they're keeping the internet. On 1/28, you told me you want to write about the system breaking down, a big investigative piece on everything that was happening.

You're holding me to things I said on 1/28? I also told my wife I'd be back soon, no need to wake my daughter for a last *I love you* . . .

This is a chance to do that piece, Rachel—a small version of it, focused, yes, but to start the process of the nation publicly thinking about the BIND attack, the botnets, 1/28, the nukes, the control of nuclear weapons, Trump Sky Alpha, where we were then and where we are now. Something real, Rachel. Something that can shape the narrative. No one knows jack shit right know. There is no history, no journalism now. Not really. The system could go in any direction. We need to start telling the story.

You should talk to Nate. Not only does he tell great jokes, but as a network engineer, he's full of theories about how the internet attacks went down. That's an actual piece. What caused all this. Not the little jokes as it was ending.

Maybe so, but we're starting with this. A sanctioned piece about internet humor at the end of the world. This is the piece.

The internet goes down for four days, when it comes back up the world is exploding, and no one will tell us why or what happened. And you want, what, Distracted Boyfriend memes?

It's a story. One story.

How about how many are left? How many of us are registered in places like this, and how many are just out there. Are we all going to die of cancer? How the central government is doing, to the extent that there is one. If you're looking for pitches.

We can't talk about any of that, not right now.

How many survivors here in this country. A million? Twenty million? How many in the world? How many in places like this?

Do you want to be part of rebuilding, or just let the last of it rot? It all starts somewhere.

I see the world around me and it's all guns and survival and control. I'm in a nice place here. There's no magic hashtag resistance position right now for journalists, there's no democracy dies in darkness or the fucking news fit to print. Just accomplices to whatever this is.

There's been a huge shock to the system, Galloway said. It's all very precarious. We give up? How about you fucking pull yourself together and do the thing you're good at and not sulk around bitching about the world fucking blew up, boo hoo. It did blow up. Deal with it.

This is a former W hotel. We have an hour of light a day. We pass the time together. I'm useful here. I sort information. I talk to the sick and the dying, I fuck a chick who is twenty-three and worked at REI and did lots of sports and canoeing before all this. We all keep each other company. It's not going to get better than this.

Rachel, Galloway said. Wake up. Get up. Just get up and do this. Your self-pity is unbecoming. They've got you in this meat locker, doing nothing. You know, we used to joke about the first draft of history? I mean, this is it. This is really when we do it.

History's over. It's the end of the end of the end of history. History stole all our shit and left the building. History fucked us. I owe precisely nothing to history.

This isn't you, he said.

I said, Time for my shift.

There were three "information centers" in the hotel, banquet halls set up with long tables and computer terminals that seated about a hundred people.

The terminals were connected to a single program, InfoGo.

There were multiple "information modules," and the system rotated you between them, adjusting for—it was said—*competency* and *fatigue*, keeping you for longer stretches on the programs on which you hit higher reliability targets.

One module had you read the automated transcripts of calls that were now produced any time someone used the government-issued "dumbphone" (as they were colloquially known), reading the transcripts the system had flagged, and that you were then to give a holistic score of 1 to 5 according to a scoring rubric and periodic group training sessions. It was rumored in my information center that a 3 or higher would get the user a visit from the authorities, but this was only a rumor; and it was further rumored that if you shaved points off your scores out of some misplaced sympathy for the users, then it was you who would be visited.

Another module: viewing aerial drone footage, ostensibly looking for settlements of survivors, signs of life.

Another module: checking documents—a seemingly random assortment of old newspapers, books, magazines, internet pages, photos of billboards, of sweatshirts with writing on them—that had been converted to pure text through an OCR program, again scored 1 to 5 based on a rubric.

But the module I spent most of my time in was Face Match. On the left side of the screen a picture of the face of a living person would appear, and on the right, a picture of the face of a dead person. You pressed *y* if you thought they matched, and *n* if you thought they didn't match, and *u* for *unrecognizable* if you felt that the pictures were insufficient for identification.

You were to move quickly, make your best guess. A few seconds per screen. Our training had emphasized that you would not be right all of the time—but there were multiple sites, other InfoGo workers seeing the faces, various pairings of the living and the dead. And gradually consensuses would emerge, according to an algorithm. They told us to just do our best, our clicks were part of a larger system that ultimately was more reliable than any of us as individuals, a system that gathered information even from our mistakes, and there was a comfort to that, making your choices, but also leaving it to this higher power.

In the days and weeks after 1/28, there had been so many millions of dead that rescue teams had been instructed to leave them, to save survivors, and to photograph and ankle-tag the dead, when possible. Drones were sent into areas where people couldn't go.

It had been explained: yes, possible matches had been provided by facial recognition software, but the software had not been intended to work on the dead. And so machines in partnership with the living were best able to ID the dead.

Just as others throughout the country were working in food production, electricity, fabrication of machine parts, we had our task.

much extinctions, such sad.

When the terminal told me to, I logged out and was through the door, moving mechanically to Andrea's room. A few seconds after she let me in we had our pants on the floor and were bringing each other off, or trying to. I was on top of her, pushing down on her neck with my forearm, and the quick movements of our hands and mouths were rough in a way that felt necessary and yet pro forma. I felt her tense and clutch around my hand, and there was a whimper, like some small part of her did not want this, but that wasn't the part that was in control, and she grabbed my wrist and thrust me farther in. It didn't matter. It was both ineffective and impersonal, and we were going nowhere. But then that changed. Her thumb was doing something to me, and she was biting my nipple. Even as I was climaxing, though, it seemed like I was pulled away at top speed; even as it was still cresting, the sensation became quite distant, and then it was done.

Then we were just there and Andrea was talking, and I let her words fall across me. Her hand was in mine, but mine was limp, hers alternately gripping and absently stroking. She was talking about the radiation curtains, and I remembered that the words I had said to Galloway were hers, not mine, and I was alarmed, because in the moment they had felt like mine.

How can it be true? Andrea asked. One hour? Sixty minutes? That whatever science—whatever medical, biological science—is going on just happens to be timed to the human calendar, to our conception of time and this very convenient one hour, sixty minutes, 3,600 seconds? I would feel much better if they said, Oh, we made a mistake, it's actually sixty-four minutes and thirty-two seconds you can have the curtains open. And what really really bothers me most of all is not knowing whether they're watching from across the street or from a hidden camera inside your room. But if you don't do the curtains right you get a knock. They're watching. But where from?

I made a sound, some murmured agreement. We were on our backs side by side, midway down the bed, feet on the floor. My eyes were closed, and I was feeling her hand, and trying not to feel it. I was trying not to feel anything.

She asked if I got the survivor aerial photography module.

I said I didn't want to talk about it, about work.

Work, she said. And she laughed. You know what our work is? Looking for survivors through drones, we're hunting for kids, families—these encampments? I mean, what do you think we're doing? I've seen the same territory a week apart, the first day it's these families trying to survive. We press a button identifying a human, then they send a team in and get rid of them. Tell me it's not the truth. They've told everyone to report in, to come in, that's how I got here. The big microphone blasting that you had to go to such and such a place the next day, and if not? What do you think?

I said I didn't know what I thought.

I said, You don't know any more than I do. You think you're seeing the same place, based on what? A tree, a road, a lake, a barn? It might not be. And they might have been rescued, then the place burned up. Or maybe they were wiped out. I don't know, and you don't know.

You're an accomplice. You've got to find a way to resist. Of course, the algorithm will catch you, and they'll take you off information, move you to a different team. You know what that means.

Jesus, I said.

I remember though how I had just said those words myself: *accomplice, resistance.* I thought I might be going crazy.

We've got to resist, she said. She flicked her golden eyes at me. This isn't you, she said.

Why'd you say that?

What do you mean?

I turned on the bed, I was pushing her down again.

That's what Galloway said. *Exact* words. Who's telling everyone to tell me that?

She was stronger, she threw me off. What the fuck do you mean? she asked.

And I was out in the hallway and moving to my room.

Then I was back in my room and the door was closed, the chain and the deadbolt. I was standing at the thick black curtains, a sort of synthetic velvet, and I pushed my face against the fabric, then banged my skull against the glass through the fabric. Then I stepped away from the curtain and stood there in what I thought of as the mathematical center of my room.

01:55:26 I have faith.
01:55:29 We shall rest to the songs of the angels -
01:55:33 [Laughing]
01:55:35 In a firmament arrayed in jewels, and we'll look down . . .
01:55:40 and we'll see evil . . .
01:55:43 all the evil in the world . . .
01:55:46 and all our sufferings bathed in a perfect mercy . . .
01:55:52 and our lives grown sweet as a caress.

What was or was not me.

To think about me in any but the most vaporous sense was to hit up against them.

Though I had been familiar with survivor guilt—though I had myself, fresh out of J-school, interviewed family members of those who had died on 9/11, Cantor Fitzgerald spouses, the brother of a bike messenger, the partner of a victim of Flight 93, though I understood the mechanics of it, the way that certain ideas are latched onto, become obsessive and unshakeable kernels of truth—I had not experienced it. I had studied it from a distance. It was a good story.

When my wife and daughter died, I was on the phone with them, or with my wife, who was holding my daughter's hand.

And I was on assignment.

I was working for Tom Galloway for the *New York Times* proper, I had been in Lower Manhattan doing a story on preparations for what was coming, how the previous days' internet attack had affected the communications infrastructure that the financial sector relied on, and trying to see how the events now unfolding might affect the markets moving forward. I was tying together threads from the mayor's office, the first responders, finance guys, heading to an interview with a contact at Morgan Stanley, the streets filling with protesters, when Trump in his zeppelin told the military to pull the nuclear trigger, to pull a lot of nuclear triggers.

And I couldn't get back to them.

I had thought I was moving into danger, leaving my family safe.

But I was moving out of danger, releasing my girls to their end.

I finally got a call through an hour later.

I said I wish I was there with you, I said I love you.

And then it was over.

If I had been there, we might have taken a different street, have found some place to hide, to save ourselves, or simply faced our end together.

I couldn't let go of that thought, the thought of a street in Brooklyn black and slick with rain, lights out, a glow on the horizon, or moving by moonlight, the three of us together, and I spot a hatch, an iron lid of some type on the street, a square, a circle, a grating, something iron. What doesn't change is the sound of it, that noise, the low resonant grind of metal on metal, and I am, impossibly, propping it open with one hand, as though it weighs no more than a photograph of what it is, and with the other hand I am helping my girls in.

In addition to the information centers, the Foshay Tower had a smaller conference room called the "media center," several terminals hooked up to a simple, text-only email program. We had all been given addresses linked to the ID numbers that had been assigned post-1/28.

At these terminals, we could access a dozen media brands that were ostensibly issuing reports through this system, CNN, Fox News, the *New York Times*, Reuters, AP.

A grid of buttons four wide by three high, CNN upper left, *San Jose Mercury News* lower right.

These had come to be known, at least among the journalists I was in email contact with, as the *functioning entities*.

There were a lot of us, reporters, editors, features writers, critics, in vague contact, wondering what the hell was going on.

It had been an early triumph of the post-1/28 world, equipping all, or most all, of the survivor camps with a media center.

An early triumph reported by means of the media brands, the functioning entities.

Functioning entity was a term that had cycled through a few of these pieces early on in moments of self-description.

"The *New York Times* is a functioning entity, and will continue to bring you all the news fit to print."

And also:

"*USA Today* is a functioning entity, and will continue to bring you all the news fit to print."

No mastheads, no bylines, you went to the news home page at a terminal in the information center, clicked the button of the media brand you wanted to access, and there you could see the most recent week of stories.

There was a general whose name appeared in a few pieces on the state of the media, the increased space for the media, under the watchful eye of the Office of Communication Oversight.

The stories disappeared after a week, as if to prevent any accountability, or to prepare the way for some larger cultural forgetting. It was unclear who was left and who was running the show, government employees of some kind, packaging limited chunks of morale-boosting news, enough verisimilitude to give it all a glint of plausibility.

The voices were wrong, the editorial slants were wrong, the pieces were vague capsules.

I had participated in some of these discussions, wondering if anyone from the *New York Times* was working at the *New York Times*, hearing from Fox people, Reuters people, there was a group of journalists dispersed throughout the settlements who had found each other, started this email group, at least until our accounts were suspended.

The media center was shut down for a week, our dumbphones were collected.

Our accounts went out, and we received vague notices to not talk about certain types of "operational logistics" for the time being.

When our phones were returned and the media center reopened, contacts among other surviving journalists were blocked, or the journalists were gone now, perhaps, it wasn't clear.

And the stories kept rolling, power was reestablished, roads were reestablished, a family was rescued after surviving underground in the Carlsbad Caverns, surviving on the cereal bars in the underground gift shop.

The president met the family. There were photos, there was a speech.

There was talk of the time when the magnificent Carlsbad Caverns, a gem of the Southwest, would reopen to the public.

In these pieces, no mention was made of any surprise from the survivors about the president's identity.

No mention of how it was explained to the family that our new president had in fact been secretary of the treasury, and that he was president only because now four people in the order of succession had been killed.

This was the sort of forgetting that came in handy in our new world.

Whether or not this new president was still in power was unclear, for a month it was always photos from the same two shoots accompanying the stories about him, the president standing in front of some ruins, shovel in hand, flag waving behind him, peering at the horizon with an oily, anxious look, or him at a desk, phone to ear, or writing something on a notepad, or listening to a general, and then for the past month I hadn't seen any stories about him at all.

We had our dumbphones, they could make calls, that was it, your hand went to your phone for news, texts, tweets, games, but those weren't there anymore, your hand would just have to forget that those had ever been there; and yet the hand remembered, and moved on memory.

That I had had a wife and daughter was another type of handy forgetting that had failed to take.

Or that outside of this, out of this hotel, we were being supported, somehow, by teeming layers of governmental life: by vast groups of governmental workers, doing, building, burying, securing, killing.

That was the best case scenario.

The system was repairing itself. It was alive, for now.

There was, there had to be, a great deal of life outside these boundaries, to support the life inside, and there was no sense in it to me. We knew there to be many such spaces as ours, holding survivors, but we had no sense if there were more of us, or of them, more in the camps or out.

But of course it was more of them that were outside.

There was a whole planet of survivors, here it was locked down, or so it seemed, elsewhere we didn't know, though you imagined them: the survivors of the destruction our country had unleashed, the rage they must have had for us, the rage unto death.

There was human circulation and human life, there were the military and government folks, and thousands of feral settlements—these were mentioned now and again in the functioning entities, how the people outside (*feral* had been used at first, then it was dropped for *unregistered*) were gradually being registered and equipped with services—and we, in our containment zones, were for now some necessary adjunct to that, which would perhaps at one point be found not necessary.

Perhaps preserving us was just some transitional step, a sort of acceptance and letting go.

But perhaps the unregistered people, they were maintaining us in some way—it was whispered that there were masses of them, whole anarchic armies being built, and so even we, who seemed useless, were being held for some war against these massed enemies who wanted to seize power, and that might be our lot, defensive fodder to be sacrificed to an untold horde.

I went and sat with Nate, who was grinning, showing his teeth, pushing his long hair out of his wide eyes and rocking a bit as I approached.

If they beat us we can join them, Nate said. You know that, right? I'm going to betray whatever and flip and roll right over. I think they'll like me. I'm fun. Or I can stay here, if the stuff continues as is. I'm easy.

It was the window hour, and there were Keebler Fudge Stripes cookies packed before the end of the world, and a pot of coffee, and the light fell across the cookies and the shiny yellow packaging was reflected liquidly by the black carafe in its spiral grooves.

Nate had been a network engineer in Milwaukee. I told him that my old editor had survived and he wanted a piece on internet humor at the end of the world.

Nate said, Did you hear about the comedian on 1/28? He received a glowing reception.

Who's out there? Who's in control? Who started this? Where are the borders between us and them? The size of the attack, the number of zero days involved, Nate said, suggest a state actor, but what's the strategy there, exactly?

We were into something that was important to him, something I could see he needed to say. His hand was on his gut, and his lips were drawn back over his teeth and releasing. He would say something to me, but after, the lips would keep moving, a shivering twitch, as though there were a second dialogue alongside the first that only he could hear, a stuttered series of reactions, splaying teeth and gums.

He said, Maybe the global internet shutdown was an accident. Sometimes you have a party and it gets out of hand.

He said, The internet got shut down for four full days. If we did it one hundred times, if we could run that experiment, how many times would the spinner land on apocalypse? Are we just in a particularly fucked-up timeline? Or is that the way things are now, the internet is some kind of magical mesh holding a horribly precarious world-system together, and a days-long system shutdown inevitably lead to system collapse, to a mass human die-off? And run the experiment again, but it's three days. It's two days. It's an hour—what happens if the global internet shuts down for a single hour? If you game it out for all possible durations from a minute to a year, how many times is the outcome likely to be the end of the world? Because we don't really know, do we? We don't have the data on that.

This is somewhat speculative, he said. My own theories, things people were saying on Reddit. IRC was back up before anything else, there were ideas going there the last day. And here at Foshay, there were some ISOC friends I found through the terminals before they closed down that kind of communication.

Speculative stuff, he said. Grain of salt.

Grain of salt, I said.

What we know, Nate said, is it started in BIND. The first day, January 23, when we still had access to the online spaces where people who had jobs like mine talked about what's happening, it was identified as BIND, at least part of it.

BIND, he said, handles a lot of the internet's addressing function—servers that essentially direct the traffic of the internet.

The attack came. There was an exploit, a zero day, a back door.

BIND servers were taken over.

There were botnets, massive botnets, the internet of things—lightbulbs, for instance, millions of smart lightbulbs—these had been hacked.

The pipes for the internet started to slow.

The capacity of the tubes, it's much higher downstream than upstream. Choke points, traffic jams, if all the surface streets are full of cars the highway will overflow. You can shut out any legit traffic to any website or network, you could topple CDNs. Akamai and Cloud Player—could you take them down? Could you take down Google? Paralyze the internet? It was happening, attempts at that were happening.

Take down financial institutions, high-frequency traders lose their link to financial.

Places that clear money can't clear, everything is frozen, nothing is moving, the traffic is coming from everywhere. And so they're trying to preserve the core infrastructure. The hackers aren't inside Facebook or Google, let's assume that. There's no evidence that they're inside. So what's happening is that there's still just a huge traffic snarl outside their gates. The normal responses to these attacks don't work. Normally you try to block stuff upstream, but there's no place that's not entirely choked off. If you're Google or Facebook, you can pull up the drawbridge, but then there's no customers, no one can connect to it. Everything times out. Google is doing everything they can, turning on as much as they can, but it's 1,000 to 1 gibberish to real people, and the gibberish can keep changing, too. Computers are dynamic factors.

Imagine that the internet, or a part of it, is a bar. And someone is acting in an unruly fashion. At some point, you have to kick that person out of the bar.

And you're ready for that. You have bouncers so you can do just that: you can kick out one person, even a whole table.

But what if it's coming from everywhere?

They're all chanting, all making noise, and no one can order a drink, if they're a legit client, they're not being served, but you can't figure out who to silence, who to kick out, because the system within the bar is modulating, and maybe even your bouncers are part of it, or some of them.

So now power grids fail, hospitals fail, and people die.

He said, Sometimes you have a party and it gets out of control.

Whatever the initial idea was, people are dying all over. Banking failures, logistics chains fail. Massive cargo ships with only eight people on board are adrift and what's on them is rotting. Walmarts empty out, all the grocery stores empty out, internet-guided surgeries are on hold, medical supplies are gone, there's no blood, medicine starts to run out, the resupply mechanisms are fucked, there's so much that's reliant on just-in-time supply chains, and all that's totally fucked, and even the people with shit warehoused nearby can't move it because there's no gas and no workers and the roads are jammed up. There's civil unrest, and it starts spilling across borders. There are people out there, even if they don't know this is what they've been waiting for, it's what they've been waiting for. If you want to kill your neighbor, kill him now. If you want to start a war, start it now. Carpe diem, baby.

So the attacks wind down, the internet comes back online, but World War III is already starting.

So there are big questions. The people who shut it down, what did they want? Was it some specific attack that got out of hand, was it China or Russia and it got out of hand, was it just fuck-up-the-system, watch-the-world-burn lulz that succeeded beyond anyone's wildest dreams? Was it individuals or state actors or something in between? Was it a US intelligence action that blew up in our face? This—the world now—this couldn't be what anyone wanted, unless we're talking James-Bond-style madman. Unless we're talking some really dark lulz. China and Russia, the US establishment, they didn't want this. This isn't good for Kim Jong Un. This isn't good for Rouhani or Netanyahu. Trump, you know, we had Trump in our particular timeline and of course he's the guy who's going to blow it all up if he gets the chance, and I'm not saying he couldn't have had some involvement in the shutdown, but I also don't see the angle there. I don't see Trump saying, Let's take down the internet. The internet is where people talk about him! The internet was where he got to barf the contents of his brain out for his adoring fans. Be that as it may, we're in Trump's timeline, and Trump is a symptom of the internet, of American sickness on the internet, he's an internet creation, this avatar of white regressive blowhard resentment and blah blah blah, so it's not clear that you can really say what if it was Obama or Hillary or Rubio? What would they have done? Because it's Trump that we chose. And maybe in some weird sense we had to choose him, we're so stupid as a country that this was in some fucked-up way inevitable. But that's just my brain making excuses, saying that it was preordained, saying we couldn't have done anything, when it was so close to going another direction. If a butterfly had flapped its wings in the Upper Midwest, Hillary would be president. So imagine: What would have happened if it was one of these more normie types when the attack came? Hillary, Rubio. Maybe all this would have been at least postponed. I mean, Trump, I think a lot of us had the sense from very early on in the Republican primaries that if Trump got the chance to blow up the world he'd do it, that was clear from his whole career, he got off on rolling the dice on big bets and seeing everyone around him get blown up, all his partners totally screwed and ruined and just leaving these smoking wastelands wherever he went. The fact that he got elected, I mean, it was a real death-wish situation for America, but then you have to ask, What would Hillary or Rubio or whoever have done in a situation where the lights go dark, the internet gets knocked out for four days, and when the lights are back up, there's some nuclear events happening, there's a global system that's suddenly got these huge ruptures. Elizabeth Warren. Bernie. I don't know what would have happened with them but these things have their own logic and maybe it doesn't even matter so much who's president, maybe even Bernie would have pushed the button. What I think about is all those old cartoons, Bugs Bunny or whatever, there's a trope where someone goes to sleep, all the lights are out, it's peaceful, and I don't know where this bedroom is—maybe it's in a haunted house, I don't remember, it's a trope, there are lots of bedrooms where this happened—and Bugs Bunny or whoever is sleeping, and then for some reason they reach for a light, they strike a match and it's all these eyes around them, staring, or it's knives and axes and guns, it's monsters surrounding their bed. I don't know, I think I'm overlapping a bunch of different cartoons here. Maybe the eyes appear in the dark, and then the match gets struck. It's a trope, the trope is, the lights go out, and then they come back up, and it's a nightmare around your bed. And how do you react? You know what I'm saying? There's monsters around your bed, how would any of these presidents have responded? Of course, we had the president we had, and the results are we're here.

That's my rough sense of it, he said. Take it with a huge grain of salt.

I got it, I said. Huge grain.

He said, Whatever happened happened.

I called Galloway back. I said I'd write his story, but first I had a story of my own I wanted to do.

I was in no real position to dictate terms but figured that too many people he trusted were dead, that he was short on patches to sew his patchwork with.

Here's the story I'll do first, I said.

I told him Nate's story, what I had heard from Nate, and like I knew he would, he rejected it out of hand.

Security issues, he said. That's not on the list of what's possible, not right now.

I'm an internet writer and you're not assigning me to write about the internet attack that precipitated the end of the world?

My hands are tied.

Okay, I get it. Security reasons. Hands tied.

Then I pitched him the story I wanted.

I said, The logistics of the disposal of close to 300 million human corpses in the United States alone. I'd like to figure out the architecture of the project, where it currently stands. The workers they enlisted from the civilian population. Lots of the bodies must still be out there, just lying where they fell.

Rachel, I like that. I like that you came up with that. I'd love for you to tackle it. Down the road, when we get back on our feet, you can have this story.

I thought you were on your feet.

We're on our feet but in a liminal period here. The *New York Times Magazine* is 100 percent legit, but for the moment we're working in partnership with the government to get our reporters out in the field, just to move them around. So a government committee is working with us and other outlets on selecting the stories. But that's it in terms of interference. How we report the stories is up to us. Believe me, they want us back. They want the media back online and functioning. They want information flowing, communication flowing, money flowing, as soon as possible. It's not ideal, but it's what needs to happen now. They value the fourth estate. They want to restore the world order. The want to restore the fucking economy, you know? These are the money guys, they can't rebuild the economy without billions of little ones and zeros zipping around, capitalism doesn't work without the flow of information and so they know that the absolute best first thing to kick-start our recovery and to ramp up rebuilding is to have a powerful and independent fourth estate.

You believe that?

I do. I really do. In a way. The world almost ended. The world suffered the most grievous fucking trauma imaginable. We're not trying to build a perfect crystal palace, here. We're not working in ideal space. We're making scar tissue. You understand that? We're putting a foot in front of another, and we're generating the scar tissue. To get some rudimentary healing going. The world has been blasted in the gut with a shotgun, and then set on fire. It's going to be a slow rehab. There is serious brain injury. There is necrotic flesh. We work. We do our work. That's all we can do.

I thought about commenting on your mixed metaphor. Then I thought: That's what you want. You're baiting me for some playful banter, like back in the day.

I paused. I would just like to know where Dominique and Verena are.

There was a long silence. I could almost see it, the man working his broad, clenched jaw, pressing thumb and forefinger to the bridge of his nose. It occurred to me that I didn't know where he was.

Where are you calling from? I asked.

He said, I'm in Modesto. That's where we're coordinating things for the moment. Northern California.

The *New York Times Magazine of Modesto*.

That's right, he said.

I said, I want to find out where Dominique and Verena's bodies are. I want to know what happened to them after they died, with an acceptable degree of certainty. If they were buried, where they were buried. You can help me. Then I'll help you.

Galloway said, You are not the only one who has lost people. I am very sorry for your loss but this jokes thing could be a great, important piece. Didn't you once write that we learn most about a system when it is breaking down?

I said, I left my wife and daughter to report a piece for you. I should have been there, but I was working for you.

You can thank me later, he said. I'm not kidding, I saved you, you fucking bitch.

A face burned off, or badly decomposed. A face rendered to the bone by animals. A photo that was blocked or shadowed or blurred. There were many that couldn't be seen, but then these were fewer as the weeks went by, presumably as multiple viewers marked a photo "unrecognizable."

They would not say how many were in the database of photos—millions, presumably—just as no one had said how many had been killed. It was generally accepted in Foshay that 90 percent of the US population was gone, which would mean close to 300 million dead, but this number was unofficial, and in fact was denied from time to time in the functioning entities, where it was said that the real number was much lower. "Closer to 50 percent" was a figure that had appeared more than once. At times it became abstracted, the faces all expressions of a single form, a face, neither living nor dead—pairs of the same face forever.

After a few hours of the work, it sometimes happened that things would flip, and you would think the living ones were dead, or the dead ones alive, and it would really be true, that the faces burned off, or badly decomposed, or torn away by animals, were vital, ready to say hello, and the smiling photos from social media or the blankly gazing government ID photos were a funeral director's approximation, embalmed and gone.

The day Galloway called, a woman stood and screamed, That's her, that's my sister, that's her purple blouse—this is her driver's license photo, and here, that's her dead.

This happened, if not quite so dramatically, every week or two.

Always there was the part of your brain looking for your own loved ones, the people you'd lost. You thought you saw them at times, ghosts of people from the office, a girl you knew in summer camp, the cashier at the convenience store, a television actor.

It was impossible to work out the odds, exactly—how many people had you come into contact with in your life, how many had left an impression, how many faces were held in a brain?

The supervisor took the woman's arm, but she clung to the back of her chair—That's her, you've got to save it, please save it, I need you to save it.

Soldiers came in and took her away, she demanded that they save the photos, tell her more—there must be more.

I was jealous of her certainty, or her ability to convince herself of her certainty, but I was mostly annoyed that she'd disrupted the flow of faces. I liked the faces—they soothed me somehow, they were the most comfortable hours of the day.

I would make mistakes on the other modules, hoping to be pushed back into Face Match.

The passage of time became something else, suspended, purgatorial, a space you stepped into and left again that had nothing to do with the slow grind of the day, the slashing crawl of minutes. You were here, then you were gone, and hours had gone by.

Of course I saw my wife and daughter, I saw Dominique and Verena.

And of course I never saw them.

I was in Andrea's bed and she was grinding her pussy against my mouth. I liked it, not seeing Andrea, tasting, moving my tongue around, lost in a world of the now.

I was thinking that, and then I was out of it, thinking of *the now*, and I started laughing into Andrea's pussy—it felt dumb and joyful and frantic. Then Andrea shifted off, she pushed her forearm onto my neck and brought herself off, and then I bit her shoulder and her breast and I brought myself off too. Then my phone rang. It was Galloway, and I didn't pick up.

Why does he keep calling? Andrea asked.

He wants me to leave here. He wants me to go out on an assignment.

You're not going to, Andrea said.

I would have said no, but something in Andrea's tone stopped me. Something needy and commanding. I felt a rage inside. I'm trying to tell you, I said.

What, baby? she said. What are you trying to tell me?

I see you so I can go back to my room and feel bad. I can think about Dominique and Verena and I can feel bad. I feel so bad when I leave here. Feeling good with you means nothing to me. Do you understand that? It's just an experience I get through. It doesn't mean anything. You're an alarm clock that wakes me up so I can do other things. You're just a beeping that annoys me enough to wake me up to how bad I actually feel. You're helpful in helping me to get to the part where I can feel bad. To think about them and everything I've lost and feel like shit. You're just a few minutes of something that wakes me up enough to feel something afterward that is real, just for a few minutes, before I lose it again.

I said: All you are is a mallet I hit myself with.

You don't mean a word you're saying, she said.

I'm going to take Tom's job. I'm going to leave here. If I stay here I will kill myself.

You're not leaving. You can't trick me.

You're a piece of wood. You're an inanimate object.

You're with them. You're one of them.

I can't leave you, not really. I can't leave a piece of driftwood. Or I can't feel bad about it. I can't feel bad about leaving a pebble.

Andrea said, Driftwood!

I picked up my pants and shoes off the floor. I stood there naked with my clothes in my hands and looked at her.

Driftwood, I said.

I'm driftwood! That's funny. What a gift you have for metaphor! she said, jaw clenched, voice pitching up, That's what I always tell people. That you have such a gift for metaphor.

Her eyes were tense and shining and her mouth was pulled back in a grin. She was on the verge of something. And then, still standing, she was racked with sobs, she was doubled over, knees bent, top half of her body swinging down, head almost brushing the carpet. And it seemed like some jokey yoga pose of grief, and I heard myself laugh, and she was swinging back up, but before our eyes could meet I was gone again.

Galloway said, I know where they are. With a reasonable degree of probability. There are three places where bodies in that area of Brooklyn were taken, but the most likely is Prospect Park. They dug up a field there, that's where most of them went within the radius you think they died in.

Prospect Park, I said.

I'm only telling you this because I think it will make a good piece. I think it's the perfect piece for you—the whole larger question of capital-G grief, of how we deal with loss on this scale, and individually, with the uncertainty of even something as simple as where a body is. Sure. That could be beautiful.

He said, Rachel, are you there? You can do this piece. I'm sorry for yesterday. I'm under a lot of stress. I'm dealing with grief, too. You know that, right? You can have this. I promise. You can travel where you need to and think your thoughts and then you can write about what you're thinking. But I need this other piece first.

I said, Our phone calls, our emails, all switched over to systems that can be fully monitored. What do you think they really want?

Okay, so sure, Galloway said, they want to know what you're saying, they'll know. But what are the options? That was already largely true, Rachel, as your own reporting indicated many times.

Which part of Prospect Park? Which field?

I don't know.

We all used to go there. I wonder which field it was?

I can find that out. But you've got to do this other piece first.

First, I visit Dominique and Verena. Where you say you think they might be.

After.

No. Now.

After, Rachel. Not negotiable. My hands are completely fucking tied on this. I'm giving you a chance that any journalist would kill for—historians a hundred years from now would kill for this. To go into the room where some part of what's left of the internet is, and poke around. Have I told you about the little room? They've got some sort of working archive of big chunks of the internet. I'm jealous! Aren't you dying to surf the internet again?

People stopped saying *surf the internet* a long time ago.

That's why I need you. You're the internet person. This is what you write about. Write about it again. You want to see Dominique and Verena? They're in there. Records of them. Trails. Traces. What's left of their footprint. You can spend some time with that while you're researching the piece.

I said, That last day, we watched *The Princess Bride*. Me and Verena and Dominique. Then we put her to bed, and it was just the two of us, we watched *Vanya on 42nd Street*. It was her favorite. Then I went into the city, and they died, and I lived.

I know that happened. I'm sorry.

You want to know what I hate, Tom? I remember I didn't laugh at all at *The Princess Bride*. I watched it coldly. And gradually Verena stopped laughing. She watched the way I was watching it, and she mirrored me, she became very serious. You know that movie. The lines about *land wars in Asia* or *to the pain*, it all seemed sad. But then near the end something changed and I was actually *moved* by it. I had this sense—I remember it—that I was watching ghosts reenact some old forgotten play. With *Vanya* I just laughed. I didn't understand why. Maybe it was the actors in their street clothes, slipping into their roles and back out. It's meant to have that effect, but the effect dissolves: you're supposed to see just the play at some point, not actors assembled for a play. But I was seeing it that way the whole time, actors slipping in and out of their roles. It was as if this wasn't *Vanya* the feature film, this was a documentary of actors in a certain production of *Vanya*.

I see what you mean.

I'm not explaining it right. It seemed like some kind of hell or purgatory. The last lines when the young girl—she's supposed to be plain, not beautiful, but she's a smart girl, and she looks totally fine, she just has the misfortune of not being as hot as Julianne Moore—in fact, I'm just realizing this now, as I'm talking: she has the same eyes as Andrea. Same face. Anyhow, she describes how heaven will come, she says these things, how they'll live a life of radiant joy, and all the world's evil will be bathed in a tender mercy. And they will rest. She says that again and again, to comfort her uncle. We shall rest. And I missed it—it's this tender and beautiful moment, and I missed it and I ruined it for me and her. I mean, I was there, but I missed it. I don't know how to describe it but I completely dissociated. My last moments with my family. And I started laughing—I was hysterical, I was laughing. And totally out of control, out of my body, or maybe I was *just* body, a heaving body with no mind I could get hold of. And she was holding me, and as I came back to myself, I thought it was both of us, that we were both laughing so hard, and didn't understand why, but I wiped away my tears and it was just me. I thought we were both laughing at once, but it was just me, she was holding me and looking down at me and saying Shhh, shhhh, shhh, it's okay, it's okay, be quiet now, you're okay, be quiet now, you'll wake Verena. I was on the floor, and I could hear back to a moment before and hear how sick my laughter had sounded. And I saw that look on her face, concern and tension and annoyance. And then you called and I pulled myself together. I went into town. She told me to stay, but I went.

I'm sorry, Rachel.

If I do the piece, I want to do it right. I want to talk to survivors, the people posting the jokes, and find out where they are now, and how they're doing. That's the only way the piece makes any sense. And it has to be in person. You have to get me to these places, to these groups of survivors, so I can talk to people whose jokes I've found.

Not in person. By phone. By email.

It doesn't work otherwise. It has to be in person. It's the government's dime, right? Public-private partnership? It's not out of your pocket.

Okay, yes, finding one or two, that would be a great story. That's a story. It's a better story. You're right. We'll try. That's why you're good at this. Maybe that can be arranged.

To do this right, I need a broad look at our life now, at how people are dealing with it.

I'll see what I can do. Let me call you back.

He called me back in an hour. A car will pick you up in the Foshay in two hours.

How many people do I get to visit?

I think we'll get you somewhere. At least one. At least that. That's a story. First you go to the room with the internet. Start there.

Is there anything you want from it?

From what?

From the internet. Anything personal?

Like what?

Something from the internet. From before. You understand?

He paused. He said, I don't have any photos of me and Jack. I don't know if that's something they would have. Certainly, we were photographed enough. But it doesn't—I don't know the details, I don't know what's left, if there's photos or what.

Do me a favor, forget everything I said about the *Princess Bride* and stuff. I don't know why I told you that. Just forget I said it.

You want me to forget it?

I felt my voice pitch up. I felt my body wanting to scream. I said, I want you to tell me that I didn't say it, you didn't hear it, and you have no fucking idea what I'm talking about.

Sure, Galloway said. You didn't say it. No fucking clue. You take care.

The man who was my minder told me *no written record*, and when I asked, with a laugh that I hoped was both understanding and dismissive, *But I can take notes off the record?* he repeated *No written record*. I would be permitted, he explained, to take screenshots at my terminal. These screenshots would be vetted and transmitted to me at a future date.

He was taking me to the room with what was left of the internet.

He wore black slacks, a navy polo shirt, a black blazer, and what I recognized as $1,200 Louis Vuitton sunglasses. I was bothered by this. The clothes were not just weathered, they were cheap, they were discount department store clothes. Which was not a problem, but the combination was suggestive in our post-1/28 world. Twenty-dollar pants and thousand-dollar sunglasses, something there didn't fit, something read to me as danger, as an implicit threat, in a government minder. In the state I was in, I thought that perhaps he didn't know, didn't understand the difference, and that was one type of signal. I thought that he might have had fine clothes at home, and that was another type of signal, one he was sending on purpose, though of course that was speculation, and doesn't alter the signal itself, what I imagined I was seeing.

In the state of mind I was in, which I understood to be paranoid, I thought the signal was:

The boundaries are gone.

Or the boundaries are not, have never been, what you thought they were.

I can dress cheap, I can parade around in what's cheap, and I can take something off someone's face that costs this much.

I can do anything I want.

No written record.

From the airport, I rode in a jeep with my minder and two uniformed army infantrymen a certain number of miles to a building whose exterior I am also not to describe, so I will begin in the cage.

"The bear cage," my minder called it, between the reinforced front door and the facility. Between the reinforced front door and the facility we stood in a cube of bulletproof polycarbonate encased in iron rods lit with blue spotlights. Outside us there was a low diffused glow that hung like a mist in the vast room whose ceiling arced over us in a cascade of dark mesh and brushed steel. The grand entryway, my minder said. Bullshit for the clients, back in the day. They needed the big entrance. The security theater. Something cool. Something like a movie. These bulbs last forever.

More bullshit, here, he said, as we made our way down hallways, ceilings fifty or sixty feet high, huge cages on either side of us run through with wires, with black and silver and off-white boxes, in some cases the cages stuffed with wires and boxes, in others mostly empty, some boxes the size of a pizza box, some the size of a vending machine.

We turned down a narrow passage between black grating, the ambient lighting, blue and white on grating and brushed steel, progressively weaker, and soon there was almost no light but blue LED track lighting. The minder took a flashlight out of his pocket and led us through several more turns in what seemed a maze, though they were all right angles, all equally spaced, and I thought to myself, repeatedly: It's a grid, not a maze. We're not lost, we can't get lost here.

But of course that depends on the size of the grid, and the obstacles you meet.

I noted that he was no longer saying anything. His pace quickened as though the vastness of the space was getting to him, a slight tic toward panic. Then I saw him check himself, a sort of hiccup in his step, as he rolled on his left heel, and he was back to a smooth impersonal stride.

I didn't look at the soldiers behind me, but I heard them, I heard the adjustment in their steps that cascaded hollowly through the space, a rubberized slap and squeak that seemed too loud, too strange, as though they were doing it on purpose, their four feet in a game—a child's game—to make the loudest possible sounds above the tidal hum of all the servers and cooling fans.

As he led me down a narrow dark passage, his flashlight played on the mesh and the blue LEDs. The two soldiers stopped behind us, and I felt a shiver on the back of my neck like a hand was reaching for me, but I didn't turn around.

He took a key from an envelope in his pocket and opened a door in a new wall, a real wall.

He flipped a switch.

We were out of the mesh hallway in what appeared to be a narrow, poorly lit storage room with a conference table and chairs, all but one of the chairs piled with boxes and cables, the table itself—water-stained particle board—overrun with what had the look of towering fungal growths, dense twists of vertical cables cut through and interworked with yellow and blue and black lines, red and green LEDs unevenly blinking, then settling into a pattern, then diffusing again, and at the end of the table a small cleared area, the open chair and what seemed to be an old entry-level Dell laptop.

My minder leaned over the chair, opened the laptop, and entered a password. He motioned me forward and—though he didn't once touch me—he sat me down. The movements of his hands ushered me forward, then turned me and lowered me, and squared me in my seat, a swift continuous arc of gestures that placed me at the screen and keyboard, and when I was really there the hands paused a second above my shoulders, on either side of my neck, I felt them falling down on me, his hands opening an endless falling, endless coming down, suspended between threat and a kind of comfort. The soldiers weren't in here with us. I imagined them posted outside the door—imagined that they would hear me if I screamed—but I couldn't know this.

And then he stepped back.

There was a new smile as he stepped back and to the side. I turned and saw it. Almost a leer. Enjoy yourself, he said. The sunglasses were gone, and this realization put me on edge, made me feel that somehow I was being had.

Of course they must have been in the pocket of his blazer.

Of course I was being had.

I placed my fingers on the keyboard.

He stood behind me, my screen visible to him, but not my face. I turned and looked at him again. He didn't smile or nod or acknowledge my gaze this time, he just watched what I was doing with huge gold eyes that picked up the blue and red blinkings of LED lights.

I began a search into what had been saved here, the portion of what was left that I was permitted to see.

trump_sky_alpha/2_the_recursive_horizon
2_2_internet_humor_at_the_end_of_the_world

On 1/28, the first commercial telephone exchange is established in New Haven, Connecticut, and a locomotive passing through Panamanian jungle links the Atlantic and Pacific Oceans.

On 1/28, a fifteen-inch snowflake falls on Fort Keogh, Montana.

On 1/28, Charlemagne, King of the Franks and Holy Roman Emperor, curses the known and unknown worlds he's left unconquered, and his dumb ass croaks and becomes a ghost.

wow, so scare.

Trump to Ivanka: Let's just do it and be legends.

On 1/28, Canuplin is born.

howdy. i'm the sheriff of we gom die. We gom die.

The jokes at the end of the world do not have time to coalesce, to gain the full imprimatur of the internet, of the parts of the internet to which and through which such jokes would normally be spoken.

Ratio alert.

GIF: *[Terrible Girl hits Bathroom Bug with shovel] [T2 clip of blasted skeleton clinging to chain link fence]*

[whispering to date during the apocalypse when the apocalypse first appears] That's the apocalypse

Trump's taco bowl pic, except the taco bowl is a globe dotted with mushroom clouds.

Video of Ivanka throwing up on herself, screaming *No no no!* captioned *Nothing but respect for MY president.*

#Resist #TheResistance #NotMyPresident

What is binch? What is corncob? but with human extinction.

#Blimpghazi

Trump's airship, Trump Sky Alpha, the obvious jokes about the palace in the sky, sprouting nukes, bags of money as ballast, the truth of it outstripping the jokes, as had always been the case with Trump, lame old cartoons of Trump Sky Alpha crashing into Lady Liberty, crashing into Mount Rushmore, etc., recirculating, *Der Spiegel*'s cover from November 2016, *Das Ende Der Welt (wie wir sie kennen)*, Trump's head as a huge meteor hurtling toward Earth, people live-tweeting his livestreamed address, widespread disbelief at the fact of the flight, of the president alone up there, and his monologue—the idiocy of it, the lies and the bragging, this terminal stupidity at the end of the world—the president cut off from what was happening on the ground, apart from whatever he saw on his video screens, his isolation from the real-world events unfolding during the flight, he is Justine Sacco, except Justine Sacco with nukes, it doesn't quite make sense, but people go for the joke anyhow.

#HasTrumpLandedYet

Feels good man.

The internet is dying, blinking out.

The internet's record of its own destruction—and that of the greater part of human life and civilization—is given in part through jokes, many of them familiar, though often modified, mutating. *People are making apocalypse jokes like there's no tomorrow,* for instance, is an old joke already available in multiple image macros, the "lame pun coon" in blue color wheel, the "bad joke eel" jutting from the ocean floor, jaw tensed, vacant pushpin eye clocking your reaction, standard bold Impact font, white letters in black outline.

That joke is one of many that proliferate on 1/28, long-dormant memes alive again for one last night, faces of Keanu and Xzibit, *woke af at the buffalo wild wings,* flowing into other memes, the available prefab containers, Trollface, Nyan Cat, Crying Jordan, countless iterations of Pepe. People were bringing back the old things, the old dead memes, it became a kind of contest, a curtain call, a last chance at everything that had passed us by, an activation of knowledge of *all internet traditions* (the "all internet traditions" meme itself dated back to a comment on a 2008 post on the left political blog *Lawyers, Guns & Money*, about the apocryphal Michelle Obama "whitey" tape).

#CurtainCall, #AllInternetTraditions.

Or it was, others said, a glitch in the Matrix, everything released all at once, a collapse of history, of chronology: the system vomiting itself forth before it expired. In any case, passing on bad jokes, ringing the last best changes on a bad joke, is how many spend their final hours. And there is a gentleness to so much of it, even amid horror: familiar, comforting, buffering the experience, slotting it into the known.

Or perhaps it was that in the four days that the internet had been down, people had pent up so much, all they had wanted to say on the internet and couldn't, and then it was all unleashed.

The internet came back on 1/27, and the world was ending a day later, and in between, there was the highest volume of social media posts ever, or so it was reported in some corners, in a way I am no longer able to verify.

Intercontinental ballistic missiles can't melt steel beams.

Where's the Kaboom?

20 minutes into Netflix and chill and he gives you this look [GIF: flaming skull]

ima wait this one out, woke af at the buffalo wild wings.

An image of a woman in a pussy hat stopping a pair of nukes with her outstretched hands.

A woman, a white woman, in fact, in a pussy hat, in the exact pose of the black woman from Baton Rouge in the iconic photo, one of the iconic Black Lives Matter images, the two riot-gear cops seeming to fall back from her, as though struck by a power, the woman in the original, Ieshia Evans, made into a white woman—of course she was, black Twitter noted, wypipo appropriating to the very end, to the grave, appropriating with the dying breath of whiteness.

This is white supremacy.

There is the struggle with finesse, recycling the old jokes, finding those slight variations, the call back to a call back to a call back, perhaps no one likes it now, but wait and maybe it will come around.

Just wait.

Just wait may be a tough proposition in a world that's ending, but, as people also note, on Twitter, on 4chan, on Reddit, what are the options?

Are we gon sit here on this site or we gon commune with trees?

Go out and commune with the treeeeeees????

```
(•_•)
<)  )╱We
/  \
\(•_•)
(  (>  Gon
/  \
(•_•)
<)  )>  Die
/  \
```

Some jokes come around.

5,332 notes for a Tumblr post with a video of Muppet Crazy Harry detonating explosives.

11,328 likes and 132 comments on a post of a cartoon Solange in an elevator kicking an apocalypse zombie's head off.

Play us off, Keyboard Cat.

Resist, #Resist, people are saying, but it is unclear what that means in the face of nuclear annihilation.

Images of animal connection are widely shared, horses touching heads, cheetah cub and baby chimp "best friends," a two-legged Chihuahua in a wheeled mobility harness paired with a Silkie, a fluffy, plush-looking breed of chicken, and still less likely combos, snakes and ducks, an alligator and an aardvark, best friends, always best friends.

Images that originated on 4chan, on Reddit, were being sucked up into Twitter and Instagram and Tumblr, and making the rounds at a frenetic pace.

Thank god for friends.

I want to send love to my friends, my community.

Stay safe, my friends.

The rush to make fun of the email blasts about impending missile strikes and other civil emergencies, or the absence of such alerts.

Waiting for my blast alert like [Vizzini "I'm waiting" GIF, scowling, arms flung out in impatience].

The hay made online about all these decentralized warning systems: they would be used only once, this was their moment in the sun, there was a ranking of them, the sharp messages that began *Inbound Threat* or *Take Shelter* and had relevant information, the one from Idaho that said *Alert Template. Information here*, the one from Pennsylvania that said: *cOrb Pulice.*

There are tweets asking for, demanding interactions.

I just need to know yr out here.

Fave if your safe.

There are tweets for the missing, photos, names and ages, locations, the missing flood the timeline, then there are too many, people stop sharing the missing.

The increasing bad joke of Facebook's "mark yourself safe" as the night progressed, flipped on worldwide, death toll skyrocketing by unknowable millions every hour.

A raw and increasingly frantic need at the end for validation, for retweets and likes, for—and this became a new joke—the LAST retweets and likes.

Hoovering up all the last likes like

Stacking last likes

Fave if your safe, retweet if your [GIF: screaming, flaming skull].

Baby pumping fist: *Just got world's last like.*

Things are being tested, workshopped, and all would soon be dead, performer and audience, or most all.

Trump Sky Alpha orbiting a blasted chunk of coal, Trump still monologuing about how well it's all going, in spite of FAKE NEWS.

Conservatives blasting Obama, blasting Hillary.

Thank God Obama spent all his time on global warming.
But let's figure out global warming, right guys?
That's a good hot take.
The hottest take.
Get the oven mitts for this hot take.
Get in the bunker and shield yourself from the hotness of these takes.
Since we have nothing but hot takes.
Since the world's a hot take.

People demanding we do it their way: don't make it political, make it political, but do so *the right way*, along certain precise vectors that reinforce certain notions.

Your mileage may vary.

And the rage at Trump, and the defenders of Trump, and Trump's last speech, the pieces of it flying around the internet, protesters overpowering the checkpoints and pushing into Trump Tower, breaking down the doors.

Long Live Resistance Auntie!

Your mileage may vary.

And a flood of racist memes, Trollface with turban and beard, Nyan Cat with turban and beard, worries about MS-13 rampages and looting, the "illegals" who are waiting to murder your family as civil society cracks.

Josh Marshall changes his Twitter avatar back to Kermit, and signs off to spend the night with his family. *We'll know more tomorrow. Or we won't.*

Mark Zuckerberg posts as Trump nears New York City. *We hope that our users—and the whole world—will stay safe today. We will be back tomorrow to give people the power to build community and bring the world closer together.*

And Zuckerberg's responders:

Bro.

Bro.

Dude.

My man.

My bro, what?

Zuck posting this shit forever in Hell.

Among the most-circulated jokes is one that begins with an AP shot of the man in a red polo shirt and white pants in the aisle of a Taipei supermarket howling grief over three small incinerated bodies. And a caption: *Actually it's about ethics in gaming journalism.*

And then hours later, the same image and caption, cropped, reframed, reworked by a larger caption: *IS THIS A GOOD JOKE?*

This call back to a joke that had died out years earlier is spreading with a kind of desperate ferocity: as the day goes on, there is more and more to see, videos of a mushroom cloud over Taiwan, of a highway on fire in the south of France, Abuja burning, Harare burning, riots in São Palo, in Natchez, waves of death everywhere, flurries of gun suicides, a mass shooting in West Virginia, then five more mass shootings within the hour, California, Arizona, New Hampshire, two in Florida, then a group suicide in Iowa, another in Belize, corpses around the world with jaws clenched, with jaws snapped wide open, with no discernable jaw, piles of the dead, screaming and fleeing humans, some actually burning as they run, dead or dying human heads screencapped and pegged to the same text:

Actually it's about ethics in gaming journalism.

And:

IS THIS A GOOD JOKE?

Ethics in gaming journalism was such an old joke, it seemed to come from another civilization, and yet it was as though that joke, those times, all of that rage, were somehow the ground we were still standing on, were all that were left, were in the end somehow really all that mattered to the system, *actually it's about ethics in gaming journalism*, that was somehow the moment, the inflection point, to which the internet had led us, we lived somehow in the wake of that, the SJWs and snowflakes, *no safe space this time*, and that AP shot of the man in the red polo, and his incinerated children, it was eventually tagged with names of women targeted in Gamergate, and the text *LOOK AT WHAT YOU'VE DONE, SHAME.*

It did not seem to be a joke, or it was a very dark one, but the account was not one that did jokes, or that was good at them.

Somehow there were people who seemed to be blaming the end of the world on the women from Gamergate, and in some places it seemed the most deadpan troll, but in others the posters seemed so upset, so sad, so furious, that they had to be for real, they really did blame them.

If SJWs need a safe space, it will be pretty safe as a roasted corpse under an atomic shroud.

A quote from Elliot Rodger that went around, *Men shouldn't have to look and act like big, animalistic beasts to get women. The fact that women still prioritize brute strength just shows that their minds haven't fully evolved.*

Still incel at the end of the world ☹

Same picture: *LOOK AT THESE SNOWFLAKES.*

Picture: *a trophy for everyone! (the trophy is the burnt corpose* [sic] *of your child.)*

Performative wokeness was to blame, women were to blame, #BLM was to blame, or Putin and collusion, *Time for Some Game Theory*, massive tweet threads, a need to make the case now, as completely as possible.

Apocalypse Twitter is exhausting.

Glad to see this continues to be a normal and very good website

There was the white supremacist who was stabbed to death on camera in Cleveland while beating an apparently Muslim American man, and Jonathan Chait tweeted about this, and only this, of the shame of it—this after thousands had already been confirmed dead around the world—and his mentions lit up:

Actually, it's good.

In fact it's good.

No it is very good.

It's good, actually.

Elsewhere, on 4chan, or Reddit, the assertion that Democrats are somehow behind it, the false flag, the new world order that follows 1/28, Shillary, *KIDS SHE LIKES AND LOTS OF DYKES.*

John Podesta, the occult, the cucks, the RINOs.

On 1/28, Jon Postel will reset the system.

Who is blue-pilled and who is red-pilled?

Beta numale faggots, haircuts and beards and graphic tees, this country is so beyond fucked, how are we going to survive what's coming, it's fucking disgusting, girls who look like dyke sluts with manic panic hair, ripped jeans, vintage band T-shirts, bands they never listened to, they destroy the world and what, we're supposed to protect them? If we survive, kill them all on site, it's our only option.

#HillaryHack, #HillarysRevenge, Hillary was widely blamed, as soon as the internet was back, WikiLeaks posted a file implicating her in the hack.

4chan: Hillary's broad grin. Stamped over it: *Best her and molest her.*

Or: *Sucking bollocks and worshipping Moleck.*

Or: *Fucking kill her.*

Stay mad cuntcucks, this is a Shillary op.

Stay mad, Stay mad, Stay mad.

MAGA.

At last the cuck world is crushed.

MAGA, my friends.

And: *Perhaps the rarest Pepe of all is friendship at the end of the world.*

"So I guess the world is actually ending now!" tweeted a former Gawker editor, and the tone there is instructive: atavistic, a return to the site's early editorial voice, at once wide-eyed and over it, giddy and etherized, a jaded and pitiless amazement, the flat relentless tone that had seeped into the water of the internet, and if the internet has moved on since then, if that is no longer quite the voice of things, on this day it is having a renaissance.

Well then OK!

YEP THEN SO WITH THE IMPENDING DEATH OF US.

One Vox writer posted a photo of what he announced was his own penis, under the headline *EZRA, CHOKE ON THESE CLICKS.*

Angela and Strawberry, Kurt honking it to hentai, people remembered the good times.

Can we all just admit now that Harambe was never funny.

Tweet pegged to a screencap of sixty-nine dead in Peoria shopping mall bombing: *me as nukes melt my face*: "nii..ce."

When bombings were reported in Egypt and Iran: *The whole internet loves nuclear apocalypse! *5 seconds later* We regret to inform you the apocalypse is racist.*

Small brain: *Drumpf killed us, as I predicted.*

Big brain: *The entire US military-industrial complex across Democratic and Republican administrations for decades is to blame, and the US people are without exception culpable for this moment.*

Galaxy brain: *Centering the US in the narrative just because they have the most nukes is colonial bullshit.*

Universe brain: *Death Tastes Good.*

Photos of kittens are exchanged in comments sections, and there is the sense among these commenters that they have short-circuited the system, beat it, at least momentarily, with kittens.

I needed that!

This too!

Awwwwww . . .

Vine: [*eight kittens in a New Balance shoebox*]

And a bulldog on a skateboard, and a black cat batted in the nose by a stealthy orange kitten, and the perfect pug, a basket of perfect pug puppies.

And the first and last tweet of a brand-new account, an egg that has just joined Twitter, perhaps for no other reason than to post this response (netting two faves, zero retweets) to a retweet of a twenty-one-month-old tweet of an etonline.com story about a YouTube video headlined "Seeing This Puppy Scared of His Own Hiccups Will Change Your Life!":

cute cute cute cute cute cute cute cute cute cute cute cute cute cute cute cute cute cute cute cute cute cute cute cute cute cute cute cute cute cute cute cute cute cute cute cute cute cute cute cute cute cute cute cute cute cute cute cute cute cute.

It was reported in some outlets that the earliest nuclear detonations had happened in Delhi, others said the Middle East, or the Korean peninsula, or Russia, or out in the middle of the ocean in an open stretch of the Pacific, the reports varied, and there was no authority, it had happened when the internet was down, and when it came back there was too much chaos, too much of the fog of war, as commentators were putting it, to understand, at least here in America, but the notion that Pakistan was behind it had taken hold in some quarters, that it was al-Qaida terrorists in Pakistan, or ISIS terrorists in Pakistan, that these terrorists had gained control of Pakistan's nukes.

On 1/28, in 1933, someone tweeted, the name Pakistan was coined by Choudhry Rahmat Ali Khan and was later accepted by the Indian Muslim extremists.

This was a fact, circulated on conservative Twitter, on Free Republic, on 4chan.

The Meaning of 1/28, a pattern, an explanation, something solid.

And then that changed, somewhere, and what circulated is the fact that Muhammad died on 1/28, that this was jihad, Islamic terror, on the anniversary of Muhammad's death.

That neither the fact about Pakistan nor the fact about Muhammad was not true did not prevent them from circulating.

On 1/28, Muhammad died. Today, his followers commemorate his death with an attack on Western civilization.

People explained that this was false and found themselves with storms of raging disagreement, they were called useful idiots for the jihadists, liberal media dupes (*pretty safe as a roasted corpse under an atomic shroud*), and then the rebuttal shifted, all at once, all across Twitter, Facebook, people were leaping in, saying that the discrepancy was explained by the "Islamic Calendar" (also cited: the "Muslim Calendar" and "Hijra Calendar" and "Sharia Calendar") and its differences from the Gregorian calendar.

What the Muslim calendar recorded as June 8 was in the Gregorian calendar January 28.

Or so people argued.

You still believe muslim lies.

It's almost satisfying to know your family's going to die because you believed the Muslim lies.

ITS 1/28 OF COURSE ITS JIHADISTS.

MAGA! MAGA! MAGA!

There were similar threads for North Korea, for Russia, for China and Iran, for India, explaining why it was them, explaining the meaning of 1/28 in terms of a historical anniversary or the cultural beliefs of the country in question.

Someone shared as a semicomic rebuttal the 1:28 Bible verse from Genesis: *Replenish the earth, and subdue it: and have dominion over the fish of the sea, and over the fowl of the air, and over every living thing that moveth upon the earth*, and this was also picked up, shared.

Jokingly or in all seriousness, some suggested that Christian terrorists had precipitated the end of the world.

Subdue it.

Have dominion.

It was unclear which of the detonations raining down across the world were US bombs, but the world was going haywire, the information was conflicting, there was no official word on which of the disasters, which of the mass kill-offs, the US was directly responsible for.

Other 1/28s emerged.

On 1/28: The space shuttle *Challenger* exploded.

On 1/28: Marty traveled back in time.

On 1/28: Sir Thomas Warner founded the first British colony in the Caribbean, on the island of Saint Kitts.

On 1/28: Henry VIII died.

Each of them appended with some variation on *Today, his followers commemorate his death with an attack on Western civilization.*

The anniversaries were scoured for resonance and clues, for patterns. Lines were drawn, connections made, causality established, certain halos of meaning.

Perhaps it was both North Korea and Pakistan, it made sense to some, an axis between them, it was Korea that had done the hacking, and the Muslims launched the first nuclear attacks, A. Q. Khan and Kim Jong Un and an al-Qaida remnant, or was it ISIS, the reported attacks with low-yield bombs, maybe it was Korea doing both, or the Muslims had hacked and Korea had the bomb, or the bombs had not been nuclear, no low-yield nukes, but conventional bombs, false flags.

False flags, stay redpilled.

Shillary will make herself president if it means burning down the whole world.

On 1/28, Jon Postel will reset the system.

It was the birthday of Kim Jong Il, or Kim Jong Un, or the first day of the Korean New Year: 1/28. And if it wasn't true, then there was so little time to learn what was.

Canuplin, one of the last memes, perhaps the last new meme to gain widespread attention.

It reaches a *reductio ad absurdum* with Canuplin, *the Pinoy Chaplin.*

A Filipino magician born on January 28, 1904, Canuplin, a Chaplin imitator, who appears in Filipino movies and the local bodabil circuit. The name itself, Canuplin, a combination of his own, Canuto Francia, and Chaplin.

Canuplin did 1/28.

In the world of the internet in which people are making fun of the jihadist 1/28 connection, there is a new account, @ApocalypsePoets, a log of 1/28s, it blends fact and fiction, states that as Henry VIII dies, his ulcerating leg fills the room with stench, his attendants too afraid to tell him he's dying, because predicting the death of a king is treason punishable by torture and death. And so swollen is he with sickness that his corpse explodes in the coffin during his funeral procession, and when his carriage overturns, it snaps the necks of several of the horses drawing it, though just how many necks (all? and how many is all?) is lost to history.

1/28 was an inside job.

Jet fuel can't melt Canuplin.

Christa McAuliffe will have her revenge.

@ApocalypsePoets is tweeting screenshots from something else, from a printed book, a list of 1/28s.

Jokes about McAuliffe and Canuplin are latched onto, but the jokes never quite connect, never make their way into anything real, it's anticomedy without charm or wit, and yet these jokes are passed around as though it is all an old joke, an old joke that will come around.

Some vague notion of McAuliffe partisans, that terror cells devoted to McAuliffe perpetrated the business that had brought about the end of the world.

And more resonantly, what really starts to lock in, begins to be shared, at least in certain corners, the magazine cover, *The Pinoy Chaplin.*

The painting of an old man, Filipino, white-gloved hand raised to mouth, a white glove of almost Mickey Mouse largeness, false eyebrows, Hitler mustache, thick but receding hair brushed back, a sort of dignity, a deep impression of time in the lines of his face, the damage of time in the pull of the lines around his mouth as his mouth opens, the cigarette held by the gloved fingers, that light emergent chaos of smoke twisting from his mouth, something irredeemably cool, and the eyes just watching you.

It is passed along.

Someone on 4chan says, *Canuplin . . . ehh?*

I mean really guys what is going on with this can we make this work or what?

By now Trump had announced it. He had landed in New York and the missiles were flying.

The weariness, the sickness.

Perfectly normal website.

Good website, here at the end of the world.

What a normal thing to do on a website this is also normal and good.

Fuck you, Jack.

The terminal weariness, the horror at how much was being de-stroyed, at the lies and bad faith, the trolls and bots and the slurp-ing of liberal tears, soy boys and snowflakes and safe spaces, the rape and death threats (*it would be too bad if some immigrant raped you*—phrasings to steer the poster clear of a ban, even now, though of course many other posts simply called for rape and murder—*pretty safe in a grave under a mushroom cloud after I've raped you and cut your head off*), the need to be heard, the need to respond, the constant chaotic hum of it.

Negative partisanship, zero-sum games, the nonstop trolling, the hate and the love, the postures that were knowing and cool and monstrously self-deprecating and panicked and thirsty and violent and performatively woke, none of it stopped at the end of the world.

The lies and misinformation, the endlessness of that.

The fundamental inability to determine: stupid or evil.

The sense that it was this, it was the structure of the internet, that had amplified the stupid and the evil, and at the same time flattened them, made them impossible to distinguish. Or made distinguishing them somehow beside the point.

I sat in the room—the man still behind me, still watching, he must have been, I could hear him breathe but it seemed to me that

he had dissolved, had become part of the wall, the structure holding me, and that the wall itself was respiring, and it wasn't quite
real. It was only this screen that was real, my body somehow moving a lightweight PC mouse, and I felt my guts turning, and forced
myself to stay, clenched my thighs, tried to breathe, because if I
left now I did not know if they would let me back in.

I took my screenshots, I clicked and typed, searching or being
led on the drift and mania.

In certain corners the damage was being traced back to Jon
Postel, his revolutionary moment, and his failure.

On 1/28, Jon Postel will reset the system.

Canuplin did 1/28.

Jon Postel, one of the individuals present at the creation of the
first node of the ARPANET, who had taken it on himself to in essence hijack the addressing of the internet, eight of the twelve root
name servers of the internet, in a dispute with the US government
over protocological control of the internet.

I thought of Canuplin, of Postel.

I thought of my daughter and wife, and I did not want to leave,
because here those thoughts could be eased or sidelined so power-
fully: it was a substance, sure it was, the internet could make you
forget so much.

Forget but not eliminate—make it more distant, send it wherever the rest of life goes when you're hitting refresh on the sites,
clicking, reading, searching.

Somewhere inside there was a part of me telling me that this
was all wrong, being here. And why was it wrong? Because I should
have spent less time on the internet while I still had my girls,
Dominique and Verena. Less here in this noise, more time with
those people I had loved, who were dead.

And I thought, no, I should have spent more time here, the mistake was not spending more, the mistake was making those memories, those connections in the brain, when the world was about
to end. And it was true, I would be much better equipped for this
world if my brain hadn't made all these connections to Dominique

and Verena, because the world was ending—it *had* ended, and yet it was an end that was still unfurling, still engulfing those of us who were left, a wave that was crashing down on us but so slowly, or not a wave, just some endless noise crashing down, a sorrow that wouldn't end, not until I was there, with them, as close to some closeness as I could be, at the mass grave and witness their resting there.

On 1/28, Canuplin is born.

On 1/28, the first commercial telephone exchange is established in New Haven, Connecticut, and a locomotive passing through Panamanian jungle links the Atlantic and Pacific Oceans.

On 1/28, a fifteen-inch snowflake falls on Fort Keogh, Montana.

On 1/28, Charlemagne, King of the Franks and Holy Roman Emperor, curses the known and unknown worlds he's left unconquered, and his dumb ass croaks and becomes a ghost.

These were lines from *The Subversive*, published years before the end of the world, by Sebastian de Rosales.

Take it with a grain of salt.

Whatever happened, happened.

Something was assembling itself. I felt the sweat on my skin from the liquid noise and movement in my bowels I was trying to suppress. I felt the mouse, its cheapness and lack of heft, the hollow feel of the plastic my body held.

01:56:01 I know you've had no joy in your life.
01:56:05 But just wait.
01:56:09 Only wait, Uncle.
01:56:13 We shall rest.
01:57:07 [Chattering]
01:57:48 [No Audible Dialogue]
01:58:01 [No Audible Dialogue]

As Trump landed Trump Sky Alpha on the roof of Trump Tower, a 4chan user said *Love Trumps Hate.*

He said, *It's true, we do, we love it, we love his hate.*

And dozens or hundreds of missiles from multiple world powers were sailing to their targets:

Oh yes, we love his hate.

Hundreds of thousands of people choking the streets of Manhattan and by the time he landed, a chaotic mass of bodies pushing up against Trump Tower, against the police and military, overrunning them, breaking down the doors, up the stairwells, soon they were out on the roof, running for him, for Trump Sky Alpha, he saw the mob running his way, and his jaw dropped, and he said *Wha-wha-wha-what?* and no sooner had Trump set down than he lifted off again, he set a final course for Mar-a-Lago.

Trump, someone tweeted, *the most hated man in the history of the world, hated twenty-four hours a day by more living humans than anyone has ever been hated by, is ending the world that hates him.*

A very US-centric POV, someone else observed, Trump the most hated—wasn't there someone, someone in Asia, maybe, who more people had hated?

Why am I spending the last minutes of my life arguing about this?

The most hated person, the person who in all of human history has been deeply disliked and hated by the most people, who has had the largest number of human animals just wishing that somehow, anyhow, he would just somehow no longer exist, no longer be among the human animals, he was still here, still making sounds, still delivering his YouTube livestream.

There were only a few moments left for the internet.

Trump, face smudged, last singed strands of hair writhing away from his scalp, was piloting what was left of his zeppelin—the secure inner vault, festooned in rotors—to Mar-a-Lago.

And there was a last irruption, millions of people pouring themselves into the social media sites.

Trump still talking, still livestreaming, sailing above the unfolding devastation, justifying and joking and raging, attacking his enemies, and then calling for a big strike, calling for it even as the internet was flickering out.

He'd announced a big one in New York, but this was an order of magnitude more, the one that would end so much of human life and civilization.

I saw it screencapped from 4chan and shared onto Twitter: *Love Trumps Hate.*

And:

A Dead Trump Pepe, *X*s for eyes.

Trump, it was said, easily, easily the most hated man who had ever lived.

A voice somewhere: *I don't want to die.*

And: **mocking voice*: I don't want to die, I don't want to die.*

A final rush of MS Paints, hasty Photoshops, Pepes saluting Trump Pepe, Pepes with *X*s on their eyes, hearts on their eyes, Trump up there in Trump Sky Alpha, the flag of Kekistan on a zeppelin, the zeppelin itself Pepe's head, Putin and Kushner and Conway appearing in different iterations, Crying Jordan and Savage Patrick, Side-Eyeing Chloe, even Harambe back again, vultures circling, enemy aircraft roaring in, all of it shuddering and flickering and trying to mutate, it seemed, trying to reach out beyond this, trying to dream up some sort of escape, the image of Canuplin there, all of a sudden, the painting of an old Filipino man, melancholy, impassive, the cigarette frozen near his mouth, *Love*

Trumps Hate, Canuplin amid the Pepes, the bombs that were Pepes, a field of dead Pepes, Pepe with a single tear, Savage Patrick at the helm, Distracted Boyfriend meme, boyfriend's eyes going from a flayed corpse head to a flayed Pepe head, the phrases *Love Trumps Hate* and *We Love Trumps Hate*, shirtless Alex Jones and shirtless Putin and Hillary in a white pantsuit and Obama in a tan suit and Canuplin staring out, cigarette in hand, in a field of Pepes that were laid out on top of the airship, something about that airship and everyone on it and everyone who surrounded it, who flew with or against it, was near some ultimate form, some joke about 1/28, about all the lies about that, all the jokes about that, all of the colossal rage and grief and fear, it was slipping toward something, it was vibrating with certain possibilities, and then the internet was dead (**universe to humans*: retire bitch*) and all that was over.

trump_sky_alpha/2_the_recursive_horizon
2_3_negative_world

A convoy of two SUVs and three larger military vehicles took me back to the airport.

I said to the driver that it had been just two vehicles when they brought me.

Dark now, he said. Good to be careful.

At the airport there was no flight, no information on why there was not a flight. I was told to wait at a table outside a shuttered bar and grill. There was a single light turned on above me, the nearby gates dark. Figures walked by using flashlights, beams splintering against the grate pulled over the bar, the taps inside, the empty rows of mirrored bar shelves.

I hadn't had a drink in over a year—not since before the Foshay. Here there was a distracting smell, beer that had turned, faint and sweet and rotten, cloying and insistent and only barely there beneath the airport smell.

I do not think of airports as having a particular smell—perhaps a neutralizing nonsmell, a kind of white noise.

This one had one.

The turned beer snaked out of something larger, a smell that belonged to a massive institutional space that was no longer being maintained, a smell I knew from the Foshay, mildew and synthetic fabrics and cleaners and too much trapped air.

The beer had flipped a switch in my brain—made the smells I had programmed myself to tune out present, unavoidable, something my mind was sorting through and cataloging.

Or perhaps I was in an avoidant mode, because I knew that I was in a trap.

I had walked into something, and I had to figure out the angle, the right play.

The Subversive and Sebastian de Rosales and Jon Postel and Birdcrash.

That these names had merged and assembled themselves in the room with the internet was a contingent thing that had involved my own searches, certain clicks, choices that were at times barely conscious—the fingers that push the planchette over the Ouija board.

The pattern seemed obvious, then perhaps I was seeing a pattern where there was none. I didn't know, didn't trust myself to know. Or rather I knew I didn't have enough information to make any determination.

Yet my mind was still humming with it, the internet, what I thought I'd found.

I wanted to go back to the internet room. I wanted a sip of the rotten beer. I wanted to be on a plane somewhere else. I wanted to be back on the internet right now.

The Subversive was a 2015 novel by Sebastian de Rosales that told the story of a boy who emigrated from the Philippines to the US, and went on to form a hacktivist collective called the Aviary that hacked various government websites in the US and the Philippines, orchestrated DDoS attacks against domain name registrars, and conducted a number of other online operations that caused a fair amount of damage, leading up to a massive attack that paralyzed the global internet. The novel received little attention when it was released, but the following year, an organization calling itself the Aviary appeared, headed by a hacker named Birdcrash, and began taking credit for attacks similar to those described in the book.

I'd interviewed de Rosales for *TechMinder* in 2017. I had even asked him about that line in his book, *On 1/28, Jon Postel will reset the system.*

And it had appeared again on the internet, in the last hours of its existence: the 1/28 quotes about Postel, and others about the first commercial telephone exchange, the fifteen-inch snowflake, the death of Charlemagne, all in a Reddit post ("2015 novel perfectly predicts today's attacks [SPOILER ALERT]") that linked a pirate copy of *The Subversive*.

It did not mean there was causation, it did not mean that the Aviary had committed the attack; the book read by more people after the publicity boost of the real-world attacks, and in those last hours, people were grabbing on to anything. The fact that a handful of people had posted quotes from *The Subversive* didn't mean anything.

I had been there at the shuttered restaurant for hours.

A flashlight came by, beam ricocheting through the space.

It was two women in fatigues.

I stepped out into their path, hands raised.

Excuse me, I'm a journalist and I've been told to wait here, but no one has come by to tell me what is happening and I need to use the restroom.

Stay right there, ma'am, said the one with the flashlight. She shined it in my face, and on my clothes, a blue button-down shirt and khakis, a little too big, that I'd been given at Foshay. My hand went to my face, and I felt how my hair was flying around my head, and wondered why I hadn't put it in its place during all my hours sitting at the little table.

She spoke on a walkie-talkie, and they took me to another wing. Use the first stall, the woman with the flashlight said. The other woman took a small flashlight out of her pocket and tested it, click on, click off.

She handed it to me. Don't be long. Click it off when you're seated and in place.

The other one said, Clicking it off wastes it. That's like a half hour of battery each click.

You know that's a myth, the first said.

I sat in the stall, I didn't know if I should click it off or leave it on. I pulled my hair back, the light crashing chaotically around the space with its walls and door as I fixed my hair in the rubber band.

I didn't like that crazy movement of the light. It seemed important to decide: leave it on, or turn it off.

It was all for show, but I didn't know who the show was for, what mattered—they were outside the bathroom—but whatever I did with the light, it was a show.

I wished that the flashlight was a gun. I put it into my mouth and everything was dark except the faint glow coming from inside my face that indicated the walls and door around me. My head was a little lamp now. Skin and sinew wrapped the form of my skull.

Who is blue-pilled and who is red-pilled?

On 1/28, a fifteen-inch snowflake falls on Fort Keogh, Montana.

I was held in a nearby facility for the next week, and I wasn't allowed to contact Galloway. Starting on the third day there were
sets of questions about what I'd found on the internet.

My interrogator was a man in his midtwenties. He wore a dark
suit, and had a look that I would have characterized in the old world
as ambitious. Every afternoon I was taken to his office to talk about
de Rosales. He would smile at me the way you smile at something
you hate, something keeping you from a prize. How had I known
to look for those quotes? What did I know about the Aviary? I had
spoken to de Rosales before—had I maintained contact with him?
Did I think he was an active member of the Aviary? Was I a member of the Aviary, had I ever spoken with anyone in the Aviary, do I
have any associations with the Aviary whatsoever?

He said, My role here is to be restrained. It is only in extreme
scenarios that we go beyond talk.

He said, What we're trying to understand is how you zeroed in
so quickly on material that implicated de Rosales.

Yes, I said, a few threads led back to *The Subversive* in all of the
noise that last day. Because of the profile I'd done of Rosales for
TechMinder, I was probably more likely to pick out those threads
than others would have been. But I can't ultimately tell you what
it means.

Did it surprise you to find the quotes?

In retrospect, no. It is not entirely surprising to find quotes from
the book circulating. The book is a part of hacker culture, online

113

culture. It was around. You add to that the coincidence of 1/28, it would make sense people were pulling quotes.

If it was a coincidence.

Yes, if it was. That's right. But you saw the Reddit post. "Novel perfectly predicts." So others were getting to the same place.

That post had what, five or six comments?

I said also there were tweets of screenshots from the book. It got around.

In very limited circles, he said.

I was told to think hard about my answers. I would not want to make a mistake in any of my answers, he said.

Canuplin, that painting of him, it was the cover of *The Subversive*, and that image definitely got around.

It did, he said. That's a very good point. It got around.

He produced a copy of the interview. He asked me to walk him through it—what I had been thinking when I asked the questions, what I thought of de Rosales's responses.

He asked me what I had thought when I interviewed him—was de Rosales Birdcrash? Or an associate of Birdcrash?

I said that at the time I had not thought so, though I had a sense he wasn't being entirely forthcoming. His presentation was very smooth, almost too smooth, and then his eyes would sharpen, he'd show himself *wanting* too much, and lose that veneer.

You felt you were being manipulated.

I wasn't sure. I wrote a piece to accompany the interview where I basically laid out the evidence—and there wasn't any hard evidence that I knew of—that he was Birdcrash. I had thought that he probably wasn't.

Do you know what BIND is?

I told him that I knew that it had to do with addressing, and was thought to be a part of the attack that had brought down the internet.

Did you know that de Rosales was one of the coders who worked on it in 1999 and 2000?

No, I said. I didn't know that.

Did you know that the Aviary—the Aviary in their Pastebin posts after their first several attacks—they would include lines pulled directly from de Rosales's novel?

Yes, I was aware of that. That's basic stuff—that was in my piece. *The Subversive* was obviously a foundational text for them. But I'm not aware of evidence that de Rosales was ever part of the actual organization. And the posts on 1/28, again, they don't prove anything, except that there was text from a novel that certain very online people liked that was relevant to the moment.

There is quite a bit here that's relevant. We seem to be in a zone of intense relevance.

Interview with Sebastian de Rosales, *TechMinder*

Have you had any communication with the members of the . . . how shall I refer to them, the nonfiction Aviary?
Nonfiction Aviary works fine. No, I have not. And I hope not to, for legal reasons.
What do you think of what they've done?
My lawyer has instructed me not to make any statements about them, or offer any opinions on them or their actions.
Surely you have some thoughts.
My lawyer has cautioned me in the strongest possible terms to not express any judgments at all about the Aviary—the nonfiction Aviary.
Can you say if you *disapprove* of any of their actions?
Apparently there could be legal difficulties in that direction, too. I'm afraid I do not feel legally competent to even outline general contours of what I don't know, if that makes sense, so I'm going to have to pass on the question.
Can we move back then, chronologically? You've spoken of the childhood portions of this as being based on your own life.
That was a mistake.
Why a mistake?
Because it's fiction. Because you draw on life sometimes but it goes in other places, for any number of reasons.
The main character in *The Subversive*, after he immigrates to America, he becomes a victim of sexual abuse.
Pass.

Pass?

Whatever the question is, pass, pass, pass.

Let me zoom out a little. The nonfiction Aviary is conducting not only the type of attacks on government websites that you described in the novel, they've also announced an operation to expose child abusers and distributors of child pornography on the internet. That wasn't in your book, but it feels like it fits with the ideas of the book.

You want me to say "I wish I'd thought of that"? That the real-world Aviary is improving on the book?

Is that what you think?

My thoughts. My thoughts. I'm afraid I do not feel legally competent to even outline general contours of my thoughts, or of what I'm permitted and not permitted to say about my thoughts, if that makes sense, so I'm going to have to pass on the question, and really anything about my life, or how my life relates to the book. This won't be a good interview. Perhaps we should just call it a day.

Okay, let's move on. You wrote this before Trump. Does the context of the Trump era change the ideas of the book for you?

No, though if I had really been thinking, I would have predicted it in the book. It's not surprising to see an authoritarian president, a demagogue stoking racial fears and other divisions, because that is where the internet has been taking us.

If you want *The Subversive* now, as a reader, how do you get it?

Out of print from the original publisher, Cyber Prairie Books, who sadly have gone out of business. Not because of any of this, but because independent publishing is hard and they were losing more money than they had to lose. If they had stuck around a bit longer, they would have been able to sell the print run of the book, rather than remaindering it.

Remaindering it?

Well, they sold me a carton of the books for cheap, and pulped the rest.

How many did they sell before that?

Fewer than three hundred.

So how do people get your book?

There are some used copies out there. I understand that it's become a collector's item.

I saw one on eBay for over $500.

Yes, there's some demand for it. Unfortunately it's under something of a legal cloud because of the nonfiction Aviary, so it's not a project a legitimate publisher can take on without opening itself up to legal exposure that would vastly outweigh any benefits to publishing it. For a time after Cyber Prairie folded I made it available for free as a PDF and EPUB file on my website. After the connection between the book and the Aviary was publicly made, it was downloaded that day so often that it crashed my site. And then there was the legal issue. Since then, I haven't made it available, but pirate versions are circulating, I understand.

What led you to create the Aviary?

The fiction Aviary.

Yes.

There were a number of things I was turning over in my head. Something that's in the book, almost twenty years ago, John Perry Barlow wrote a manifesto called "A Declaration of the Independence of Cyberspace." It's beautiful and important and quite short, and I encourage everyone who hasn't read it before to google it and read it now. It's also, I think, fundamentally wrong. What it does, in rather visionary prose, is carve out the internet as a space that existed somehow after or beyond government controls. The opening runs—please correct the quote for your article—it says, "Governments of the Industrial World, you weary giants of flesh and steel, I come from Cyberspace, the new home of Mind. On behalf of the future, I ask you of the past to leave us alone. You are not welcome among us. You have no sovereignty where we gather" [*ed: he had the quote perfectly*]. This has become something of a punching bag in the years since, for a number of reasons that could and have filled several books. For one thing, the internet isn't some ideal mind-space—it's physically embodied. It is physical architecture, it's cable, it's fiber, it's massive data centers warming the globe. It runs through countries. I researched the first global telegram for my book, and the final piece of the cable ran through Manila, the transpacific cable itself, it was a copper cable layer, insulated by a layer of gutta-percha latex, then a sheath of brass, then a layer of jute yarn, then a final layer—the exterior—woven from iron and steel wires. The steel wires alone weighed nineteen million pounds. So today it's fiber-optic cable, it's maybe lighter, but it's not really different. It's a vast work of engineering, it's objects in space, and people in different parts of the globe have vastly different experiences of the internet and vastly different amounts of political power when it comes to how the internet works. That's one thing. For another, the ideal that Barlow embodied—what I would call the technocratic hippie libertarian ideal—pretends to a kind of neutrality, and it's not neutral: it benefits America, it benefits capital. The bodies that control the internet, you'll see much greater representation there from commercial stakeholders than noncommercial stakeholders. I'm not saying all of the technocratic hippies that created the internet as we know it have gotten rich, many could have cashed out in various ways but chose to labor on behalf of this ideal, which is great—but whose ideal is it? Even something basic like top-level domains—you know how each country has a domain, *dot us*, or *dot fr* for france, a *dot ph* for the Philippines. These were developed from a list by the European-based International Organization for Standards. The list is itself contested, which I won't go into here. But then to delegate the authority to administer the country code, you have to have someone that the Internet Assigned Numbers Authority considers a trusted partner in that country. And they don't always certify such a partner, so for instance there's a guy, a white guy who lives in Japan, a guy who's been working on the internet for a million years, he controls the domains for a number of what they call orphan country codes in Africa. And, you know, he's not doing it to make money—he's not making money—he's doing it to keep the system running. But you see what an unequal system it is, for people in different parts of the world. So let's say you're trying to take back authoritative control there for a new government to set up a means of getting, I don't know, resources about vaccinations to the people of the country. Or forget that—you just want to use your country's top-level domain in whatever way you think appropriate. You're the country, you're trying to take some authority, and you're stuck petitioning some white guy living in Japan, proving to him who you are, that you deserve the authority. And maybe you get it and maybe you don't—*you*, in *your* country. And that's just talking about the country code TLDs. Power reproduces itself throughout different parts of the system in different ways.

I'm going to read you a quote from "Birdcrash," the leader of the nonfiction Aviary.

Please don't. I won't be able to talk about it. It's better to stick to the book.

Okay, sure. John Perry Barlow isn't the only whipping boy in the book. There are some interesting, contrarian takes on the *Whole Earth Catalog*, which is usually regarded very fondly when people talk about the history of the internet. Steve Jobs, in his famous commencement speech at Stanford, quotes the final issue, on the back of which there's a picture of a country road and the words "Stay hungry. Stay foolish." Is it fair to say that you don't like the *Whole Earth Catalog*?

It's fair to say that the narrator of part 4 of the book doesn't! His point is how the *Whole Earth* catalogs are these revered countercultural objects, but the generation that grew up on them became the worst capitalists of all time—or at least, the richest capitalists. So where are their hippie ideals now? And just look at the language of it: the whole earth! What an American demand! It's not enough to call it the American Catalog—it needs to take in the whole earth, under the guise of, you know, some hippie-dippie-new-age-let's-change-the-world stuff, peace love dope, but what it really ends up being is let's control the world, exploit the world, sell things to the world. To the whole earth!

You're a network—

Hold on, hold on, I'm not quite done yet. This idea of "the whole earth" is very different when you're from a country that's been subject to multiple colonizations. As a person with that history, when I hear white people talk about "the whole earth," even in a positive context, there are alarm bells going off. And this *stay hungry, stay foolish*—it's just so perfect, it assumes such a different shading if you're from a country that's been colonized. Isn't it clear that this is the logic of a swarm of locusts? *Stay hungry, stay foolish*. I don't want to put too fine a point on it, but what this really is, is the voice of blind, endless consumption, a consumption that doesn't care who it rolls over and destroys. In my book, I have a character rephrase *stay hungry, stay foolish* as *Remain ignorant of all your hunger makes you do*. And the whole earth, that's what it has to be—the whole thing, *everything* has to be consumed, that's the logic of capitalism, and that's the same logic that's accelerated by the internet.

So it sounds like you're pessimistic when it comes to the growth of the internet.

Of course! We have to be pessimistic. But you know, there's also hope. I'm from the Philippines, and the founding father of the country is a revolutionary writer—a novelist, I don't think there's any other country where that's the case. I should say that this is canonical, if contested—some intellectuals today would say someone like Bonifacio was the true bearer of the revolutionary spirit. Be that as it may. Rizal, he learned to rebel because of the same global colonial networks that were oppressing him. I recommend a book, a very good book, Benedict Anderson's *Under Three Flags*—it's a book about Rizal and the Philippines and worldwide anticolonial revolution, and Anderson talks about how Rizal met revolutionaries from Cuba and other colonized powers, and they learned to resist together. There's a part in my book—and I feel like I'm overexplaining things here, but since *The Subversive* is no longer available, I hope that's okay. There's a part in *The Subversive*—the title comes from Rizal, from his second novel, *El Filibusterismo*, and there's a part in Rizal where his greatest character, a revolutionary and con artist named Simoun—he wears blue-tinted glasses and deals in gems and jewelry, he's an adviser to the governor general of the Philippines, he's just incredibly cool—this character, after traveling around the world, he comes to a provincial town and he's showing off his wares from a box he has with him, and he keeps opening drawers and compartments in the box, revealing better and better gems, jewelry that's more and more rare, necklaces of Cleopatra's he said were discovered in the pyramids, and rings of Roman senators and knights, found in the ruins of Carthage, and you realize that this impossible box must be honeycombed with secret drawers and compartments. And I would say that it suggests that Filipinos can be very good at that thing—secret compartments.

So any time you're colonizing people, you're also sowing the seeds of your own demise?
That sounds like a bit of Marx. Which I of course approve of. And I'd say yes, you certainly could be sowing those seeds. You're sowing those seeds, if people learn how to respond. You know—and this is another kind of writing—the first major global computer worm, ILOVEYOU, was written in the Philippines.

And you see an analogy there?
Well, I would say that between Rizal and the author of ILOVEYOU, you can't tell a Filipino that writing doesn't matter. Writing can change things. Of course, that connection is somewhat tenuous. You have to separate between the Spanish colonial period and the American colonial period. In the Spanish period, people were deliberately kept from the Spanish language. In the American period, English was forced on them. All this is common knowledge to some. So the dynamics were quite different, and Rizal, you know, he's read in English in the Philippines, not in Spanish. What you have to understand, what it's very hard for Americans to understand, is colonial power. And the system that the Philippines has been brought into, this whole process, it's a colonial process. And the internet—if you want to talk Marx—it's dialectical. It's both produced by the economic conditions, and it produces them. In the Philippines, you have a country that went from a hacienda-based, big-house oligarchic system to a period of postcolonial economic nationalism when the country attempted to integrate

itself into the world-system on its own terms, and failed—or lost. Manufacturing was stifled, ultimately, by international markets. The primary exports became not things but people—a distributed system of labor under Marcos, in which the country became reliant on remittances, people working abroad, so-called Overseas Filipino Workers, sending money home. The Philippines would make larger and larger financial bets on this distribution, relying not on labor at home but on remittance flows, bundled and sold . . . And so we have a situation where the Philippines provides labor to the world, and acts as a connector between power centers. This is nothing new: the twenty-first century runs through the Philippines. The revolutionary moment at the end of the nineteenth century, when the revolutionary spirit and tactics in the Philippines spread to other countries across the world. The anti-insurrection tactics of colonial powers—waterboarding was practiced here by the US extensively, and you can draw a line from there to the Iraq war. At the beginning of the twentieth century, Manila became the final link in the round-the-world telegraph, and one hundred years later, ILOVEYOU was the first ultramassive computer worm, also linking the world. For all that time, forces of global connection and disruption have been originating or running through the islands, and that is why I say that the world as we know it today runs through or is disrupted in or by the Philippines.

These technological forces, you also write about how they've disrupted our perception of time. There's a striking section that almost sits apart from the rest of the narrative, called "Notes for a Philosophy of Time."

I don't think of it as "apart from." For me, that's the center of the whole thing.

What will your next writing project be?

I am 90 percent sure that I'm done with fiction.

No! You're just getting famous. Whatever's going on with *The Subversive*, surely people would be interested in the second.

We'll see. I think that I may have said what I need to say. Writing is hard, and ultimately, I'm lazy in certain ways.

I understand that in real life you're a network engineer. Have you had to face down any hackers in that capacity?

Well, I won't answer that question directly. I'll just say that I am very happy with my job, but it is not one that will make headlines. I do back-office networking for a fast food chain based in the Bay Area. I run their intranet and do basic IT.

What do you hope for the future of the internet?

Well, this is a question of great interest for our species, one that my novel was curious about, and I think the question is something like: Where does the internet stop, when is it enough? You see that with the internet of things. Millions of new connected devices. And the significance is not the objects themselves, the things being connected. The objects are in a sense mere pretexts, conduits through which the force and essence of the internet moves and exercises its power. Again, it is not the space of freedom that it was once billed as—that was itself already controlled and regimented in the '90s, and then since that time, there's been a mass consolidation of the experience of the internet in the hands of a few sites. Facebook, Amazon, et cetera. So I hope that people become more mindful of that.

I have to ask. Are you Birdcrash?

Of course I'm not.

Any last words for Birdcrash or any members of the nonfiction Aviary?

None whatsoever.

The morning of the eighth day the ambitious young man walked me to a room with a desk and phone and several filing cabinets. A guard indicated for me to sit at the desk, and as soon as I touched the seat, the phone rang.

It was Galloway. He sounded abrupt and hearty and frightened.

Galloway said that he understood that I'd been inconvenienced, and that everyone was grateful for my patience.

They've asked me, he said, to express to you that your cooperation is important to our project. It is very important for the *New York Times* and for both of our jobs that you be frank with them. They've also asked me to explain that it's not a confidentiality situation. With old sources. Not in the new world.

When the old world blows up, I said. Then the old confidentiality agreements are nullified.

Something like that.

I'm not protecting anyone. I've told them what I know.

They need to understand your relationship to Sebastian de Rosales.

There is absolutely nothing I haven't told them. He was an internet person of considerable interest for a while. I set up an interview with him via email. I did the interview in person at a café in San Francisco. We spoke. There was a profile in the magazine, and the full interview was made available online. The interview as posted was essentially our whole talk.

Was there anything in the interview that wasn't included?

Edited for length, no big crazy revelations.

Did you ever speak to him after that interview? Think. This is important. Emails, social media, whatever.

We talked for an hour, a little more. There were follow-up questions, maybe three or four emails. I may have emailed him a link to the interview when it ran, I don't remember. That's it. I am interested in getting to Prospect Park. I will burn whoever I need to to get there. That is a promise to you and whoever is listening in on this call.

Galloway thanked me and hung up. Ten minutes later he called back.

They're going to take you to the place they've got de Rosales. A prison. They'd like you to talk to him.

I told him thanks but no. They surely had people better equipped to talk to him. I said that if there was information they needed to get from him, they must have had ways of getting it.

Well that's the thing, they're trying, but he's dying of radiation poisoning, and he won't talk. He's very ill. He might die any day. You've talked to him before, maybe you'll have better results.

I'm sorry. It's either Prospect Park or send me back to the Foshay. I think I'm just going to go back to being a Foshay person.

That's no longer possible.

Make it possible.

There was a pause. The Foshay Tower is no longer in government hands.

What does *that* mean?

I'm afraid that's all I can say.

The phone began to shake in my hand. I pressed it against my face. I said, You're not serious. This is a tactic. You're trying to get me to talk to de Rosales.

It's not a tactic. It's good you weren't there.

What happened to the people?

We don't know. *I* don't know. All I know is it's not a place people can go right now and it's good you weren't there.

What the fuck, Tom.

I know.

126

Okay, I said. Okay. I'll do it if they take me to Dominique and Verena.

Hold on, he said. I heard a muffled exchange, Galloway and someone else. He got back on the line. He said, De Rosales comes first. He's here, he's on the West Coast, afterward, they'll fly you to New York. And one more thing—if he is Birdcrash, there's a way to prove it. Birdcrash left an encrypted Pastebin document on 1/28. They need the password.

So what is it? I see him and I go to Prospect Park? Or I have to get this password?

Get the password. Think of it as the password to Prospect Park.

He said, Just do your best.

Sebastian de Rosales turned the title over in his mouth. *The Subversive*, he said. *The Sub-verrrrr-sive.*

I was led through door after door to get to him, down staircases and cinder-block corridors painted institutional yellows and grays. I felt the heft of all those doors accrete within me, all those points that could stop you getting back to where you'd come from. I had a sense of one-way burrow—that I was not only lost, but deeply lost, positioned in a trap within a trap within a trap, and the only way out was to keep going deeper.

Here in the final room there was a mirror across one wall, a chair, a standing lamp, and a hospital bed with a small, emaciated man in it.

I had thought I knew who was in control, what I was doing here, but I held the bag with my notes, and wondered.

He had been at this location for nine days, according to the Office of Communication Oversight. In other words, ever since I had found the quotes from *The Subversive*.

When I interviewed him in 2015, de Rosales and I had met at a café on the Mission. He had worn a white shirt, tapered and pleated burgundy pants, and dark brown leather sandals without socks. He had a tattoo of a burning ship on his forearm. His hair had been up in a man bun. He drank a matcha latte.

Now, in the prison, he was greatly changed. He was around my age, almost forty, but his skin had become withered and drawn, and his silver-streaked dark hair seemed shocked by, flung out from, his golden, drifting eyes—he was deep in radiation sickness, his pupils floating under a layer of gold, almost completely occluded.

Sebastian, I said. I told him my name and reminded him where we had met.

After a time, he turned his head my way. He spoke slowly and without connection between thoughts.

The world around us was gone, it was just the two of us in the room, and I was losing the plot, I didn't know who controlled anything, if he had stood up and walked out and left me locked there in his place, I would have thought *Yes, this is what is happening.*

If they had brought me here to be tortured and murdered by him, if he had tools at his disposal, if hurting the woman who had found him was the cost of his cooperation, I would have thought *Yes, this, of course this.*

He said that everything that happens, happens twice.

He said that death is followed by a dream of death.

Maybe it's a simulation, he said, maybe it's that.

I could not tell how much of the disjunction in his speech was willful, how much involuntary, a mind actively evading questions or simply carried along the currents of cognitive loss.

I thought about Prospect Park, tried to remember its contours, where the fields were.

Sebastian, I said, it's very important that we talk about *The Subversive.*

The Subversive is divided into four parts. The first part begins in a classroom in an unnamed city in the Philippines, where the narrator, ten-year-old Benjie, begins to shake. It seems to be coming from inside him—he believes that he is being visited by the Holy Spirit, or dying, or both. Then he sees the nun pitch over her desk and curse. A seriocomic scene follows: the nuns telling children to keep calm, be orderly, get into line, get onto the stairs going down, reciting Hail Marys—nuns leading their students in prayer in strident, drill-sergeant voices, the various nuns and various classrooms staggered, waveforms of prayer falling further and further out of phase as the prayer loops, nuns seeming almost to compete with each other, leading the children in tones of barely controlled fury at what the Blessed Virgin has allowed, *Mary* and *grace* and *thee* and *thou* almost shouted, nuns dragging their lines down the stairs two or three classrooms at a time, children clogged and tripping even as the stairs themselves roll in waves—and it is as if the school is on the back of a great bird that is flying away. Later, Benjie helps his aunt and uncle and cousins clean up the spilled merchandise at their sari sari store—jars and bottles have been smashed, the floor is sticky with orange soda—and on the TV, there are people in other neighborhoods that have been squished in collapses. Benjie has never seen anything like it. They've been squished! he says. He says, Ewwwww! His cousins shout, Squished! Squished! And his aunt sends him to his room. But he isn't joking: he saw them, they had been squished, the meat and organs of them squished, and now they're dead.

A few days later, a balikbayan box arrives from his mother in the US: clothes and imported candy for him and his aunt—two giant Toblerones—and in a wrapped package labeled *For Benjie*, a Nintendo. His aunt sets up the video game system in the back of the store, and she charges five pesos a head for boys to sit in back and play it. The boys will remain in front of the screen in a small shifting group all afternoon, day after day. They are playing *Super Mario Bros.*, and they are in the infinite loop of Negative World. Benjie is older than his three cousins; he tends the store while his aunt is gone. Sometimes he takes a few pesos from the register. He has a ceramic statue of the Virgin Mary with a red felt bottom that peels off, and he can hide bills in it.

Benjie teaches all of the boys how to get into the glitch level that is Negative World by crouching on the pipe at the end of 1-2, jumping and sliding over—it is deeply frustrating to get there, but there is nothing more satisfying than when you land right, and start to slide.

There is a way out of Negative World.

He thinks it has to do with the coins—with which ones you grab and which ones you leave as you swim through the level.

If you beat Negative World, the Nintendo company pays you a million dollars.

Later in the book, the narrator will spend some time ruminating on this question: Where did that belief come from, that you could win a million dollars? To what extent did he ever believe it? He did, in some part of him—he is sure of this—believe it. It is this belief that fuels the action of the first part of the book—he orchestrates the boys to try various strategies for beating Negative World. His aunt is pleased with the money they bring in, and the candy that they purchase, and she gives him more responsibility, leaves him in charge for a longer amount of time.

But one day, his aunt discovers the stolen money (he is not the first person to hide bills in a statue of the Virgin) and as punishment, she sells the Nintendo to the parents of another boy down the street. She is tired of having all these boys hanging around in her store anyhow. That boy's mother sets up a similar situation, but the boys have lost their belief in Negative World and the million dollars, they just play the game like anyone would. Benjie and his cousins can't play it anymore. Why would I give you money for that? his aunt says. His cousins beg her. She tells them to get the money from Benjie. He is a thief. Who knows how much money he has stashed around?

He tells the other boy, the boy who now has the Nintendo, that he has learned how to beat Negative World—his mother has a friend in America who works at Nintendo. Benjie says that he won't tell the boy, though, not unless the boy promises to split the million with him. Benjie gets 75 percent, that's only fair. The boy does not think that it's fair. At last they agree, they will split fifty-fifty. Benjie says there's a chip—a simple rectangular black chip. It lifts right off. If you take it out and turn it around, rotate it 180 degrees, and replace it, then you can beat Negative World. It's the biggest chip, and you have to use a little force but then it lifts right off.

The next day his aunt slaps his face.

You convinced that stupid boy to break the Nintendo?

It is not my fault he is stupid.

You are both such stupid boys. Susmariosep! Now his mother is telling me to give her her money back or get a new Nintendo! Where am I supposed to get a Nintendo? Where do I get the money? Do you have the money? You had better write to your mother and get the money.

The truth is, he does have just enough money, hidden in the spine of a Bible that sits on the shelf downstairs. He thinks: All his aunt wants is the money. She won't care where he got it. That is what aunts want. They just want money.

His mother is in Minneapolis, where she works as a nurse for him and his future, working herself to death for him, she tells him every month or two when she calls.

He won't call her for this.

The next day he gives his aunt the bills.

She counts the money.

She tells him that he is not living under this roof anymore—his mother can take him, or he can live on the street. She won't have a liar and a thief living here with her children.

In part 2 of the novel, Benjie goes to the United States, where calamity descends almost immediately. He is never able to quite untangle it, and he doesn't feel he can ask his stepfather which came first: the marriage, or her lung cancer diagnosis. There is a photo of the three of them, after the ceremony in their backyard (his stepfather isn't a Catholic, and there's no time to make him one, so it can't be a church wedding, which Benjie is told not to tell anyone back home), and his mother looks beautiful. She poses, hip out, head back, long dark hair suspended straight down from her angled head, in a short, shiny blue dress and heels with buckles with shining blue and silver gems. His stepfather wears a brown suit. Benjie wears silver pleated pants, a white shirt, and a silver bow tie. His mother nods approvingly at the photo when it comes in (she is happy with the photos as long as she looks good, the lighting is okay, and it's her good side): she says, You know, Benjie, how you look in this photo? You look *pensive*.

This is a word that she uses over and over to describe him in the coming months, always with a little flourish, as though she's just plucked it out of the air (You know how you look? . . . *pensive*), and he comes to dread it. He is embarrassed for her—it is a vocabulary word she picked up somewhere, and it is overly mannered like her shoes and her lipstick. He hates himself for thinking this. Perhaps he is pensive, if it means a bad kid, ungrateful. And things are moving quickly. Within a year she is dead, and he and his stepfather are left together, baffled and a bit shy, moving through the house like two boys stuck together in a house without parents. They eat in front of a television playing *Star Trek: The Next Generation* or *MacGyver*. On TV commercials, people open a can of Coke and money pops out. People buy a car and they get a "cash back rebate"—stacks of bills are ejected from the AC vents and the glove compartment and ashtray, the new owners gasping in delight. There is an arcade that Benjie's stepfather has taken him to that ejects long strands of red tickets from the Skee-Ball machine. His stepfather encourages him to get a prize, a pencil topper or an action figure, but Benjie carefully hoards the tickets. He wants the top prize, a television of his own.

His mother had insisted that he call his stepfather Dad. Now that she's gone, that has fallen away, but Benjie does not know what to call him, and it seems that this is at the root of their problems—he finds it embarrassing to talk to the man he lives with, because he doesn't have a name. He has heard other children call their stepparents by their first name, but the idea is so wild, so altogether out of the question, that it might be a custom of alien beings. At night sometimes he hears her saying, *I worked myself to death for you.*

His first week in America, they all went out for Arby's. They ate it in the car, driving out to a lake. Benjie threw his wrapper and cup out the car window on the highway. His stepfather yelled at him: What the hell are you doing?

His mother shouted back, He doesn't know! She explained that in the Philippines, sometimes people just throw their trash, no big deal. She tells him not to do that anymore, but she's laughing as she says it. Benjie at first has a hard time quite believing the prohibition, and he tries it again the next day: his stepfather pulls over to the shoulder of the highway: this is as angry as he will ever see him: his face is bright red. It's a $100 ticket, he says. And more than that, it's wrong.

You need to get this straight, right now. We don't litter! Do you want to be a litterbug? It's disgusting. It's primitive. I'm sure the Philippines are wonderful, but welcome to civilization.

Benjie watches *Star Trek* and reads Dragonlance books.

He likes Data and he likes Raistlin. They both have gold skin.

They don't fit in. Data is very quick at calculations, but humans don't relate to him. Raistlin is more powerful than anyone: he controls magic that will be able to destroy the world. He has a delicate stomach, he eats bread dipped in a few drops of red wine. Data has a daughter, but she dies. In another episode, a new life form is created in the holodeck when the computer is told to make a being smarter than Data. When Raistlin sees people through his hourglass eyes, he sees them dying, their skin withering away.

Every morning Benjie eats white rice and four microwave sausage patties. He drinks a glass of SunnyD. He is gaining weight. His stepfather sets him up with computer games. He is a network engineer, he shows him how to access bulletin boards. He stands with his hands in his pockets watching Benjie at the computer, then goes into his bedroom and closes the door.

Benjie likes the computer, but doesn't like to be in the house. He often goes to a park and sits on a swing or walks in the woods. There are things under pieces of wood when you turn them over, ants and grubs and beetles. In the woods one day he meets a boy, who invites him back to his house to play. He and Benjie take their bikes there. They're playing with two yardsticks and a tennis ball. He has seen other boys' places before, and they all have plastic bats, plastic toys—real toys. This is something different. The boy is poor. He is in a low house that doesn't have aluminum siding like the other houses, it is wood, and the paint is bad. After a while playing (he can't remember the game, the game itself never really coalesces . . .), the boy's father is there, and he tells them to come to the toolshed. He turns a padlock on the door, entering the combination—Benjie tries to look, but it moves too fast. It smells inside like paint and rot and something warm and sweet. There is a wheelbarrow hung on the wall, and saws, and hammers, and a screwdriver set: the wood there is full of holes in neat—he wonders what the word is—grids? If you drew vertical and horizontal lines between the holes, they would be grids. The father has a calendar on the wall. There are women in it without shirts. They have big tits with nipples on them. Do you like this? The father asks. I bet you like this. The other boy is gone now, it is just the two of them, he has been maneuvered, he is sitting, in fact, on a lawn chair next to the man, and their knees are touching. It might be an accident—it is just how the chairs are—he is looking over his left shoulder at the grids, the tools there. He feels the man's hand touch his chair, the armrest—and like it's nothing, like he's not even in the chair, the man pulls Benjie's chair so that they are next to next and the sides of their legs are touching.

A month later, Benjie sees the man again. He's walking to the 7-Eleven when the car pulls up beside him. The man tells him to get in. Benjie can't move. The man talks to him, and Benjie is able to move at last, but only into the car.

In part 3, Benjie is older, he's gone away to college at USC, where he is studying computer science and engineering. It opens with him watching the movie *Anak* in a class on Southeast Asian cinema. It's the story of an OFW, an Overseas Filipino Worker, a mother who's taken a job as a nanny for a wealthy Hong Kong family, leaving three children behind with her husband, who is killed years later in a workplace accident, leading to her return. He does not feel much of anything, but he wishes his mother was there to watch it with him—he thinks that he would like to watch her feel something, watching it. He would like to see her cry. She went away when he was one, and then he had her for another year at the end of her life, and apart from a few visits, that's all he got. He would like to ask her why. He doesn't think that the money is enough. He would like to understand it, he would like for some kind of understanding to emerge. He would like for her to weep and hold him and beg forgiveness. He gets hung up on a scene where the mother buys a Kermit the Frog stuffed toy—a big one, two or three feet in length or height—it flops around, neither length nor height seem quite accurate. It is clearly unlicensed, a knockoff. The proportions are wrong, it seems like someone's bad idea of Kermit, a cheap idea of him, which is what it is—and he thinks, *I* can see this, the characters in the movie, they can't. They don't see that it's unlicensed. I see that. He knows if his mother were alive, she would not have looked at the Kermit and understood that it was a knockoff, or why it mattered. And he finds himself flushing with shame at his dead mother for her not knowing, and at himself for thinking this thought.

At USC, Benjie also meets Jon Postel, who runs the Internet Assigned Numbers Authority and was the editor of RFCs (Requests for Comments), thousands of documents going back decades that describe the protocols on which the internet is based. Postel is a big deal, one of the grand old men of the internet, Walt Whitman beard, a serious *aura* around him and his office at USC's Information Sciences Institute in Marina del Rey. There was no chance for a freshman to meet him or study with him, but Benjie became quietly obsessed with him, reading RFC after RFC, spending hours lurking in the ISI, and finally he hacked Postel. He wrote a few lines of BASH that he slipped into Postel's .profile on the main server. Every 300 to 1500 seconds, the script would flip Postel's keyboard mapping to Flemish and back. Postel could be heard cursing in his office, for days, and then one day he started to laugh. He stalked out into the hallway, shouting, Okay, who did it? Who did it? And Benjie was there, he was on the floor, he stepped in front of Postel, his whole body trembling.

You? Postel said. He spoke matter-of-factly, without anger, with a mild curiosity.

I'm a student. Benjie could barely speak—the words were stuck in his mouth. I wanted to meet you. I only had it do it for two to eight seconds at a time.

Only two to eight seconds at a time. He seemed mildly amused, wavering on the edge of something. Why don't you help me make up for some of the time you've wasted. Your first job is to figure out how to distribute IP addresses to Central Asia. Do you think you can handle that? Or are you just here to make my life worse, two to eight seconds at a time?

Benjie becomes wrapped up in Postel's unfolding struggle for control of the DNS system. He takes a world literature class where he reads José Rizal's *Noli Me Tangere*, and on his own he reads

Rizal's second and final novel, *El Filibusterismo*. He befriends another student, Apolinario, who is involved in WTO protests.

This part culminates on 1/28, when Postel grabs control of the root authority for the internet, a watershed moment in internet history. However, the authority claimed by him on behalf of the small group of technocratic elites who had always run the internet is superseded by new, global concerns, the stakeholders. By the end of the year, Postel is dead.

If the book had ended there, it seems unlikely that it would have had much of a life after the initial, modest round of attention (a pair of mixed prepublication trade reviews; no national or regional print reviews; and a smattering of online mentions). It was published by short-lived Nebraska micropress Cyber Prairie Books, the second of four titles the press released before folding only a year after its launch.

However, in part 4 of the book, the form changes radically. There is no longer the attention to psychological realism and to the story of Benjie. Instead, we have short chapters, philosophical or ranting, taking on a diverse array of subjects, including:

ILOVEYOU, a computer worm that originated in the Philippines and infected tens of millions of computers across the world;

the first cable to go around the word, which was sent by Theodore Roosevelt, on completion of the transpacific cable to Manila;

a riff on how Magellan was killed in 1521 in his attempted circuit of the globe, and now, almost four hundred years later, the cable was completing his mission;

a massacre of the Moro people in the Philippines in 1906, about which Teddy Roosevelt sent a congratulatory telegram to the general in charge: *I congratulate you and the officers and men of your command upon the brilliant feat of arms wherein you and they so well upheld the honor of the American flag*;

a long riff on the *Whole Earth Catalog*, a counterculture magazine that inspired a generation of those who would transform the computer industry;

an explanation of the inverted tree structure of the DNS;

a quote from a newspaper documenting the fact that the trans-pacific cable had a section welded from the great electrical circuits of history, the very wires used by Samuel F. B. Morse and Alexander Graham Bell; a section of Atlantic cable laid by Cyrus W. Field, through which the first cable message was sent across the ocean; a piece of wire over which Thomas Edison lit the first incandescent bulb ever lighted from a central station, and another through which the current of electricity was sent by President Grover Cleveland when he opened the World's Fair at Chicago;

the creation and control of country code top-level domains across the third world;

a contextless quote, *Later, three Colt "potato-digger" machineguns with 8,300 .30 caliber rounds were added to the mix; one manned by a nine-man Army crew and the other two by eleven sailors from the gunboat USS Pampanga. Supporting were three surgeons and seven hospital-corpsmen, five Signal Corps, six HQ, and 150 mules driven by American civilian packers. A composite company of approximately 40 men were held in reserve in Jolo, but never called upon*—the end result of the battle was a one-sided, nearly complete massacre of the seven hundred to nine hundred defenders (two-thirds of whom were women and children);

a ten-page riff on history, temporality, and repetition, "Notes for a Philosophy of Time," that begins with the beheading in the third century of two men who would be made saints, and ends with the death in 2012 of Lonesome George, the last living Pinta Island tortoise, the end of a species;

and the creation of a hacker group called the Aviary, a group that is behind an escalating series of attacks, including data thefts, hacks of government and military websites, a DDoS attack on Amazon that takes the site down for the better part of an hour, and, finally, a Stuxnet-style attack on a nuclear power plant located twenty miles from Loudoun County, Virginia, in which the country's internet architecture—or vast parts of it—writhe.

It becomes clear only at the end of the book that the narrator of section 4 is Apolinario from the previous section, and that he and Benjie have founded the Aviary.

This still was not particularly remarkable, except: a year after the book was published in 2015, a hacker group—not in the book, but in the real world—released the credit card information for half a million MasterCard holders.

The group that posted the data called themselves the Aviary.

The Aviary—the real-world version of the group—would go on to claim responsibility for a number of actions, including crashing government websites in the Philippines, the US, Slovenia, and Mexico; a DDoS attack on GoDaddy; doxing of hundreds of alleged creators and traders of child pornography; the attempted defense of an uncontacted individual in the Amazonian rainforest; bringing down the SpaceX rocket with the Facebook satellite on it (this, in particular, is disputed by both Mark Zuckerberg and Elon Musk, who attributed the crash to a technical failure); and replacing the home page of the United States Air Force with their own logo, a bird, wings extended, with one leg removed, and the motto *fractus dominium*, broken power.

That logo was the same employed by the group in the novel, and while there may have been differences between the fictional group and its real-world counterpart—this became the subject of online debate—the philosophy underpinning them was, at least ostensibly, the same, and went back to the Aviary in the book, RFC 1149, IP over Avian Carriers.

The internet allows for communication between different types of networks, as long as they use the protocols that govern the internet. RFC 1149, published on April 1, 1990, presents a scenario in which data packets are carried on a pigeon's leg. There was obvious humor in mixing the anachronistic homing pigeon technology with the internet. But the author also pointed out that it would allow the internet access to places where other communication technologies couldn't reach. Where there are no wires, no satellites, even there the birds can fly.

The Aviary was ostensibly formed in resistance to this: the logo of the one-legged bird symbolized an animal who would not be part of the system: the information-carrying leg was sacrificed in order to resist what the Aviary called the totalizing power of the internet.

The growth of the internet had been, as the Aviary saw it, a project of colonialism and control that had been ushered in under false pretenses: the initial drivers of what we now know as the internet (survivability of communication or the sharing of resources between research institutions, depending on who you asked—always that tension between the military applications and a beneficent increase in knowledge in the fight for the story of the internet, and some truth in both directions) had seemed clear positives. If survivability of communication infrastructures reduced the odds of a first strike wiping out the entire command and control of the US government, then that reduced the chance of a first strike happening at all. A system of packet-switched, distributed communications—where a message was cut up into pieces and sent through multiple nodes to its destination, where the pieces were reassembled—allowed for this.

But it also meant no limit to the ground the technology might cover—an address space that was created in 1980 with over 4.3 billion addresses was not enough—not enough for all of our computers, phones, and devices. And so a new space with 80 million billion billion times the capacity was created.

The Aviary wanted to stop the internet from "totalizing"—from taking over every scrap of the known world. They thought we needed to scale back the internet, to slow and eventually reverse its growth.

The internet's freedom was illusory, and if drastic action wasn't taken, the internet would lead us into a situation of mass control, if not, indeed, the end of the world.

The birds, they believed in the birds, one leg amputated, resistant to all protocols of the internet, no IP, no DNS, just birds flying free, one leg lost.

I had been with Sebastian for an hour or more, and I had nothing. I moved the lamp, I tipped it over the bed, turned up the shade so all of its light was directed at his golden eyes.

I thought that the guards would come for me. I touched his face and turned it to the light.

He smiled vaguely. He said, What type of bulb? It's Edison. One of those bulbs in hipster bars.

I told him that he was correct.

I can't really see, but I feel it, the quality of the light.

Do you remember when we spoke? I was with *TechMinder* then.

Who are you with now?

New York Times Magazine.

They still have that? That's very nice.

Mr. de Rosales, I know that even when I spoke with you, you felt very passionately about the growth of the internet, and resisting the internet's colonial tendencies.

He released an acrid, wheezing laugh.

Resist! he said. Resist! Hashtag resist. Were you a member of the *hashtag resistance*?

Under Trump?

Yes, under Trump.

Well, there were policies for journalists at some of the places where I freelanced. But no . . . I don't think that anyone would have considered me a member of the resistance, hashtag or otherwise.

You just let it happen?

I did what I felt like it was possible for me to do. I wrote about net neutrality, the spread of fake news, Cambridge Analytica. I covered stories in the Trump era.

So you just let it happen.

You think I should have marched more? You think that would have made a difference?

I think that someone should have done something . . . more.

Then he began to drift, to make sounds . . . he said *resist* again, and laughed.

When he woke next, I said: Birdcrash.

His face looked as though it had been slapped.

You're Birdcrash, I said.

I'm *not*, he said, with something like disgust.

I see, I said. You're not, are you. You know who is.

They've been interrogating me for days with more at their disposal than you've got.

Okay, I can see this is useless.

I agree.

There's one more question, not about this. One I'm just personally interested in.

A last question, he said.

Why did you get in the car?

What car?

With the man who molested you.

Sebastian tensed in the bed.

I said, I assume it was flawed writing. First book. Maybe a mistake in the plot. It didn't make much sense.

It was an ugly thing to say. Sebastian rolled his head to one side and he shivered. I wanted to take his hand, to apologize, to withdraw the question. Instead I looked down at him, thinking of Prospect Park, thinking of the password, and I sat very still.

He said, It wasn't a mistake. It happened. He pulled over. He just kept talking. He asked me why I was looking at him like that— did he remind me of someone? He said whoever I reminded him of, that man must have been a bad man who had done something wrong to me. He told me to get in the car, we'd find him, and we'd make sure that that never happened again.

Why didn't you put it in the book?

I couldn't write it! Listen to how crazy that sounds—I couldn't make it seem true! And even at the time, I couldn't believe it, it seemed like a dream. I knew it was him. But also another part of me said no, it's not him. Getting in there, I could prove it, I could fix it, I could erase what had happened, if I just did what the man said and got in the car. And then I was in. The locks—automatic locks, they popped down, and then went back up. Sorry, the man said, and I remember that he giggled. I knew it was him, but I was also sure it wasn't. I was just a kid. I was from another country. I was ashamed. You weren't supposed to question adults. But then we were driving, and everything was out of my control.

I reached out and took his hand through the blanket. He didn't move it away.

I said, People liked Birdcrash because he took on the people who preyed on children. He wouldn't let them get away with it.

Yes, that was a reason that some people liked him. He let out a breath, a rattling whimper from somewhere in his chest. All right, he said. All right.

When did you meet?

He found me just before our interview—a week or so before that.

You worked on BIND in '99. Did you give Birdcrash some information that he used in the attack?

People think there's nothing they can do, and it seems that there really isn't, but there's people, people at various points in the system—he wheezed, and then under his breath he whispered— who can do something.

What did you tell him?

Sebastian turned on his side, away from me. I need to go to sleep now. Jesus Christ will you people let me die!

I remember you said, Stay hungry, stay foolish: it's the logic of a plague of locusts. The BIND attack slowed them, didn't it? It slowed the locusts down.

They eat everything up. If someone wants to stop that, or slow it down, that's not a bad thing. Remember, C is a language so obscure that there is an annual obfuscation contest, where people write code whose intent will be opaque even to the most sophisticated programmers—if they were that good, they might put in a back door, one that you could kick open by, say, searching three unusual terms in a row.

Why would you do that?

Hmm, he said. One wants to resist. Tell me, he said, you said you didn't march? Against Trump?

I did actually.

You marched in the marches? You wore a pussy hat?

I told him that I had.

He smiled in a sort of abstracted blissful pain. He said that Americans were so dumb. He asked why I had worn it—the pussy hat. He said, You were . . . resisting?

I told him the truth, which is that I hadn't liked the pussy hats. My wife, I said. She bought them for the three of us—my daughter came to the parade, too. I tried to beg off, I couldn't wear it.

I told him the story, and I felt my voice growing sharp. I wanted to take the pillow that was under his head and press it to his golden face, but I let the story happen.

Dominique put the pussy hat on my head when we joined the parade. Come on, she said. You're so worried about authority.

I told her there were policies against it from the *Times* and other people I worked for.

They're going to blacklist you? Dominique said, mockingly.

I told her it wasn't about that. It was disrespectful. To them— what if a picture of me showed up? It wasn't giving Trump the bird. It was giving my editors the bird.

I said this, I told Sebastian, but I didn't believe it, really.

And our daughter Verena marched between us.

Pulling off the hat felt so good. It felt like I had won, holding my pussy hat in my hand, then pushing it balled up into my coat pocket, leaving my other hand free, feeling the pussy hat in my pocket while I took my daughter's hand with the other.

I said, Sebastian, the truth is, I hated that pussy hat, and I was thinking about that in the parade. I was looking at the other pink-hatted women—white women taking selfies, white and pink, this massive intersectional failure—it was the other white women I was so furious at. And then I'd turn back to them, to my wife, my kid, and feel good about them, and feel good about the movement, and at the same time I felt so righteous, keeping that hat in my pocket.

I had tried to argue with her the night before that pink was wrong, because—and I paused. She said, Because my pussy isn't pink? Because not all pussies are pink? Because you read that on Twitter, and now that's your excuse? My pussy is not pink. And the movement can sort that out later. But tomorrow we'll march. The hats are the fucking hats. For tomorrow, they're the hats.

My wife is chanting and holding my daughter's hand, and my daughter is looking around at all the signs and she's just heard what happened, and I take her hand. I say, because of my job, I can't hold a sign or wear a hat, but I'm so glad to be here with you today.

And I'm holding her hand and Dominique holding her other, and Dominique says, It's okay if your mother's a wet blanket! She has to be! It's her job! We'll be the revolutionaries!

A wave of chanting sweeps up to us: this is what democracy looks like. Verena exhilarated but frightened. The signs with curse words and body parts and the chanting and the anger and force of will out there.

Are you feeling it? Dominique asks. Are you experiencing it?

Verena nods happily, and then tugs my hand. She says, Are you experiencing it?

And I feel how not into it I am—how my hand is communicating that, and why should that be communicated to her, to my daughter, when objectively, the revolutionary spirit is what should be instilled in her, and my wife is the one giving it, and I'm giving something else, just giving her worry.

So, I say to Sebastian, no, I wasn't so good at the hashtag resistance.

Sebastian said, You want your body to be both counted among them and kept wholly separate.

Sebastian said, You want the movement without the display. And ultimately you have to take the movement, flaws and all, or you stay at home and feel worse.

Did they die? Sebastian said.

They died, I said.

When you said it was an Edison bulb in here, were you telling the truth?

Yes.

Are these the last lightbulbs left? Is this what they're down to?

Maybe. I don't know. It could be they're the easiest to produce.

Sebastian said, CFLs in the hallway. Fluorescent in the infirmary. And this here. It draws a lot of power. So they're down to the scraps. Or they're making them again and this is what they can make. Where are they being manufactured? What happened to the supply chain? Is this the last leftover? When it goes out, what happens here? They'll abandon the place. What about the inmates? Do they leave us screaming in the dark? Though I'll be dead before this lightbulb.

I don't know what they'll do, I said.

There's a story, though.

People keep pitching me stories. I just want to go to my wife and daughter. If I can get what they want from you, they'll let me go to see where Dominique and Verena are buried. They're in Prospect

Park. I need a password to the last Aviary Pastebin posting. It's encrypted.

I don't have a password. I'm not a part of the Aviary.

You're lying. And you're about to die.

I could give you a hypothetical about the attack. About how it happened. Would you like that, dear?

I'd like that, I said.

Sebastian said, It could have been lightbulbs that started all of this. Let's say a Chinese engineer working on the smart lightbulbs, he raises an issue about vulnerabilities, and this very smart guy who's actually doing exactly what he should be doing by pointing this out to his superiors, they're embarrassed and want him to shut up. He gets exiled to monitoring internet comments about Xi Jinping. Suddenly he's got something very valuable, and he's . . .

Disgruntled.

Hypothetically, he's *highly* disgruntled.

He might be bought.

Or even have ideological reasons to join up. With . . . whatever entity was behind the attack.

I asked him what else he thought—hypothetically—would have been part of the attack.

Tell me what you want from me. Sebastian locked me with his flat golden eyes.

I need the password to unlock the last document Birdcrash posted on Pastebin.

I'm not Birdcrash. And I don't have the password.

But you do know who he is, don't you?

I hope so. We used to date.

You helped found the Aviary.

No. I just wrote it. He made it a thing in the world. I met him after—after we talked, after it was a thing. He reached out to me.

How, how did that happen?

Sebastian patted my hand. Do you know about the loneliest man on earth?

Who is he? It was an action of the Aviary, but well after your piece, and well after the world stopped giving a damn about the Aviary and what they were doing. Attention had moved on. And they hadn't done anything in over a year, this was their last action, or it was until 1/23.

The loneliest man in the world, an uncontacted man in the Amazonian rainforest, believed to be the last of his tribe, language unknown, tribe unknown, but pressured, hunted, all alone. Occupying valuable land. He dug holes. The purpose—or purposes—of the holes was not known. Trapping animals or something religious perhaps. After he was discovered, and logging interests made concerted efforts to harass him, drive him out, even kill him, he was safeguarded by a public-private partnership, drones used by remote supporters, donors, monitored the borders of his area. The loggers got the idea, they sent in their own drones—they wanted to kill him, you understand. End the protection of this land. Birdcrash became obsessed with him, and he used the force of the Aviary to bring down these drones, sent their own drones with offensive capabilities, they used their networks to try to protect him, it became a distributed defense, but then something changed. The internet did not respond properly. The internet had no desire to protect this individual when there were lulz to be had. The mission was perverted and some wealthy white expat started helping people to equip drones for pure lulz, and the drones were no longer protecting him, they were piloted by people online who started bringing him memes by drone, laminated printouts affixed to drones, Nyan Cat, Crying Jordan, Pepe, a second drone to catch his response, and the next day it even progresses to points where the man was looking at a photo held out by a drone of Pepe riding a drone and delivering him a meme, but the heads of the two of them had been swapped.

What happened to him?

I assume he was killed. He stopped appearing on anyone's radar.

Birdcrash had good intentions.

We dated. We had some good times. He was insane. We broke up. I stopped contact with him. I wondered why I had ever gotten to know him—why I'd ever written the book. I stopped opening his emails, I blocked him where I could.

What do you mean where you could?

He still sent messages. There were the attacks. There were Pastebin postings that referenced my book. And there was the final message.

The encrypted Pastebin.

I don't know what that is. I never saw it. I'm talking about the attack.

1/28—you think that was a message for you?

No, let's say it was omnidirectional. It was a broadcast message.

I told him that he was right, it was. My family had received the message. They had taken it to their deaths.

I said, Tell me who he was.

You're ready to kill me in my bed, aren't you? You have crazy eyes, you really do. I'd let you kill me, but I think they'd stop you, and our talk would be over.

Sebastian smiled. He said, I'd like for you to be able to visit their graves. Your wife and daughter. That's a very nice idea.

The building beside the airstrip had a coffee machine that dispensed instant coffee into paper cups. It was coin operated, but the coin box was open, and four quarters lay in it. There was a sign taped to the front of it: *DO NOT USE*. And in a different color ink, scrawled below: *If you do use, do not steal the quarters*.

I saw three men get coffee, one of them twice.

I got coffee. A while later, another man came by with a sandwich for me.

You didn't take any of the quarters, did you? he asked.

No.

We need those to make the machine work.

I didn't. I raised my hands in a *what do you want* gesture.

He nodded. He said, Better safe than sorry.

Something in it, some irony verging on menace. Safe than sorry. Some inside joke I didn't have the key to. Hostility, anyhow.

Or maybe I was just tired.

I kept my mouth shut.

Better safe than sorry.

Galloway landed after dark in a C-12 Huron, empty apart from him and the flight crew. An army officer materialized, asked me to stay in my seat. He sat beside me, staring blankly ahead. Galloway was seated several banks of seats behind us. I turned and waved—too emphatically, ridiculous, like the start of a parade float wave, which I arrested instantly, and my hand was just there, up. Galloway nodded.

Please face forward, the officer said.

This is silly, I'm going to say hello to my friend. I started to stand. Or that's wrong: I did not stand, and I was not physically restrained, so it would have been more like when you are ready to leave a party and you start making testing gestures, not standing but shifting weight, positioning yourself to move, communicating intent.

But now the officer was standing: above me, looking down. He folded his arms. He said, My instructions are that you don't speak until the general is present.

And when will that be? I asked.

He sat back down, said nothing.

What general? I asked. Who are you? Where are we?

He'll get here when he gets here, he said. No more talking.

.

The general in question was the head of the Office of Communication Oversight. The man, I thought, who had been dogging us, watching us, controlling us the whole time. He was pale and bald, with a round face and broad, downturned lips. He had a gut, and his soft, deep voice seemed to rumble up from it, catching and rasping in the machinery of his throat—something choked and distressed. There was as well a high-pitched, singsong note that would break into his speech at odd moments—almost the sound of someone soothing a baby. And a hand would jump up and smooth the lapels of his jacket, or touch his throat, or just flap in the air.

We have a predicament, the general said. The car the dog caught. I understand that what was approved was a piece about *internet humor on 1/28*. I'm a bit perplexed how we got from there to, ah, a conspirator in the attacks. That wasn't the assignment, and yet here we are. And so. And so. We are placed in an odd position. I'm afraid that this information can't, we are not prepared for it to go out, and it is, ah, it is very sensitive. Very sensitive indeed. You have to excuse me, my first stop was the facility with Sebastian de Rosales, but he passed away—just a few hours after you visited, Rachel, I'm sorry to tell you. So how do we move forward? It is information of such a sensitive nature that those who have it, they would almost need to be quarantined.

Quarantined, I said.

Galloway said, I'd like to speak with my reporter alone for a few minutes. How can I talk about this when I don't know what it's about? I have been out of touch with her for almost three weeks—this is not an acceptable situation.

Well, the general said. That's also delicate. We don't want to have to quarantine *you*, Tom. Not you too, Tom, if it can be helped. As you know, I'm overseeing a number of reboots of marquee news outlets, and we're happy with what you've done. Tom, we're very happy with you, with the issue you've lined up. The piece about the endangered birds nesting in the ruins, making a comeback. The crossword puzzle. The word hunt for those less intellectually disposed, thank you for accommodating us there, Tom. The profile of the cellist playing out there in the middle of some danger—I hope I never oversee a disaster recovery where there isn't a cellist playing somewhere dangerous, what a story. You're putting together something real and worthwhile, and we don't want to jeopardize it with this sort of mess.

If Rachel found something, she'll write it up. We'll be happy to work with you to make sure that it doesn't damage security. But a true narrative of 1/28 is something we should be working toward. I don't like this word, *quarantine*. The truth isn't a sickness, Bill.

Well, Tom, that's where we part ways. The truth can be a kind of sickness, under certain circumstances. Sure it can. Or we could say that *the people, our people* are a bit sick right now, and the truth must be administered in some cases judiciously. The truth, you see, the truth is really whatever helps the system, that's what the truth is, the truth of and for the system, if you understand me. For a person who's dehydrated, one might think of intravenous fluids as having a certain truth value. A person with cancer, chemotherapy—again, that's a kind of truth. Isn't it, Tom? That's the truth we need right know. Of course the historical truth, the actual accounting of what happened on a more granular level, that *will* emerge—it's of great importance that it does, it's essential, no question—but when should it? We have built certain ideas here, around the notion that it was foreign powers that caused the internet attack. Now if it's a domestic enemy, then that means a shift of emphasis. It's still a narrative that can work. But if people have been saying foreign powers, foreign powers, and now it's this? It's not entirely flattering to the system, you see, to think it was just some kids, essentially. Now, there's the Philippines angle, that's something we can work with. A sort of hinge piece. The Philippines, I think people will remember something bad was going on there near the end, but it's a bit of a blank slate for America. It's something, at least. I've got teams who can help us figure this out. What works, though, with the nation's image of itself? That's in a sense the truth—what is real, and what the people will accept. Where those meet.

There are Filipinos living here, Galloway said.

I'm sorry?

It's not a blank slate to Filipinos. There were millions of them, surely many thousands now.

Tom, don't be so literal. Speaking of the way a nation sees itself is of course not an exact science—yes, on some literal level there are as many ways of seeing the country as there are people. There might be a, uh, a viewpoint of pansexual first-generation Finnish immigrants who work in the Forest Service that is quite distinct from this more general image I'm speaking of. Pardon me, but you know what I mean. And even in any little microgroup, division, contestation. But every nation has an idea of itself, something larger and more general, and even if we can't fully pin it down in its particulars, we know what we're talking about.

Mom and apple pie, Galloway said.

Johnny Appleseed, Apple computers, mom's apple pie with the lattice crust. You understand me, Tom. Meanwhile, out among the unregistered, there are whispers, there are low-powered radio transmitters, old-fashioned—it's really remarkable, the ingenuity—old-fashioned hand crank letterpress devices, *analog* bullshit, these really distressed and confused people who don't understand what we're doing here, or have a sense of how if they could just listen to our plans they'd find themselves in a position where they could be integrated into this new world, a world that's going to be solid and have the potential to *last*, these people—it's awful, really—circulating their own news, rumors, lies, with absolutely no standards. Do you know, they say—this is more widespread than you can imagine—they say that there's no food left anywhere, and if you register, you're actually going to be slaughtered and eaten up? That we've resorted to mass cannibalism?

Fake news, Galloway said.

Precisely.

I said, So what is the bottom line? I've been promised a trip to Brooklyn. My prize for getting Sebastian to talk.

The general pressed his fingertips together and let out a small laugh.

Well, yes. I know about that. Prospect Park. I think it's a fine idea. Something I'd like to happen. But we don't know where this is going. And we do want to reward you for your find. So. Let's table the grave stuff for a moment. We are going to take this individual that de Rosales has identified as Birdcrash into custody. We've got people watching the place now, drones out there puttering around. There's a little house—a cabin—it could be something.

The general rested his chin on his hands, elbows braced together on the desk, and smiled broadly. So, he said, that's where we are. There's a real possibility that it was de Rosales—I don't think he's as innocent as he claims. Perhaps this person is just some no one that de Rosales fingered for whatever perverse reason.

He *is* a novelist, Galloway said. He's used to lying.

The general gave Galloway a look that seemed at the point of crossing into annoyance before the grin restabilized on his face. That's right, Tom, he said.

For what it's worth, I said, I didn't have the sense that he was lying.

Thanks for that insight, Rachel. I'm very glad to hear your opinion. Because we're going to take him in, this fellow in the shack, if there really is anyone there—the heat signatures are ambiguous, I'm told—and we'd like you to come with us.

I got the information out of Sebastian. That was the deal.

Rachel, I admire you so much. You have been a wonderful help. Though technically, we asked for the password—the password to the Birdcrash document.

So what do you want?

We want you to come for a ride-along. Tom, no objections to one more assignment for Rachel? Watch our brave men pick him up. If the story gets told—and that's still an if—this will be a part of it. Rachel, Tom, I leave it to you, but I think you'll have to agree that this is a good plan. In fact, Tom, if you don't mind, I'd like to speak with Rachel alone.

After Tom had left—with a mixture of reluctance and obsequious-ness, a pain in his face and defiance, before he turned on his heel and was gone—the general said, Rachel, I'm glad we can talk one-on-one.

He said, Tom is a wonderful editor, but he is also a bit of a true believer, if you know what I mean. I feel like you're a different personality.

You feel that, I said.

So we've got you quoting Marx and bantering with one of the people who caused the end of the world.

Yes.

I've also, and this just happened to fall into my lap, just rou-tine background stuff, you know, I've got you—the general checks his notes—saying that the idea of the mass slaughter of the ultra-wealthy helps you sleep better.

I'm not sure what you're referring to.

Oh, it's right here in one of the transcripts, a journalist friend of yours, she was apparently at the *Washington Post*. You said: You hear what happened to the rich people, the billionaires, I mean the super rich, luxury custom bomb shelters and compounds and all that? And they thought they were making themselves safe. And you explained that you'd heard how there was a clamoring for these rich bunker spaces, the whole system wanted them. And then your friend asked: What happened to all those billionaires? And you said: Killed like pigs in their ultraluxury slaughterhouses. Hunted and slaughtered, or starved out, or suffocated, in the safest little crannies in their beautiful ultradeluxe bunkers. Shot or stabbed or beat to death. And your friend said—oh, this was in a discussion about how to get to sleep, did I mention that?—your friend said: And that helps? And you said: Every night. And she said: Them dying. And you said: Beats counting sheep.

What's the point? I said. If I do this, will I go to Prospect Park, yes or no?

I like you, Rachel. I think we can partner on this. You're a good writer, and I think you're a very pragmatic person. And if not . . .

What if not?

C'est la guerre.

So, Prospect Park?

The general pressed his fingertips together, then opened his hands wide. Prospect Park, he said.

We were four Humvees (one with an armored turret) and two tactical vehicles moving into undocumented space. Drones had been sent ahead of us to check for obstruction in the road. There was an arbitrary quality to the decay, what had been burned down and what remained. We passed a farm—soybeans—with several military vehicles parked outside of it.

What happened out here? I asked.

The soldier beside me said, It's fucking animals out here. They go for the farms—you have to protect those first. Do you know how hard it is to protect a whole farm from ambush? But we've got to have the farms. For civilization. And it's hard to fuck up a whole farm. A whole field. Do you know how hard it is to fuck that up without an airplane dropping a shit-ton of fire? And yet they creep in somehow and fuck it all up.

We were winding up some hills as the sun set—the roads were overrun with fallen branches or branches that had been put there. The vehicle in front of us had something like a cow catcher that knocked the debris aside. Then we were deep in the hills, and coming off the road to a long road through the trees, just two ruts. Tree branches banged against the side of the vehicle.

It should be here, the soldier said. This is where it should be.

We pulled up to a low structure—an old wooden shack—when the ground started to incline there were pipes emerging from it, and a grinding beneath us. Go! the soldier shouted.

But we were already falling—the earth beneath us dropped away, and we were crashing into a darkness.

I heard sprays of automatic gunfire, and then I was gone.

So you found us.

Through all the stuff of life, and control of life, through all the nodes that had assumed the power to give life and end it: you are here.

It's your life we have and we have it here and we won't end it, no not now.

They say we live in a universe fine-tuned for life. We say: for death.

The universe was fine-tuned for you to find us, just as it was fine-tuned for us to do all that we have done.

It's our hope that you see. To be bound up like this. It's not special. It's all of us.

Nod if you agree, Rachel.

We are not all bound up in tape and dangling from chains from the ceiling, tape over mouth, head taped and pulled back, suspended, held there with our tummies down, and yet: we are.

The universe has been fine-tuned for the internet in its forty years to set the conditions of totalization to make the world's end possible. To circumvent the controls of the bilateral mutually assured destruction through distribution, through the insertion of the network into everything.

It spread through the benevolent technocratic California hippies, through hobbyists and web commerce and great military powers.

It gamified microloans and monitored dreams, and every night it cleared fifty trillion dollars in transactions.

It would do what it needed to do, to extend itself into every corner of the globe, and then overlay those corners, further control them, subdivide them.

Did you see The Mist. *The scene in the pharmacy, the layers of webbing that overlay everything, it becomes almost a blur, a softening of edges, that overlays, that holds the humans in place.*

While great alien beasts bestride the world, and little ones, and humans hum and bicker and doubt.

Cucktards, ashtray fags. Those words, that time.

And then the wind came, the great withdrawal. Poland and Hungary and Brexit, a rush to abandon the world markets, the totalizing systems.

In the Balkans and Kosovo, teens crafted fake news and sold it here, millions of clicks worth.

And now destroyers were in charge, floor-shitters and fascists, failsons and large adult sons deconstructing the administrative state.

We think of the collision management of the ALOHAnet, the primary masters and slave servers of BIND.

We think of RFC 1149, the birds who would be made to serve, who would carry the information on their legs, through the 3-D ether space.

The universe was fine-tuned for Trump to become president, just as it was fine-tuned for him to end civilization as we had known it here on this planet, this little bit in the universe.

What you are feeling, what your body is revealing in your face, we can't tell you what to do, but we think: Don't do that.

Stop squirming. We don't like the rattling chains. We don't like them, all those chains that are rattling. We don't.

RFC 1149, IP over Avian Carriers. There is no outside to the internet. In this network of networks, even the birds will work.

We think there are parts of you fighting right now that are no longer useful parts.

And we understand. They probably protected you, when you were a child, these good parts.

And how do you feel to them.

And can you ask them to step back.

It's okay if they won't step back, but struggling now won't help, we can't give you our information while you are struggling.

Or we can, but we can't be sure that the parts that have to take it in, all the information we have in our mind, our mind free at last of the old blockages and entanglements, will be heard and processed and remembered by the parts of yours that need to do that.

But perhaps we have to simply trust those parts, yours and ours.

We wish you would take a moment to breathe, to understand your breathing.

It is not what your body's used to, being bound up in tape and suspended from the ceiling by chains, but real calm and deep breath is possible in this position.

Damage is growth, or can be. We will damage your brain so it can grow. All the tools are right here.

We have gathered birds, you see the birds throughout this room, we do operations on birds, and now on humans, on you, a human, just like we did on our own head, we'll do one. We're making an internet of birds, little wires, little chips, new protocols, new ways of being, a sort of freedom, it's all new.

Avian carriers, it was a joke, but shouldn't the internet survive us. Shouldn't it be turned over to the birds. And this time the birds lead the way. We drill into them, but only so they can lead us, and we at their service.

What will you miss. There is nothing much worth missing.

We remember Kool-Aid Man in Second Life, the toading of Dr. Jest, faggots and cucks, Shill4Hill, the collision-avoidance systems of the ALOHAnet, the shitlords of Kekistan.

We remember the blue-pilled and the red-pilled, Ivanka's side hustles, christfags and MAGA and a new home of the mind.

We remember the glorious subtweets of the deep state.

We remember . . .

We remember . . .

What do we even remember.

We remember Sebastian, our love Sebastian, the love we lost, and we remember the dead birds in our pockets.

And we remember . . .

Hum hum hum . . .

The rarest Pepes.

Yes we remember them best of all, the Pepes, the ones that were so rare, how rare they truly were, how good to be alive in a time of such rare Pepes, all of us in our places, but unseen, we and the Pepes, waiting among the weary giants of flesh and steel for the life of the world we knew was nearly here.

All that's back there somewhere and gone.

The internet was designed to survive an attack from multiple points. Nothing can survive an attack from all points at once.

Rachel, it is so good to see you.

We will drill into your head and give you the new world.

We are Birdcrash in the age of gold.

Enveloped in some screams I felt a gasp building. The chains said *no*, and there was rattling, and a letting go that couldn't be sustained, because to release the core, to relax my midsection and let it fall, would arc pain into the lower back so it felt my spine would snap, and I had to pull back up, pelvic floor locking as though it were itself becoming ungainly steel.

I tried to take in the space I was in, to understand what was happening.

There were floating stairs leading down into the dark hall from the floor above. Brushed steel steps in the walls of a black enamel. Birdcrash pressed a button on a remote and the stairs retracted into the wall.

There were dead birds scattered around the floor, small songbirds and crows and two herons, necks curled around each other. The air was alive and thick with decomposition. His voice, when it came, came from a distance, an underwater sound burbling and self-satisfied. And he moved as though he was not a creature of the land. He was extraordinarily tall and slender, and he moved in slow motion, loose limbed and almost cartoonish, rocking from side to side as he spoke, and he would hold the drill over his head, and pump the trigger, make it whir, to punctuate what he was saying. His skin was pale and glistening. The eyes were huge, golder than any I'd ever seen—sprung, and rolling. Tufts of hair stuck out, and there were big round scabs on his forehead.

Then his arm was around my neck in a headlock and he was

drilling, boring through the broad bones of my skull, a shrilled sharp pain that lit me up, my whole system, it rattled my teeth down into my pelvis and seized my legs and feet, my body shot through with shattered teeth.

The doors in Inspector Gadget *opening.*

The doors in MST3K *opening.*

Have you seen Jurassic Park. *The girl hacking a system that never existed, a 3-D environment built so that the movies might stiffly swoop through.*

The girl: I know this! I know this!

We gathered up our zero days, our lost boys, the boys of the Aviary.

And we kicked the door in.

Security is a feeling.

We see from your face that you don't feel secure.

Rachel, we will describe what we are doing so that you feel safe.

All the drilling is done. The three holes in your skull are done. A neat row, forehead to crown.

There's some bleeding, we're sorry, relax your face, the extreme and constant movement of the muscles of your face keeps wiggling the sweatband off. And then blood gets in your eyes.

Aqua regia, the juice of kings.

Aqua regia, nitric acid and hydrochloric acid, in a molar ratio of 1:3. We will dropper that into you, right into the holes we've made in your skull, and damage your brain, so the damage can be routed around.

Here comes a little droppy droppy droppy.

Now see you moved.

You can't move.

You don't want this in your eyes.

If you are waiting to be saved, all your friends are dead, we must tell you that. Once we dropped the cars into the chute it was quite a simple matter to dispense with the soldiers.

We would have brought more down, we would have spoken with them as we are speaking to you now, but they all died.

Two trucks in the pit, and the one above, we blew it up.

The universe wants us dead, all of humanity, it is quite a small matter to help a human animal accede to the will of the universe.

To give them a little boost.

We can't see the system. No one can. Politics, economics. The global nodes, the connection, the roar.

Did you see The Matrix. *The underside of the cubicles, one of the first systems shots in* The Matrix, *the screws revealed, the prefab holes, the uniform screws, it can be taken apart and put back together, no problem,* it's in this configuration now, but that can change, within certain very precise limits.

The cubicles, the ceilings have descended, the modular desks, the cubicle systems, we have assembled these, these desks and cubes, we put them together once, long ago. Hauled the parts and made a system.

Ceilings are systems moments, so are cubicles, and the grill of the truck that strikes the phone booth, that's one too, these are systems moments, but they are not the system.

We cannot understand the system of the world, we cannot understand the system of even a single human animal.

The suffering of the people. The peace that is found in a single life, and the suffering.

We come into this world sucking some order from the chaos.

Hum hum hum.

Each human, the totality of humans at any given moment, the human and nonhuman animals who have lived on this planet since our time began, our solar system, our galaxy, all of it sucking a little order from the chaos for a little while.

Four billion unique IPs in the IPv4 address space, they thought it was nearly infinite, and so soon they were running out.

We suck order from the chaos, more and more, we wrap our lips around the tailpipe and we suck, and one day the chaos says no, stop it, no more, this is too much, you can't do it anymore, you can't have your order anymore.

Of course you can't.

You can pull on that rubber band, make it some shape, make it all the shapes you could dream of, that you've been trained to dream of, but one day it snaps.

We humans weren't more than a moment, not more than a blip in the cosmos, then back to entropy, and isn't that fine, and how nice that we should be present for all of this winding down, and witness, and be glad, as it snaps, or simply loosens and turns to a loose pudding with a taste that has no information in it.

We are the Aviary.

We contain many.

But so do you.

The lost boys, they brought us a harvest of zero days.

Lost boys with Kali Rolling, seeing what could be penetrated, systematically testing the barriers. Did you see Jurassic Park. *Like velociraptors, hunting in packs, testing the fences for weaknesses, scanning ports, clever girl. The lost boys and Kali Rolling and money and blackmarkets and secrets and time.*

Sebastian, he brought the BIND backdoor.

He never said he was quite one of us, one of the lost boys, but he wrote what we'd become, and he was our love. And he told us about the backdoor, but then he wouldn't give it to us.

He said that he couldn't be with us in love and also be in the Aviary, if he gave it over it meant it was the end. He said, I can't explain, but I can't give you that. If I do, it's the end of us.

But we were already planning. We thought: We can have Sebastian, and the backdoor, too.

We thought: If you want to poison as much internet as possible, look for BIND servers in an autonomous system. If you're not an autonomous system you're more likely to rely on upstream.

Start with a thousand BIND servers in a thousand autonomous systems spread out through all the top-level domains, include the rinky-dink country code TLDs.

Set up hundreds of simple web servers connecting to Amazon Web Services, Microsoft Azure, DigitalOcean, set up fake user accounts with providers that connect to their infrastructure and spin up or tear down servers whenever you want, you can do it in minutes at a massive scale.

You control domain servers, poison ones you don't like, and since it's a zero day, there won't be a malware warning.

If you have a backdoor in BIND, you can do it, sure you can.

They think they're at CNN.com, they go to a site that looks like the error page or it mirrors CNN, but they're served a web page that is designed to trip an exploit in IE or Chrome or Firefox, in OS or Android or Windows 10, Windows 9, Windows 7, Windows XP. You'd need a harvest of zero days, and we did have a harvest of zero days, but it is ultimately only a handful of operating systems that are 90 percent of users.

Our lost boys brought us zero days. Or we bought them with the money from the blockchain heist.

It came from Sebastian, from his backdoor to BIND, after the end of us. It came from zero days we bought, and other zero days that came to us through our network of lost boys, all the lost boys of the Aviary.

We left a final Pastebin post, it has all our plans, our plans for the next phase, for the internet of birds, the networks we still have in place, the new world after the world.

Selves were hurt, boys were hurt, and now here we are.

Will you be a lost boy with us.

We would give you the password, Rachel, but we don't trust you yet, we don't trust that you understand. How can we make you understand. How can we. Another droppy droppy. The password is quite simple, but it is also very complex. It's one of those things.

Maybe we contain more for now, the boys, the lost boys of the Aviary.

Selves were hurt, boys were hurt, and now here we are.

We are building the internet of birds for them, so that all of that can be registered in the system before it dissipates.

If that's what the birds want.

But why were the boys hurt in the first place. Well, that's not a question we can answer.

Our father would come and visit us, my mother would let him in, let him come to our bedroom, as a little boy. A dark suit and low-hanging red tie, our father.

Our mother . . .

Our mom was a smol burb.

The system shattered, the teacup broken, it always runs that way, disorder of waste energy always outstripping the order we create, but we try, don't we, to make a system, when there's no real system, there are just nodes of cruelty and control, and hate, and yes, and love. We did love Sebastian.

There was that father. Who was he.

Here come some soldiers. They're on the screen, they see the dead there. Maybe they were their friends. They are using things on the front door to blow it open. That is fine. They have found us. That is fine.

There are so many. They are taking three routes. Only one gets here, and only after some branchings.

We are sick. We are filled up with cancer. We knew that there would be others, many, who might make their way here, to our door, to the little shack. That people would be seized by an impulse they would not understand and they would make their way to us.

We had prepared several bays, it might have been you and some soldiers bound up in tape and chains, but the soldiers all died. We only need one, now you will be us.

We would have brought the soldiers in, but they resisted in such a way that the only way to keep you was to give them a boost.

All the unresting thoughts of humanity stuffed in our skull, and even we can't see the system. Even we can't see even a single person, not really.

No one can.

But you can help us. You can help the remnant remember what we can and can't know about the system.

If Postel had succeeded that day, if the root authority test had turned out differently, maybe history would have changed, have opened into something new.

We have only so much time before more are sent, or before they get here.

We are deep in the mansion and we know that they are coming, even now, but we know they won't find us, no not for a long time, not unless it's what we want.

A little shack from above, but from below a mansion built underground at great expense.

There are turns and false ends and secret passageways, a whole underground Winchester House, mirrored and turned upside down, algorithmically elaborating itself over the months, no expense spared, we are deep here in the burrowing heart of the mansion, but it is where no heart's expected, no heart anyone would look for.

Or it is not a heart, a vast underground mansion, no heart to speak of, there are just messages moving, or waiting to be sent, in a series of rooms and traps.

A whole lot of information waiting to be transmitted into bodies. Mostly to give them a boost.

Yes, we had a three-dimensional map made of the Winchester Mystery House, we mirrored it and iterated it, feedback loops, spontaneous breakdowns, growth, damage and growth.

Lights still on, juice drawn up from the earth, the unremitting earth, electricity sucked directly from the earth, and from all the creatures under, the worms and moles and monocellular life, we can suck it from the bones of boys, from the bones of dead boys and posthuman animals, oh yes, it has long been possible, as Tesla proved.

Tesla proved it, and Morgan wanted to know: If anyone can draw on the power, where do we put the meter.

And Morgan destroyed Tesla.

A Morgan is always looking for a Tesla, to destroy him.

There are bones of boys, there's that, too.

When new soldiers come, as they must, there's lots of rooms for them to die in along the way, lots of electricity to power the ways to make them die along the way, to give them that little boost.

The knife room and the lime pit and the room where the oxygen gets pumped out.

So there is time for us to talk, time to do this work, this necessary work, and at the end, you and however many others who join us here will be free to go, and you can return to the world and lead the people, the remnant of the people, and the birds, you can lead the remnant of the birds, or they can lead you, or you can enter into some kind of reciprocal relationship, a sort of grace.

We will damage your brains, and make your brains better.

We've started our recorder, we have a backup, we want you to know and remember everything that we say.

We'll just wrap your head in our left arm so you stay still.

You are resisting in your tape, and in your chains, like a fish.

Do you think that you are a fish now.

Oh my dear, look at how you wriggle, do you think you are a wriggling little fish. If you are a fish, you are a fish with a brain that's stuck, and the brain needs to be rebooted.

A little damage to the brain to make it stronger.

Here comes the droppy droppy droppy.

Shush now. Let it happen.

There. That wasn't so bad.

DNS is totalizing: an addressing system for all things.

Totalizing systems give way, they first accrue as much order to themselves as possible, and then they glitch out, they fail, they lose pieces.

A man in a suit. A rich man, a powerful man.

Our father would make his hand into a claw, draw it in swooping circles above our thigh or stomach or neck, he would say, Here comes the chicken hawk.

In his car, or limo, in the back of his limo, as he drove us to school, or had us driven, the morning after he'd flown in and got in under the sheets with us.

Who was our father.

Trump, we think it was Trump, it must have been Trump.

Wasn't it Trump.

It was a man who came. Why wouldn't it have been Trump.

He would say, You know what the chicken hawk does when it sees a chicken.

Then the hand would swoop down, and the fingers would dig like lightning into our thigh or stomach or our neck.

He strikes.

The chicken hawk.

We would be laughing, we couldn't help laughing, our whole body lit up and tensed with it, but we laughed.

Who was our father, who was he.

And his hand would be moving, digging in, exploring the texture of the muscle beneath our skin, and he'd just be watching, watching the work of his hand, of our body, as our body shook.

We'd clench our muscles, all of the muscles of our body, and hold so still.

And still we shook.

We were so shook.

Don't they understand for everything there is a cost, there is a debt that accrues. To them and to the ones they've touched. They understand. Don't they understand.

Maybe they don't understand it, but there is.

Maybe they don't understand because they don't have to.

Maybe they just do their thing—they work their need—and then they're gone, and the debt is what they've left us.

Totalizing fathers, they give way, they glitch out.

Hum hum hum.

They've left us a debt.

Do you remember the emperor in Star Wars. *How energy shot from his hands, how much pain it made in Luke.*

And how his father saved him after a struggle. But where was our father to save us, where was our father, he was the one hurting us, watching with a mystified look as his hands did their work.

And where was our mother.

There was a billboard outside the San Francisco airport that said Write Code. Save Lives.

It was for Taser, trying to entice programmers to Scottsdale, Arizona, to code for them.

Write code. Save lives.

We were driving Sebastian from the airport when we saw it.

Have we told you about Sebastian.

Have we told you about the birds. Have we told you how we're building an internet of birds, we mean, for the birds, for whatever they want from their internet.

Look at all the birds.

We don't think they'll be okay.

Hum hum hum.

The birds on the floor who won't get up might not be okay.

Once we had birds in our pockets.

The day we drove out and showed him the holes. Have we mentioned the holes.

We showed Sebastian the holes we dug out there in that remote public land.

He was puzzled but he was going with it, he had a bemused interest, he was going with it. He said it's okay, it's okay.

He said You know, those could be dangerous. Some hiker or a child could fall in and get hurt. You may not want to leave big holes in a public park indefinitely.

We were glad we were out in the dark, we didn't say anything, but we felt a rage at him, and he stopped talking, and we knew he could feel it too. We walked back to the car in silence. And we said, You know, the cocaine you love very much, the cocaine, that's what's causing the pressure on the loneliest man. The narcos are literally killing the indigenous people so you can have that stuff.

We said, You talk politics, and yet you fear it.

Think of the fear of politics, think of the Gates Foundation, we said. They stay away from politics and shame on them. That's why we have Trump. The political can't be quantified and measured directly, can't break down human beings to numbers, so the Gates Foundation stays away from it.

Hum hum hum.

Trump, we think it was Trump, he would come down to our basement room, in his suit and tie, he would take his shoes off and climb into our little bed, it was some sort of man, that was our father, and he would just hold us, and stroke our hair, or he would goof around, he would touch our thighs, our stomach, kiss us, I'm just goofing around, he would say.

People say it wasn't Trump, but maybe it was Trump.

We were digging and we fell in a hole and that was the end of Sebastian with us.

That hole, it's getting crusted, the one in you, let's open it back up and get a droppy droppy.

When the bit stopped, my whole body shook, and the silence screamed as loud as the drill. I didn't know if I was screaming or if I was just screaming in my skull—trying to scream through my nose, my mouth taped over, the blood running down my face and getting sucked into my nose so I thought I would choke on my own blood. I was desperately sucking air and bubbles of blood.

I was bound in tape, but it was looser now at my wrists behind my back, my skin so slick with sweat. I focused on the wrists, turning them slowly but insistently, trying to find some give in the tape before I blacked out again.

We we were at a party, some start-up, some venture capital party, lights and glass and DJs and the dark, and we sat at the bottle service and sucked it down. We sat by a billionaire, knowing his money. This was years before the Aviary, and yet, we owe it to him, in a sense. The billionaire was talking about life and death, how to sustain life, how to keep it going forever, we said no. He spoke of minds living on, how his mind might somehow, in a box, we said no. We said a mind in a box, it would not have continuity of consciousness. It would be like how in Star Trek *the transporter annihilates its human animal and that human animal is dead, and it rebuilds another, one who believes he is the one who is dead.*

But the one who is dead is dead.

The billionaire said he understood the problem.

A boy came with the bottle service, and offered the billionaire his blood, and the billionaire's head swung back, and his mouth went wide, and he brought his mouth down to the boy's neck and drank of his blood.

The billionaire said: Mortal corruption, to live on anyway, to live on as the one destroyed, or to know someone was. Or the chance to simply live in a box in the internet.

We listened and tried to understand.

A rich man, a powerful man, he could do such things, he could drink a boy's blood.

We said: If we had to choose between death and imprisonment forever in the box of the internet . . .

We said: To live anyhow is better than not at all.

The billionaire said: I'll bet you twenty million you won't stay in solitary confinement for ten years, with nothing but the internet.

We told him we didn't have twenty million to bet.

He said that was fine, if we lost, he'd take our blood, he'd drain us.

And we said Good. We had been working then in the valley for a while, doing this and that. We didn't want our blood so much then anyway. We said It's a deal.

It's not our fault.

We took the bet. We lived in a cell deep in one of the billionaire's homes, for almost ten years we did, with the internet, and a toilet, and the food we were brought.

And we learned such things, and saw such things, and we read Sebastian's book, and we had our bank heist before it was over.

And we were free, and we started the Aviary, in the real world we did it.

We shook the tree, and what fell down wasn't juicy peaches, but nuclear devices.

A huge botnet, IoT, plus devices, computers and phones.

It started with BIND, with the back door Sebastian gave us, and from there it spread.

The largest botnet ever activated, harness them, give them the malware, and it all falls down.

And what fell down was bombs.

We did not make them fall, but they fell.

We remember terrible things done to children, children who were used and wrecked without a thought, they would one day join the Aviary, some of them would.

You are trying to scream, Rachel. You should not try to scream.

You're in the Aviary now. You might be. If you say you want to be, that's all it takes.

We'll take the tape off soon, and you can tell us you're in the Aviary, if that's what you feel.

Another drop of aqua regia, nitric acid and hydrochloric acid, in a molar ratio of 1:3.

It is eating through brain tissue, yes, but it is causing damage to set you free from damage, and neuroplasticity is a real thing, so remarkable.

And there are always trade-offs.

No ethical consumption, they say, no ethical consumption—it's really true—under capitalism.

Trump, what is a Trump. A vast ungainly hog who has scalped a lion somehow. And staggers around in it. The rotting mane and pelt. Day after day, and year after year, eyes clenched, chin jutting, squealing and snorting and wheezing, daring you to say it, to tell him what he is.

You're not a lion. You're a dumb bad pig. A mentally ill pig, and no one likes you, you're the worst, the worst one ever.

He was such a bad dumb little shit pig wasn't he.

You are bound up and suspended and beautiful.

Here comes a droppy.

Hum hum hum.

But we all are bound up and suspended. You know that don't you. We're all just what you are now, we all are, all the time. The universe has strapped us all into the most elaborate Rube Goldberg death machine. Do you remember the poor monkey.

The density parameter, the cosmological constant.

Um, um, the Hoyle state.

The poor monkey.

Everything ever, all of history, all of the systems, millennia of piss and shit and betrayal, science and greed and the wars for standards, all of this to heave the monkey up out of our atmosphere into space to die.

Hum hum hum.

Midcentury spaceflight was a slaughterhouse, from the point of view of the monkeys. Alberts II and IV, Bonny the pig-tailed monkey, Gordo the squirrel monkey, Able the rhesus monkey, death from explosions and splashdowns and the sheer stress of it all.

All that evolution, all those millions or billions of dollars sucked out of the system, just to kill a monkey or a dog in the most elaborate possible way.

The abattoir of capital, the abattoir of science, the need for an addressing system for all things, so that we might make the whole earth, the whole universe, our abattoir, or reveal it for the death house it already was.

What we did with the Aviary is we yanked away a sheet and revealed what had always already been there, the clouds of radiation, the poison, the vast spinning wheels of excrescence that was our world.

Fathers want everything, they think they can just have everything.

Some soldiers just reached the knife room. Ooh, the front guy is getting all cut up. Ooh, the others are retreating.

But they are in the knife hallway and there is no retreat. And they are not even in the right branch.

They are dying quite awkwardly. It's gross and we don't like it. The blades that flew out of the wall didn't do their job well enough, there's too much human squirming in the blood that's opening beneath them. How long will this last. How long will this last. Shut it off.

The other two groups are safe for now. There are more soldiers at the door.

What were we saying. Fathers. Fathers want everything.

The man is gone and then there's your mother again, it's just you and your mother again.

And you are left with wiring all askew, going to the bathroom wrong, digestion wrong, everything all activated, all the muscles tensed.

For months or years, for a whole life it will be like that.

You wet the bed, you touch yourself in class, you faint in a bathroom stall, and no one sees it as a sign of anything.

We had a mother, of course we had a mother, but where was our mother.

Enveloped in some screams I felt a gasp building. The drillings were past, but the reaction kept cascading through, pain and electricity and constriction and a slight sense of movement, and rattling chains, a sense of . . . cantilever? I heard that word, *cantilever*, in my head, it echoed there, my body held up at three points, bands at hips and feet and chest that hooked to chains.

I surfaced and it was the wave pool at the water park. I was in the water with Verena. She liked to swim underwater. Dominique was sitting on the edge. Verena said: *Tell me I'm a fish.* I told her. She was back underwater. She'd swim a few strokes and surface. Sometimes she had me go with her, sometimes I was supposed to watch. *Tell me the password. Tell me my fish name.* She broke the surface and sun twisted itself through water chaotically all around her. Dominique wasn't playing with us. *Tell me I'm a dolphin.* Tell her she's a dolphin, I said. She wants you to. Dominique had the look of someone who wanted to be somewhere else. She had the look of someone thinking about a cigarette. But her hands were squeezing the sandpaper edge of the pool. I was having a conversation with her and another one with Verena. Dominique's and mine happened when Verena was underwater. *Tell me I'm a sea turtle.* Dominique said: *She has more fun with you, but she loves me more. Kids love the primary caregiver more.* This was an old conversation, but we were into it sometimes. I said: It's not a contest. *I didn't say it's a contest. I'm just saying how it is.* And our girl: *Tell me I'm a dolphin. My name is Finslip and you're Flapper. We're dolphins.* I pushed off and went under with Verena. Underwater I was tuned in to the screams of children, which above I didn't really hear, or I heard but filtered into the background. Down here it was different: they screamed slowly inside a bass drum—the water was a big whale heart that we were in, and the vibrations pushed Verena into me. I held my dolphin daughter to my chest and stood. I lifted her over my head, breaking the water into golden parts. We were at the water park and everything was fine. *Tell me I'm a seal.* You're a seal. She was under again. Dominique said: *She wants me when she's sick. She wants you to tell her she's a seal.* She wants us both to, I said. I wanted to say: Real play is pure and beautiful and makes everything else worthwhile. Play is the best thing Verena gave me. I knew I should say this. But I didn't. Dominique did a cough laugh. She said, *What do you want me to say.* I said a line I'd said many times to my wife, a laugh line, it relieved the tension a little, usually. Let's get a divorce, I said. Dominique: *Let's.* We laughed at the laugh line. I ran my finger from her knee two-thirds of the way up her inner thigh. It was slippery under my finger—I saw my white finger on her light brown skin. I saw the wrinkles on the skin of my finger, and the oiled smoothness of hers, and the tension of her posture, the hands gripping the sandpaper edge, and black hair falling over the lime green swimsuit. *You're Flapper, you're Flapper.* I held my daughter and fell back with her. We crashed into a new kind of hearing. I heard her forcing out her air for the effect of the bubbles we could see in the blue, the too blue water, in the whale's heart with the bass-drum screams. My feet were slipping and I couldn't get us up—my daughter was in my arms and I slipped a second—a panicked crash—and then my legs were under me, thrusting us up, too hard, and I was holding her too tight, my nails in her chest, digging under the line of the top of her swimsuit, in the air. Flapper, I said. Flapper has Flippy. *Finslip,* she shrieked. *I'm Finslip.* But she was testing something—if there was still fun in it. And there wasn't—she could feel that there was no more fun in it, that something had changed. That something had happened that she had to evaluate, and that she should probably feel bad about. She kicked away from me, she pushed off my right femur and my right index finger hung for a second in her left swimsuit string, and I had a horror I would pull it off, some-how, embarrass her, expose her, but it snapped back, without pain I think—she took no notice. She was underwater again. Dominique: *A divorce for me would mean I have my life back. Kids have bottomless want and need, but no one will ever love you like a kid. But I would have my life back.* I love you, I said. Bottomlessly. *No, you love me superfi-cially because you want to fuck me. You're compromised. She needs me 100 percent of the time.* So, I said. I ran my finger up her thigh again. Only partway, and pressed it in, and watched the skin change. Let's get a divorce. Let's have some peace. At least half the time some peace. *You know you're wrong. You know that's not how it works,* Dominique said. *Now I'm Flapper,* Verena said. Dominique leaned in close to me. She said: *A divorce is a good deal for me, and a bad one for you. Why would you want to spend 50 percent of your time focus-ing on her 100 percent, when you can now spend 20 percent focusing 80 percent? I'm Flapper,* Verena said. She said, *Who are you?* Then we were in the car. Verena slept and Dominique and I listened to the audiobook of "The Sign of the Four," narrated by Stephen Fry. We listened and we heard *We earned a living at this time by my exhibit-ing poor Tonga at fairs and other such places as the black cannibal. He would eat raw meat and dance his war-dance: so we always had a hat-ful of pennies after a day's work,* and Dominique said she hoped her daughter was really asleep because that shit was racist. And I said it was, but it was still important. And Dominique said, *How is that important for her to hear?* And I felt a panic because I didn't know, or couldn't remember then, why it was important, I knew in some part of me that it was, but I couldn't explain it, "The Sign of the Four," the racism there, whether it was important because the au-thor knew it was racist, and was commenting on it, or because he didn't know, and that's why it was important, I just didn't know, it was swirling inside, but I couldn't explain. Then we were home. I made dinner while they sat together up on the roof. I came up with a bowl of watermelon salad with mint and feta and I saw through the door to the roof the two of them side by side watching the sun go down over the uneven roofs and the new glass towers of

Greenpoint and Long Island City. I came up with a big yellow plastic mixing bowl with pink watermelon and bits of green and white, and I watched them, facing away from me, bodies aligned, sitting on the outer bench, looking out at the roofs, across the boroughs and to Manhattan, very still, Verena far more still than she would ever be with me—or so I thought. And I looked at their shoulders, Dominique's dark skin, Verena's less dark, closer to mine, but not mine either, both so different from me, from what my skin was, or what it looked like, what it did for me, holding things in, and what it did, presenting things, and how those were uses that no longer had a real distinction, I thought, in that moment, but I looked at them, those girls, both a part, I believed, somehow, I thought, a part of my skin, my wife and daughter, but I couldn't have explained that any more than Holmes and what was said in that. But I felt it. I went back down treading so quietly. The recipe didn't call for sugar, it didn't need sugar—Dominique might be annoyed by it, but Verena would love it, and her happiness would increase Dominique's net happiness, too, even if she was annoyed with me, and I felt more than anything that I wanted to increase our net happiness—I shook sugar all over the salad and brought it back up, and when I came out my girls were still looking out at the horizon, but there was something new now, a keypad on the door, and I rapped the window, and I held out the big yellow bowl and said *Hey*.

Look at all these poor birds. What have we done. Oh no oh no what have we done.

Sebastian, have we told you about Sebastian. We met him after the ten-year bet, we met him online, we did, we liked his tattoos. He had a tattoo of a ship, of a burning ship, and a schematic of a ship, the same ship, and it was turned over on his body, different slices of the ship, the burning ship.

Sebastian had the best tattoos.

Heart heart heart.

Oh this heart, oh Sebastian.

We read his book, we read in the billionaire's cell, and we loved it, more than any book we'd ever read we felt a kinship and a love, and we carried out the first heist, the DAO hack on the blockchain, seventy million worth, a smart contract bug, we were still there in the billionaire's room, getting rich, even as the billionaire was losing his own fortune for other reasons, his start-up with the blood and boys under scrutiny, stakeholders suing him massively, the feds closing in, he said to me, I'm so ashamed, I don't even have the twenty million for you now, and that night I carried out the blockchain heist, and I escaped from the cell in his mansion, and I put something up on Pastebin claiming credit for the attack in the name of the Aviary, and I quoted the line from the novel about it being a time of noting and binding together. I knew that night that I would make the book I loved, Sebastian's book, a real thing in the world, and when I'd done it I'd find the author and say, What do you think.

He had diagrams that were burning all over his body.

There were sharp lines, and the slices of that boat, and the burn.

Kek kek kek, do you remember kek. We said kek on date one, we met in an online space where hackers were, he talked about kek, we spoke about that.

We said: We are pretty sure we hate that, hate the saying of that.

He laughed, he said that he hated it too, the saying of that.

We told him that we'd been at the bottom of the internet for a long time, give us time.

It was all different, the way we said things then. We're doing our best to tell you about Sebastian, of how it was said, but it was all different.

We told him one day we were the Aviary.

This was months after we were out, after we had begun assembling the lost boys, the men or human animals of all genders who would be the Aviary, and had made a half-dozen attacks.

And he said he had guessed, he had wondered.

He said everything that happens, happens twice.

We hadn't drilled the holes. This was all before that.

We brought Sebastian home and we jacked off, side by side, while kissing and touching.

Also we ate his ass, I think we ate his ass.

And we drank wine and we did blow.

And we fucked a little, we got in there, a little.

And he got in there, a little.

There was cum, yes, there was cum, on our bodies, also going in them, cum shooting into the bodies, from the bodies, shooting right up in there.

And there were poppers, there was the smell of that, that smell like poppers, a sharp sweet gasoline, and letting go and pounding, or just lying there, but it spins.

Kek kek kek, he said, and he laughed.

And we were so drunk.

And we told him we loved him, and it was still right there, right that night.

We think of that night: how it spins. And how we said love, how had we said it.

And he didn't say it.

No he didn't say it.

We talked about ILOVEYOU, and kek, and ILOVEYOU, the virus, and he laughed and called us crazy guy.

We were lost in the burn.

The burn of his ships.

I think this was right before you met him. I think this was only a few days before.

Here comes a droppy droppy.

We loved him. And somehow love died.

Did you see They Live. *The glasses that reveal the messages BUY! OBEY! CONSUME! Now we could see the messages, but even these revelations were just ways of spreading the system into every nook, so those earlier signs could fall away and we could see the real message that had been planted there for humanity, and that message was DIE!*

The universe was clear on this, it said WON'T YOU DIE ALREADY! WON'T YOU DIE! DIE! DIE! And yet here we are and we haven't died.

There is so much metaphor. We cannot describe massive systems without resort to metaphor. Meaning is no longer centralized, it is distributed, and the metaphors must be replaced. DNS is a way to get to this, to create a practice, a protocol, that constructs meaning even as it erases itself, it's real work, which is not fully cognizable by any one person or any one machine—hence distribution, hence metaphor.

Protein folding at home. SETI@home, blockchain.

What we think is: We have more in common with the loneliest man on earth than with the rest of the human race.

We understand that there are inadmissible racial dimensions.

Nonetheless it is what we feel, or what we felt then. For this last member of an uncontacted, or barely contacted, tribe, in what we call the rainforest, of what was Brazil.

And it led us here, to the holes in the system, we drilled an internet of holes.

We had a mother. Yes, of course we had a mother, we did have a mother. She was there, she was there every day, she just wasn't there where we're talking about.

We've got all the unresting thought of humanity stuffed in our head.

We dove to the bottom of the internet and came back with the dankest memes.

Turn the dials the tiniest smidge on any of dozens of constants in our universe, less than 1 percent of 1 percent, there is no primordial ooze or bellowing mastodons, no TV, no duct tape, no Styrofoam or computers or us.

Be liberal in what you accept, and conservative in what you send.

We shook the tree, the poisoned tree, that's all. What happened was the system happening. We had all kept the airplane up, the airplane of human civilization in the postindustrial neoliberal world-hum, we were keeping it up with our thoughts and wishes and now we said that the emperor has no clothes, the plane has no wings. It's Wile E. Coyote stepping out on air, a leap from the lion's heart. We pointed at the narrow reed Wile E. Coyote was walking on, we said This is not secure, this is not it, this is not the best thing to be walking on. And someone else took advantage of our words, and they stuck a dynamite stick in the hand of a coyote who had been expecting a bouquet meant for . . . for someone. And it blew, and the coyote fell.

The internet was designed to survive an attack at individual points. Nothing can survive an attack from all points.

The internet sees damage as censorship and routes around it.

Hum hum hum.

We were always children, always—the system—in our ignorance of the lives of the people we exploited, we were like little kids, we saw the people to whom we had granted space, but to whom we had not granted life—they built their lives, they made their spaces, and they had so little to do with us. The arrogance that we could place people in this space, and then wish also to what—to be their friends. But we were kids, and we had our thoughts.

Some soldiers just reached the lime pit. See the first one sink—his buddy has pulled him out.

But the floor of the hallway has tipped up, and they are all falling in.

We don't like the choking and the screams and the fingers and arms trying to pull themselves back up, up the inclined wall of what was the floor, which is now boxing them in. We think what's worst about the screams is there's no noise, it's just the faces on these little screens with the mouths and faces contorted in horror, and no noise, and you imagine the blub blub blub as they get pulled down, as the burn overtakes their bodies and they can't keep themselves up above the surface of the lime pit.

And they are not even in the right branch.

A horror in their panic, but also an acceptance at last, how utterly unavoidable this is, we see that too, and that is their animal grace, right there at the very end.

204

Goodbye, boys, goodbye.

The loneliest man in the world. We tried to save him, but we were his death.

The other two groups are safe for now. There are more soldiers at the door.

Once upon a time you could grab a spade and dig . . . almost anywhere. You were afraid of what. Bears or wolves or snakes. Certain other humans, from within your tribe, from without it. The whites, all the terrible whites, settler colonial genocide if you were indigenous. But still, whoever you were, you had a certain wide berth. In the broad center of humanity, you did, as a human, have a right to dig. Or not a right, not something inscribed in law. No laws applied. You just could. And then it became very difficult.

One had to go to the middle of nowhere to find a place to dig. But private property, the theft of land from those who had worked it for centuries, where was the space.

A colonized people, they couldn't see it the same way—the openness of space that had been stolen, had been regulated and been the site of killing after killing. This was a discussion with Sebastian, he told us this.

Nowhere was shrinking. The middle was shrinking. The white, imaginary middle of nowhere was gradually regulated out of existence. Barbed wire cubing up the prairie. For thousands of people the first telephone lines plain old barbed wire. It conducts. It cuts, but it conducts. Massive party lines, old whiskey bottles for insulators, voices in metal, everyone listening in and all those voices buzzing the land like excited ghosts.

Smash cut to helicopters, high-tension power lines. Police, federal agencies. Private businesses with watching employees, with cameras whose feeds were watched by employees. The real ghosts gone, replaced by private businesses whose surveillance feeds were monitored by cheap labor in south Asia.

Add more cameras to the chain, outsource all that watching. Consult the satellites.

We all have a notion of these massive satellites, keeping an eye on the earth, keeping an eye on us.

Have you seen Moonraker. Diamonds in the sky. Available to governments and private citizens both, at a certain cost. But they aren't or don't have to be these massive works of space architecture. Big hunks of Roger Moore's space junk. Sputnik, *remember* Sputnik, *remember the idea of* Sputnik. *Size of a basketball.*

Satellites, they're not even that, they're the size of the spatula that slipped out of the hand of some guy. The size of a flash drive. Somehow they point the right way. Or they point all ways equally and that's okay.

Closer to earth, the drones. Eight million drones sold in the US alone the year before it ended. The proliferation of drones, each with a camera. A new encircling net, taking things in, taking note. Danny Dunn's dragonfly. Buzz buzz.

Do you know Danny Dunn. So good. So good.

Right here on the surface, right here among us, the proliferation of citizens who might see a man digging and take a picture.

So back to the dig.

For Instagram, a man in the desert digging a hole. It might suggest a narrative. We were all recruited, all our opinions were valid, a photo-

graph posted online of a man out there simply digging—that was sug-
gestive, that might bring in some likes, some comments.

A white man with certain trappings could dig in many places, for a time.
We're talking land. The way it was. Public land. Land, in American
space. Yes, you can dig a hole. But a hole two by three, and five feet deep.
Imagine digging one of those. A system of those, a dozen, more than
a dozen, twenty or more spread across a space, let's say thirty square
miles. Let's say thirty-one.

That's what we needed. That's the land we needed to find.

Let's say in the Bay Area. Now that's hard. Where do you do it. In farm-
land, grazing land, public parks. A regional park or a state park. Where
can you dig.

The boundaries. Their erasure and re-creation. The regulation of space.

Hum hum hum.

At first it was going to be just one hole. That's what we told ourself. But
we also said: We need to do our own hole, but in a space where we can
imagine our way to twenty holes, thirty holes. We wouldn't dig them.
But we needed to know there was that potentiality.

Of course once we'd dug the first, we needed to do a second, a third. It
was very hard, very hard to stop in the space we had conceptualized,
it was hard to just hold the virtual holes in our head, and not take our
spade and dig them.

BIND 9. BIND 9 is everywhere. It's been through the wash.

The obfuscation, C++.

The internet of things, that was part of it.

Do you know how hard it is to dig a hole in America. How hard it was, when America was in its last form.

Some soldiers just reached the dynamite room. Ooh, it's all blowing up. And they're in the right branch, but not the right subtrack. And there's the way that their limbs are.

Their limbs that are something else now.

The other two groups are safe for now. There are more soldiers at the door.

Hum hum hum.

We made our fortune in a famous blockchain theft, like a heist in film, but consider it as a Lucite bank, completely clear, and every motion legible. And all the depositors outside: they are there, looking in, if this has caught their attention, and they can see it. But they can't move. They can't move to the bank. They can talk to each other about the rules of the bank, as their money is being stolen, carted out, and it becomes clear that this is a rule of the bank, that this can happen, and the only thing they can do, standing out there, is change the rules. But there's not time. And so it's others who come in, the good guys, the white hats, to steal the money that's left, to keep it safe, to return it to the rightful owners before we can steal it, and we're all racing. The money is still pouring out, gym bag by gym bag. The good guys, the bad guys, taking this money that everyone can see.

We thought about the Aviary, about the book of Sebastian, and what we might do with it, and so we said it was: the Aviary. That that's who had done the theft. And there were so many more things that followed, all as the Aviary.

We stole from Sebastian, from his book, before we ever met him we made his book real.

208

Fractus dominium.

We're not getting the order right.

You need a droppy droppy.

We were digging and we killed the internet and that was the end of the world that used to be.

Let's start with how we fell in a hole we dug. All that year we had been digging holes, because we wanted to understand the loneliest man in the world. His thing had become our thing. The loneliest man in the world, in Brazil, uncontacted but pressured, hunted, all alone, last of his tribe. He dug holes.

We dug holes too. We fell in one. We had just broken up with Sebastian.

Let's start with love, the end of it.

We had been in love with Sebastian, and he had wondered where we went at night. At last we drove him to the holes out there in the country-side. We explained the holes, and the connection to the loneliest man in the world. We expected Sebastian to freak out.

It would have been right of him to freak out.

But he accepted. He said, Okay. Well, I hope you're careful. I guess it's exercise. He said, It's okay, it's okay.

We realized we were screaming at him, and he was saying, It's okay.

We hadn't expected this, no we had not. We hadn't wanted this.

We were out at night digging holes on remote public lands, and he was saying it was okay. We screamed and threw the keys at him and told him to go home, to pack his things, to leave us. We would call an Uber later, we said, he should just go.

He didn't understand. This was our secret and he treated it like it was nothing and we got very angry.

It was unbearable, the electricity buzzing through us because he just wouldn't understand.

Maybe we said other things, and maybe he did too, we can't remember.

We hadn't, you see, we hadn't processed things. We made mistakes. Our brain was still jammed up. We had dug holes, but not the right ones. The right ones were the ones we'd drill *not dig. We'd drill them right in our own skull and then we'd see and process everything, all at once. We'd reboot our brain and see how to reboot the system.*

When we had first started seeing him, he had wanted to know were we always attracted to Asian guys, why were we with him, what did we want, what was inside of us that drew us to him. And we didn't know, we couldn't tell him, we tried to be honest, we couldn't say. But his anger had been comforting, had kept us in a place we found comforting, a place of reason, a place of understanding that he was angry, irrationally so, and it wasn't our fault, but we could understand, we could communicate that.

Here we wanted anger and we got acceptance.

We were a couple and what we needed was anger, but we got the wrong thing.

We stomped around in the dark after he left and we fell in a hole. We tripped and fell headfirst in a deep and narrow hole and we were a quarter mile from the road and we injured ourselves. We thought we were paralyzed, we thought our back was broken, we fell in and we were folded up like a billfold, somehow both our head and *our feet were at the bot-*

tom, face pressed to ankle, no room to move, no adjusting, deep in a hole, body folded over, butt up, dirt and worms falling all around our face, and little ants.

We were stuck in our hole like a chump.

We stayed in the hole like that in the cold with insects crawling and somewhere coyotes making their sounds for hours we think.

The coyotes got so near and loud we thought they were circling the hole, or digging through to us, or up above, sniffing up near our butt and haunches. We thought the bugs and worms that touched our face were the little feet of coyotes who'd come down in the hole, we just made little noises, moaning into the dirt and waiting for the end.

Then the dirt shifted, and our phone fell next to our face, and we got a hand down and called Sebastian, our boyfriend, now our ex-boyfriend, and asked him to come back for us.

He hauled us up by our butt, enough for us to get our arms out, to scramble our feet up out of the hole, we popped out and swayed in the headlights and fell again on the dirt. After a time, we were able to walk out and get in his car.

We thought we were paralyzed, but it was just the muscles of our back we'd hurt, it turned out.

He turned on the heat and we stuck our hands in our pockets.

All the birds in our pockets died. Did we mention we had birds in our pockets. Our pockets were full of birds and they all died.

We remember the birds.

The pockets were dead, have we mentioned these birds.

There were birds.

We have always had a thing for birds.

Yes, there were birds in our pockets.

We had brought birds, we were going to show him how we placed birds in the holes, how that was part of it, how we so gently and lovingly placed the little birds in the holes, but we had forgotten and they were dead now, perhaps in our fall, or from our wriggling around in the hole, folded up like we were, all those little tiny baby birds, we had started to have the idea about an internet of birds, we were working toward that, we knew we couldn't tell him.

We rode back to Oakland in silence. The pockets of our windbreaker all bird guts, beaky.

We couldn't take our hands from our pockets or he'd see or smell the guts of birds, and we'd have to explain the birds.

But near home we sneezed and our hand came out, slick with bird guts, and we blew them everywhere, and Sebastian's eyes went wide, and we were really and truly done, we understood this, as he took us in, when we were about to sneeze he looked at us, and we at him, and we sneezed, and he wiped his eyes, and turned back to the road, with his bird-guts face.

And Sebastian said we would never see each other again, we were over.

And we said we wanted BIND, the backdoor he'd put in, but wouldn't give us the magic words for.

And we saw him thinking, If I do this, then truly it is over.

And he said, Okay, I'll never use it.

He said, Use it for something good. He said, All yours.

DNS is an addressing system for all things.

The doors that they stack up, one after the next, in Zelda, in Marathon.

How we used to love the doors in video games, opening a series of doors.

We'd like to give you the password, we really would.

This town will follow you around.

How we loved the doors in the internet, the rooms inside the rooms, inside the rooms. Link layer, internet layer, transport layer, application layer.

Our little room in the basement, our Nintendo and PC. The blue couch, the bed, the desk with the owl lamp, overhead light turned off—Let's just rest a minute, he would say, and crawl into bed—play of light from the CGA, then EGA, then VGA, as the years passed.

There were doors he had to push through to get to us. And we think: There were doors he pushed through inside of us, doors to rooms that weren't there before.

Doors to new levels that we hadn't been to before, deep down inside of us.

We contain all the unremitting thoughts of humanity, we broke things and made new things, new places, that's how it works.

The doors and our father.

All of this kept within certain limits, or we think so, when building his doors.

We mean: He didn't touch our genitals, or did so only glancingly, in a way that could be excused as accidental, incidental to what else was going on, goofing around.

His hands, what they touched, what they erased was the memory of what they touched, of the possibility of that memory. Those hands took away something, and meanwhile they were building something we didn't find out about for years, though we heard it, a high-wire whine in a room in a basement behind a door we didn't have the key to.

Maybe one more. Maybe one more hole in your skull.

We drove out to Sailor Gulch, near Telegraph City, and that's where we started to dig.

The ceiling is always the system, in movies. It often is. The system, the grid, hovering over us. The camera pans up to reveal what we always knew. The ceiling reveals the truth of the land—the grid, subdivided, tended, glowing.

The murder of buffalo, the treaties with the Indians—familiar stuff. Glass beads for $800 billion worth of real estate. The way land is stolen. The way a house is stolen. The bureaucratic so-called accidents at banks. The punitive desire to never renegotiate a loan. Everything always clawing and scraping to take away. Take, extract from life. To be sure that cradle to grave value is created, and then juiced, extracted. How land and home are defined. How they are distributed.

It is not an accident when there is a ceiling. They have to build those. The movie people. They have to build them, they cost extra.

The system of the coffin, the great fear of being buried alive, the string clutched in the hand. Ring the bell.

Did you see The Matrix. The real truth—the reason Neo can stop the squids in the real world, otherwise barely acknowledged—is that there is no outside to the system in The Matrix, they're all in there all the time, it's bedtime stories or lullabies, this dream of resistance. The metalevel, the outside of the real matrix, in that, their head jacks aren't removable. Why would they be. You want out, you die, that's it. Perhaps that is a less interesting movie, which is why they buried it so deep.

But here we can. We can do something about it here. We are drilling in your head. Here comes a drop.

Here comes a little droppy droppy droppy.

You can scream into tape, but also: you can't.

We can plug up your nose, we can pinch your nose: like this.

We're sorry we did that.

But we hate your screams.

And no you won't die. And no you are not outside the system.

The unremitting horror of having a body.

Here comes a little droppy droppy droppy.

But it will be better.

Did you see The Matrix II's exploit, SSH, secure shell, she ran sshnuke, which was a program, an actual program that existed at that time, that would go into a particular computer, 10.2.2.2, that IP address, and she hit the z10n0101, and we cheered, or Sebastian did, we heard from him that he and his friends he saw it with cheered. It was not perfect, but it was good for the movies.

And BIND, the zero day we put inside it, that Sebastian put in, that lay hidden and untampered with for almost two decades. BIND has been through the wash, private industry, US government security, but no one found it, in all the hundreds of thousands of lines of code, it slipped through.

And we kicked the door in.

Security is a feeling.

Some soldiers just reached the hungry hungry lions room. Ooh, here come the lions. Ooh, there's a retreat.

But there are lions behind now too. We don't like it, we don't like the screams, and the way they cower, how they cower and scream and how fast the lions are. And the soldiers are not even in the right branch.

The other two groups are safe for now. There are more soldiers at the door.

We have heard the stories of fathers here in the Aviary, what they have done. How they gaslight you. What they did to you was nothing. For seeing it that way you're the pervert. And your motherboard is now fucked up, so it really does seem it must be you who's the pervert. The sight of children can glitch your system, even if you never act on it, and that in itself allows the narrative to be rewritten: you were the pervert, you were always the pervert, nothing was really done to you, it was just affection, there's nothing wrong with affection.

Mothers, where were mothers.

Sometimes they play I Spy with My Little Eye.

Sometimes our mother played that game with us, surveying the space, telling us what we should see.

Where even are mothers.

What is the deal with mothers.

Some soldiers just reached the machine guns on swiveling mounts room. Ooh, they're getting so shot up, the ones in front.

But the floor of the hallway has tipped up, and they are all falling into getting so shot up. And they are not even in the right branch.

The other two groups are safe for now. There are more soldiers at the door.

We had terrible spasms in our groin, in our asshole, our penis hurt terribly, it hurt when peeing, we could never seem to get it all out, all of the pee. We woke up screaming with muscle spasms in our asshole, attacks of electricity seemed to cut through our balls, through the shaft of our penis. We went to doctors, they didn't know, and didn't understand. They didn't seem to believe. They jammed a catheter down our peehole to check if there really was urine that wasn't getting out, the worst pain, the worst pain we've experienced, it ruptured something, something that was holding on too tight, imagine a peephole in a door, the glass lens, imagine a screwdriver going through it, imagine it shattering through lens after lens, all down the urethra.

How to describe the pain.

Imagine having nettles driven into your penis. Or imagine having a penis, then that. I'm sorry, Rachel, imagine, though. Let's say on the back, slightly on the right side. Then imagine a spined rod being shoved down your urethra, then imagine a static—an odd tingling, that static

TV noise except it's inside your urethra. And it's pain. Throw all of that all together. Imagine it as a 10 on the scale of the worst pain. Screaming. Kicking. Wrecking around. Imagine all that, and then imagine that someone took hold of the dial, and turned it down to 3. Even 2.5. There is pain and it is constant. It is forever pain. Forever pain. In your urethra, the thistle and the static and the rods. All at once, forever, then dialed to a 2.5. Not a 10, sometimes less. But here.

Of course your body recoils, of course it tries to pull stuff in, for safety. The shell, the turtle, that life.

That is what it feels like, all the time. How do you deal with that all of the time.

You blur it out somehow. You learn not to feel it, even as you feel it.

So many things are invested with an urgency you have to repress when you have that pain. Something in you is screaming DO THIS, DO THAT, DO THIS, THAT, GO, GO, KEEP MOVING, and another part of you knows you can't present yourself that way, so you throw a big blanket of cotton batting over it, two, three like that, over your whole life. You wrap it up, the voice becomes far less defined, sort of fuzzed out, just as the screaming figure comes down to almost nothing—a bit up at the nose.

We hid bottles of Smirnoff Vanilla around the house. Sebastian snooped, and we hid our half pints of Smirnoff Vanilla. We hid them all around, we drank them, they took down the activation, the pain. They really helped with that.

At night we'd smoke weed and play Wii Play. *It was two console genera-tions before where we were, but we liked it. He was really good at the escalators, and we were good at space.*

Then Sebastian left.

There is a ghost body within our body that has these experiences. Or a semitransparent body that mostly conforms to us, that is slowly vibrating at the edge of us, just trailing us, and this body is the one that raises the handgun to the side of the skull—right in the middle of the skull, perpendicular, right where the most meat of the brain is—and pulls the trigger, and the bullet goes through in slow motion. We feel this in our own body. But it is not us, or it is somehow other. Because we can feel that bullet dozens of times a day. We can feel it a couple times a second, three times a second if we're so upset. Blam blam blam. Sometimes thousands of times a day. That's how it was for so long.

We drilled the holes in the head and all that stopped, or it came way down.

We still drink, but not nearly so much.

Perhaps we will have a drink now, we have so many cases of them, the half pints of Smirnoff Vanilla.

Ah gug gug gug gug. Ah gug gug gug gug.

Ahhh. Tasty.

We have butt cancer. Did we say it was butt cancer. It's butt cancer.

We can't remember. It's so hard to remember.

Ah gug gug gug gug. Ah gug gug gug gug.

We love our Smirnoff Vanilla.

Why is this happening to us, what did we do.

Did you see The Matrix.

We're dying of cancer!

We're working on our internet of birds. That will be our gift to the world. Or to the birds. That will be our last sucking of order from the chaos, but a system that embraces chaotic flows. Birds wired and whole, no need to snip a leg off.

Don't snip a leg off.

Do you hear me.

We just need to get these birds wired right and then the protocols.

Did you see The Matrix.

The screens when Neo is taken into captivity—they are not flat, they are curved cathode ray models, the archaic technology, the tiles on the wall, the grid on the front of the notebook, grids everywhere, a systems moment.

Keanu's abs are a systems moment, the creature crawling inside him.

When Trinity does the hack, Sebastian said, sshnuke, he and his friends all screamed. They loved it. We wish we had had friends like that.

Our father used to lie in bed with us, we were washed by those low steady lights from the computers ratifying everything, or simply bearing witness.

It is hard to know, it is hard to know. That we were personally a vector of history that killed so many people—sometimes we think that.

Hum hum hum.

Everything turns to shit.

And alongside that, ILOVEYOU, the worm from the Philippines, per-haps the greatest worm of all time.

We miss him.

Oh my gosh we miss him.

Where is our world that was ours, that had our futures in it.

Don't blame Sebastian. Maybe we wouldn't have kicked the door in if he was still here. But you shouldn't blame him.

If anyone, blame us.

Or just the universe.

It's always women, mulattoes, queers, minorities who are the points of exception, the instability that brings the system down.

Have you seen Tom Cruise movies. He is always out there because of a woman. Fixing things because of a woman, saving a woman.

Have you seen Smiley's People.

Vast powers, the great systems, the West and the Soviets of old, Karla and Smiley, the greatest minds of the greatest power, and all of that brought down by a woman, a crazy woman, Karla's daughter.

That is what the system is.

We do not ask why she is that way, why she is insane, hypersexual, seem-ingly incurable.

No one asks, it is not important, they want us to believe.

It is not important to the work of the system, of sustaining it and dissolving, or that's what the system tells us.

Systems moment, the grill of the truck in the opening scene of The Matrix—*arrayed like a drop-tile ceiling. The replacement of the individual with this brute system.*

You look a little whiter than usual. Do you remember when they said that to Keanu in The Matrix. *A certain type of ethnic ambiguity is the right screen for our projection.*

Have you seen the lobby in The Matrix.

Have you seen the lobby in The Conversation.

Have you seen the lobby in Three Days of the Condor.

The lines, curved or straight, the elevators or spiral stairs.

These points of access, these choke points, the protocol required to get in, to advance, unless you can beat the protocol, unless you can blast your way past it.

We like doors and we like lobbies.

But the internet is quite different. There are choke points, yes. But every packet, you see, every packet of the trillions sent down their twisting routes each day, every one goes in and out of that lobby, TCP/IP, the protocols, controlled by the system, even as it follows its distributed logic, each packet being routed its own way, it is timing and congestion and the vicissitudes of protocol.

Ah gug gug gug gug. Ah gug gug gug gug.

Ah we miss Sebastian.

Ah gug gug gug gug gug gug gug gug.

We live in a universe—it's perverse—a universe fine-tuned, they say, for life. We say: for death.

We remember Pepe.

The rarest Pepe.

All expressions of humanity, and it's Pepe, he's the one we see, he's the one who confronts us.

The things in us, the space in us that we created, to draw all the things into our body—the space, the things, are warmed, made tender—and then burnished—brought to a beautiful heat. Out loud it is cold, yet everything inside burns with a big heat.

What happens to those of us whose lines are subtly redrawn, who are gaslit, who must hold in our heads the notion that everything is okay, that nothing is happening, when in fact there are parts that are screaming Stop, we hate this. The abusers off the hook. Perhaps the abusers fooling themselves, even believing that nothing is happening—but no, of course not, they know precisely what they're doing. And perhaps with the best possible motives. They are getting to touch a body in a way they want to—within certain limits—and believe that they are doing no harm. Believing they get away with it. Not knowing or caring that within this supple and compliant body there are parts that are screaming like they are in hell. And of course, you can't have parts screaming and lie there, supple and compliant. So those parts are sent away, they are sent to the very edge of the horizon, and they can scream there. Yes, to have your father lie in bed with you, under a pretext—his back, his plans, spread out over his own bed.

Day after day, year after year, the screaming exiles off at the horizon, the surface on which all is calm, all is bright.

It wasn't a thousand, we think. Maybe dozens or hundreds. We just don't know. It happened. It's as blurred out as everything else. We had fathers.

There were fathers.

Were they Trump. Who were they.

Do you understand that at age eight, we had such a cultivated sense of . . . we had an exquisite self-hating inside of us.

We broke toys and sipped on Drano—just wet our lips in front of our mother. We jumped up and down on grates.

Ah gug gug gug.

The car was another space. Inside and outside. He would kiss us. On the lips. In front of the school.

There was the life with our father, then a job in computers, then our ten-year bet, then the holes and Sebastian, then the end of the world. And now we're here, Rachel.

The universe fine-tuned.

The internet has given us wisdom. All that the unresting thought of man has created in the ages is compressed into a small space in our brain.

We know that we are wiser than all of you.

Some soldiers just reached the electrical current snapping through the air room. There are so many soldiers in so many rooms, we cannot keep updating you. No one is safe now. There are too many lions. There are too many guns. There is electricity everywhere. There are more soldiers at the door.

*Treating children like meat. We do not mean as we were treated, arms
and legs maneuvered, touched, handled, the pliable child we were, without concern for the thought of the child, who was meat. We mean in our
ten years in the billionaire's cell. At the bottom of the internet, people
literally treated children like meat, images and videos of children who
were being prodded, torn, torn apart, children trussed and sliced and
done up, and like all human endeavor, the untimate shittiness of it—
these people are going for the supreme aesthetics of* Hannibal, *the loin
with a Cumberland sauce of red fruits, kidney pie with yellow beets and
chèvre, the famous roasted ortolan. They reach for that, and end up with
the opposite.*

Have you seen Cake Wrecks. *That was what the little children looked
like. You had a child. And a cannibal has made of your child a cake wreck.
Which would be worse, we wonder. To have your child prepared with ele-
gance, plump and succulent, well lit, drizzled with sauce, perfectly photographed in HD, or to see your child as a cake wreck.*

Have you seen Smiley's People, *how a woman is what breaks it all,
how it's always that way in these scenarios.*

*We're talking about protocol, diplomatic protocol, and it's showing the
whole system, and it needs . . . what. It needs a crazy woman, it needs a
plot point, and it's a crazy woman. But why can't we just show the whole
system without that crazy woman.*

We're going to put in a little drop now.

*Your screams and thrashings are loosening your tape and you know what
that means.*

More tape. More tape, more tape. Wrappy wrappy.

*A woman breaks or a mulatto breaks or a faggot breaks—there's the
whole history of art. But why should they be the ones to break.*

We met a Filipino coder poet and we fell for him. We fell in love. We got high and played Wii. He had written a book that we'd made in the world. Then we took him to our holes.

But see the soldiers, see what they're doing. Even when the soldiers are in the right branch and subtrack, and the right sub-subtrack, there is still so much left for them. Door that's a bomb, door that's a wall, door that reverses you, door that shrinks down when you touch it, door on a door on a door.

Stairs to windows, stairs to dirt, stairs to the creatures that live in the dirt, window to wall that's in fact a stair to a window to a wall that's in fact a stair to a window to a wall.

The sharks! sharks! room, the poison foam room.

How does China control a government. Pays a ton of money for resources, not direct political intervention. State- and non–state-controlled companies, no one makes money without the Communist Party, all the leaders and all their families deeply involved in this.

Microsoft with open standards, embrace, extend, destroy.

Imagine your genitals being chewed at by fire ants. What would you do. You can't rip it off, that can't be done, and the ants can't stop eating, they will never be destroyed, and they are chewing on your butthole, too, going up in there and chewing.

Our butt hurts, our whole body does ah gug gug gug gug.

Okay we feel . . . we feel better now.

About ourself but not the system.

But you are here, we are talking to you, the system, that is what we should talk about.

Let us get some wires in these birds. Get the juice flowing. It's a different drill bit of course, very delicate. We're going to change the drill bit.

You hear them getting close. You are jumping and choking. You should stop that.

Here's a droppy.

Ah gug gug.

Have we mentioned the decade we spent in the rich man's basement. He bet us twenty million dollars we couldn't spend a decade in his basement, nothing but the internet to keep us company. He came down hauling his blood helper boy, blood flowing from the boy to him, a boy in a hospital gown, pale and silent, the rich man looking in on us. Of course we could spend a decade there. We left the day before the bet's end, we had made the Aviary, we had carried out the blockchain heist, we didn't need his money, we didn't want it.

But why didn't we free the boy. Or boys.

Surely we looked back to his mansion and said, Hey boys, the ones who help with blood, surely we said to them, Boys, let's get out of here.

But we were, we think we were the sole survivor.

We built a distributed network of people who believed in undoing the network, or holding it back. And we had our small victories. We met Sebastian, and we were in love, then love was over. Trump was elected president. We said fine, it's fine, we will stop, it doesn't matter, we will stop. And one day we saw a mother in the airport, and we said no.

We said it's time now.

Hum hum hum.

It is so simple. To request three specific and highly unusual domains in a row, and that kicks open a back door on a BIND server. Three domains that had never been requested in the history of BIND, or they had, and no one had known, no one had known the power of requesting them in that order.

Request these three domains in a row from a thousand BIND servers at once and that gives access. That one can ask all upstream and down-stream, when infected, script, Morris worm–style that helps it spread. Kicks open a door. Gives you root or superuser control over a BIND server.

You could scan every AS out there and map what their servers are, then try to query them all at once. The hacking is happening in the same channel as DNS resolution, so it's hard to stop, because you can't shut off DNS resolution—that would stop the hacks, but would itself break the internet.

We are explaining because we want you to know, to understand.

Google has its own name server. We knew Google would be tough, Google tried to keep domain name infrastructure running as everything else blew up. Anyone can use the Google server, ask it for name info—three-fourths of people, the BIND users, had phone books that were complete gibberish, but Microsoft and Google had phone books that still worked.

If you have the right DNS servers in the hierarchy you don't need to get all of them. If we don't know an answer, we ask upstream. So as long as an exploited BIND server is upstream, eventually we'll get there, and bad servers are also querying downstream.

You need certificates, and that's hard. But we got certificates. We bought them, we stole them, the lost boys got a harvest of certificates.

Compromise a top-level certificate vendor, think of the DigiNotar attack, Google certificates fooled every browser in world, except Chrome, because Google is Chrome's mom.

Rush off to a suborned provider, gin up a certificate, slap it on in time to get a response, while also grabbing the CNN page—everyone would find the internet very slow, but only the first time they visited the site.

Distribute further, there are scripts to spin up proxy servers, each server a printing press for certificates without sending too much traffic back to the certificate authority. And it's hard to fix, you need a browser patch, because browsers trust the certificates.

Uh Rachel are you listening.

You seem to have passed out and we need you.

Ah gug gug gug gug.

We would like to trust you with the password.

The acid is working in your brain, productive of damage, clearing and generative damage. Perhaps a drop more. Perhaps more tape, you are flailing and ripping so hard.

A bit more acid. Now you can't do that, you have to hold still. Now you see the acid eats right into your skin.

Let us take our knife, your holes are clogged and clotted.

There now there, and now more acid.

It won't eat up your brain. Not all of the brain.

Huge botnet, you can use it to attack anything. You can use any of the computers to spread malware, they can all spread email with malware, attempt to attack other computers, try to harvest all the passwords on all the computers, but if going for stuff that happens fast, shut down the internet by DDoS attacks.

Huge botnet, and it all falls down.

Little pigeons, paper rolled on the leg, it's just code, that's all it is, that's all it could ever be, all these centuries, all these scratchings, all of writing, all of speech, the stuff we're made of, DNA and its replication, subatomic agitation, it's just code, just instructions, that's all it is, all it ever could be, you could fit it all on pigeon legs, given birds enough and time.

Then the end comes, and it's the age of gold.

It's all there in the documents of the time, the last speech of the last president aboard his zeppelin.

Given birds enough and time.

So now it's birds, in the last world, we said: No birds. Here we say: No, birds.

Do you understand.

An internet of birds, it's possible, it's what we're working on, it's what's next.

We heard a man once speaking of an internet of trees, that's possible, an internet of trees, we really do think it might be true, but we said, Why not start with an internet of birds.

Look at all these birds, they're not an internet yet, no not these birds, but there are so many birds.

We wish these birds were feeling better, they don't seem to be feeling well, but it's out there, it's already out there, our internet of birds.

We felt liquid sliding out of our left eye. It was not tears, or not crying, it was simply a liquid flow. And in the right eye, twitching, a crazy beat, like the heart of a trapped mouse stretched over the right side—for our point of view—on the upper eyelid. You could touch it and feel it. And we, we felt distant. Our eyes were doing things, and perhaps we were a bit sad, a bit tense, but that wasn't it. The board our eyes were plugged into didn't seem to be our board.

We drilled into our skull and reset the motherboard.

But the world was ending.

We drilled into our head, and then we shook the tree.

The doors in Inspector Gadget *opening.*

The doors in MST3K *opening.*

Ah gug gug gug gug gug gug.

We like a substance abuse, we like a fresh substance abuse inside of us.

We have our reasons.

Some systems are highly controlled, within us, some are distributed.

Some things get locked in, very controlled, in the body of a human animal, and others move far away—the control, the system, living apart from trauma. And the internet, emerging from the trauma of recent wars, the threat of nuclear wars, the need to find survivable modes of communication, just as a body that has been assaulted and threatened with assault will find ways to make its communications survive.

Your body is not a body, your body is a distributed network, some pieces communicate the end of the universe back to you, so many hops, but their messages still arrive, eventually, the packets inside of you, the messages will arrive someday at their destination, they are out there in the network, moving, looping, trying different routes, but they find their way home.

This is of course a metaphor, you can't see the system, can't truly see or know a single object, a single atom, but there are objects and atoms, they are embodied, and it is only by metaphor we can get there.

Every thought is a metaphor, every idea is a metaphor, every image we see a metaphor, the image and the thought, they refer to things that are real, but we can't get at them, we have no access, but if you want to shed a few layers, make it almost immanent, you can drill the holes.

You can at least see the images, the metaphors, for what they are, and they are bad actors.

Every person you see, every idea you've ever had, it's a bad actor, a trauma actor, a crisis actor. They say that every film is a documentary of the actors in it, and the actors are all bad, in every movie, they have always been bad, in the documentaries where we see them for what they are, they are paid crisis actors trying to fool us, and their payment comes with death, to die, to be freed from the role, that's the payment.

But grasses are much better, more natural, than the paid crisis actor, the birds are better, and the trees, though they often move too slow for us to truly take in what good actors they are. This is why they try not to shoot actors in fields of grass, because the authenticity of the grass, the naturalness of its movements, make the actors ridiculous, and in real life, too, we increasingly avoid fields of high grass. A woman went on a long vendetta against the grass, she called the police repeatedly, to get rid of marsh grass in a park, she said that women were being stalked there, that they would be raped, and this you understand was in a highly manicured urban space with a very small patch of marsh grass, a swath of tall grass ten feet long and half that wide, but it was the grass she hated, and she triumphed over the grass, they mowed it down.

They are near now. The soldiers. They will be here any minute now. We can't be here forever with you, though a part of us would like it.

Our childhood, our childhood, it was so many doors opening, and yet one we can't see or remember closed tight.

To make your peace with protocol, to accept distribution, and also the most rigorous protocol, a contested zone, rules, freedom, and yet it's not talked about.

And you just roll over for it.

Because it's how you make a system, how else can you make a system.

You just roll over for all the protocols you can't see, or that you have allowed yourself not to see.

Some soldiers just reached the lime room. Ooh, the front guy is falling in. Ooh, the others are retreating.

But the floor of the hallway has tipped up, and they are all falling in. And they are not even in the right branch.

But others are almost just outside, or they are up another stair and around, and it's windows of brick they'll see, and feathers, and a deep calm.

We don't know, we really can't know, where they are, they seem to have cut it, the cables to the screens, we have the light here, we do, because we have the generator here, but out there it's dark, it really is.

It really really is.

What finally made up our mind.

We saw Trump and we said okay.

We said okay, this is what the universe wants.

We said we would leave our mansion, we wired it up with bombs and we went to the airport, we would go somewhere else, another country, we would leave behind everything we thought we might do, we would abandon the plan for the big attack, the harvest of zero days, the months and years of planning, the internet of birds, we would get on a plane, go to another country, leave all that behind.

We saw a woman at the airport. She's playing I Spy with My Little Eye—and her voice, you understand, her voice is really much too loud, it doesn't have to be pitched this way for her son, but they're playing, and she says, I spy with my little eye something red. And the boy finds something. Something with lots of circles, I spy with my little eye. And it's really aggravating, this performance—this performance of motherhood, it's obviously a performance, it's outwardly directed, and it is going on and on, and you understand why the boy won't stop shrieking and crying when his mother stops talking, his mother has acclimated to this as the norm, and this is her default, this terrible woman hollering about the color red and a soccer ball and a drill, a tool, all the things she spies with her little eye. And we look around and we see the other mothers, they're giving a bit of side-eye, so we know it's not just us, they're put out as well by this self-aggrandizing performance of motherhood. And we realize, it's not just a performance, it's not just trumpeting her own mothering skills, the fact that she's building her son's neural connections as we speak, stimulating him, forcing him to learn, it's actually something more than that, she's bullying us, the others in line, this is an aggressive act, an attack, but one that you simply can't call her on, she knows she has immunity, and she's glorying in it, she's picking more things, glasses on an old ugly face, the face ducking down, turning, hiding itself, then it's a brown bag, and the brown bag is falling apart, it's an old suitcase, the suitcase of a poor person, and she calls it out, this bullying white woman, dragging along her son. And we realize what she's actually saying is I spy with my little eye structural racism. I spy with my little eye white impunity. Because imagine it. Imagine if she was black. How that would change things. If she was Asian, a Chinese American mom loudly educating her children on the backs of everyone in that line. A Latino woman. Think of it. Two femmy gay guys, two big dykes. Because part of the problem, in truth, was the nonreaction. Plug them in, one by one, imagine. That's white privilege, that space of utterly obnoxious performance that also somehow gaslights the whole culture, that makes criticism impossible— criticize that woman with her kid, and suddenly you're the crazy one. But we weren't.

We weren't crazy.

Imagine it was an Arab woman speaking actual Arabic, can you imagine the reaction. This woman educating her child in some foreign tongue, pointing at one passenger after another.

We thought of the kitbashing of Joel Hodgson. We thought of the weary giants and the rarest Pepes. We thought of a thousand white women calling the police on a thousand women of color for no reason whatsoever.

And the next day we kicked open the door.

We reached into our bag of tricks. We set up our Rube Goldberg device, all the zero days, all our long-dormant plans.

The next day the world fell through a trapdoor we invented.

And Trump came tumbling after.

We hear them, they are only a few doors away. We will give you a last big squeeze of the aqua regia, and you will be better, your brain will be.

Let us gather some birds, let's see if we can get these birds working, wouldn't that be wonderful, a fully functional internet of birds.

Some more aqua regia, and then some birds, Rachel.

We're so glad you joined us, Rachel.

Let's find some birds.

Let's go get the birds that will be our future.

And then my hand was free and wrapped around the drill before I knew it was free. The duct tape was tearing and I had the drill. I ripped the tape from my mouth. Birdcrash was facing away, he was at his desk across the room, digging through a heap of dead birds, and I put the drill to the tape at my ankles and pulled the trigger. But my feet were chained too tight, even with the tape cut through I was still suspended, so I cut the tape binding my other hand.

I could barely think, barely see.

He was coming toward me, and I was drilling at the tape that bound my midsection, and it broke and I slammed to the floor, my head and shoulder hit the concrete, feet still suspended, and he was above me, moaning *Noooo, noooo*, and wrestling with me, he was yanking the drill from my hand.

But I wouldn't let him have the drill.

He was standing over me on the floor, we struggled, and he wrenched my arms back and forth, my whole body swinging back and forth, but I held on.

I was the stronger—I felt my body lit with a wild crushing strength.

I ripped it away and drilled into the top of his foot where it met the ankle.

His fists came down hard twice on my skull, and lights flashed, but I was still going into the foot, and then he was on the ground, and staring into me with his dark liquid eyes, curled up on his side, crying *Nooooo, nooooo*, pulling himself into a fetal position, and I put the drill to his temple and bore down, it went through,

I pressed both hands on top of it and gathered my weight up over my hands, feet still suspended behind me, I arched my back and pushed down and felt the drill bit go through, ripping hair that spun around the bit and the drill bit stalled, and I leaned in, and I said, What's the password, what's the password for the document, you want people to have the document, and he whispered it to me, and I was pushing the drill and it hit something hard on the other side, and I kept on until the bit could go no farther, buried to the hilt, and I put all my weight on it and his eyes went wide and dry and I felt the little bit, the one he'd changed out for the birds, whirling and whirling in his brain.

trump_sky_alpha/3_resolver_daemon

trump_sky_alpha/3_resolver_daemon

3_1_zone_transfer

You opened your eyes. There was light and sound. People were there and then gone. Everything is fine. We shall rest. A man was speaking, but it was wrong. The words were words with no definition. It was night and day. There were people. You couldn't move. Everything is fine. They brought apple juice. The man was back. He was speaking. You wanted to say, *I pity you.* You wanted to spit the words at him. Words were a gold ball in your mouth that your teeth were locked around. You can't get air in. But you resist. At last you breathe. You opened your eyes. It was night and then day. There was a man. He was speaking, but it was wrong. We shall rest. He was holding your hand. You moved your hand from his. Words were a huge golden thing your teeth were stuck in. We shall rest. We shall see all evil sink away. Everything is fine. It was night and then day. A man was reading. We shall see all of our sufferings bathed in a perfect mercy. Your hand moved. Your blankets were soaked and cold. Everything is fine. The blankets were dry and tucked you in. A great compassion shall enfold the world. The meat of rotting apples filled your guts up with burn. You moved your hand away. Your mouth was full of gold. Your blankets were clean. It was night and then day. We shall rest. You vomited gold. You puked out golden apples. You opened your eyes. You opened the envelope. You tore the bandages from your scalp and found the holes. Blood pooled under your nose and above the lips and was running through your lips and in your mouth and under someone's tongue. Blood flowed into your nose as you breathed all night and all of the day. You were holding his hand. You were holding some blood. Gold apples tumbled from your mouth. Gold apples tore the corners of your lips. Your jaw unhinged. Blood flowed against time and gravity and ran up into your nose, as you breathed, and how did it—solid gold? How did blood and gold flow back into you? You choked on golden fruit and you choked on whole words. You choked on blood and the sweet liquid of the words your mouth threw up. Words were a sweet gold fluid and you loosed them. You spat the words you knew and have known forever—

My poor poor dear one you are crying. I know you've had no joy in your life but wait dear one wait.
We shall resist. We shall resist.
We'll just resist.
Yes dear one.
We shall resist.

—and you puked your blood and apples.

trump_sky_alpha/3_resolver_daemon

3_2_dumpdb "[-all|-cache|-zones|-adb|-bad|-fail]"

It's been great, it's been really amazing, the extent to which we've had the biggest response by far to the threats we've faced, and that's something to me that's very exciting. In the history of this great nation, you look at FDR or Eisenhower, as you know this is a substantially greater response, and that is why we've been able to contain threats that are much bigger than any we've ever faced before. It's a record breaker, this was just certified, it's a record breaker in terms of how fast something this big could have ever been contained.

The loss of life, it's always tragic. But it's been incredible. The results that we've had with respect to loss of life. We have little Rocket Man and the crazy disrespect and Iran and China and it's all been contained beautifully.

I've been receiving calls, mayors, governors, big guys, all thanking me. Everyone agrees that my first responders and military have been amazing. It's a fabulous day—they say it's the greatest aircraft of all time, they call it the Crystal Palace of the Sky, but it is a very tough and very safe ship and it is going to do very very well today, believe me. I went up to New York, now it's down to Mar-a-Lago, and everything is going beautifully.

In New York, what was happening in New York, it should be banned, the things that people were marching for in New York, or really, rioting, many people have said that it's treason. And what's the punishment for treason? Isn't it death? It has been, at times. Of course I hope everything's fine in New York. New Yorkers, they love what I'm saying about many different things. It's the fake news, in most cases, who are the bad people who are instigating this.

There are things that the last guy set up that were so dumb and so weak, everything with cyber, with the military, with our missiles, it's just dumb, dumb stuff. But you look at what we're doing—I can't talk about it all, but believe me, we've been doing very well. There are some really beautiful organizations of people in the military and they tell me they're so happy that I'm the one here when it happened. And all the experts are saying how much worse it would have been if it was still the last guy.

I really need to thank the generals—can I take a moment to thank the generals? These generals we've got, they are amazing, and they've said to me, We're so glad it's you. In every single branch of the military we have, we have these generals, and what a job they are doing. What an amazing job. And what they're saying to me is that this is a very small little bomb that's being used over there, a small nuclear device, and what we used, and can use, it's so much bigger. Would I be up here if it was any real danger? You run down the line with what's happening in these places around the world. These are almost all very small little bombs, and even the ones that are a little more serious, even those, ours are much, much bigger, so people can understand that we are in control of the situation, and everything that's happened in these last hours, well, we are going to have a very, very successful number of days.

You wouldn't know it from the press, just how beautifully it's going. But where I'm standing in Trump Sky Alpha, you see them, all these beautiful cities, beautiful towns below, and they look fabulous. It's been happening what, a few hours, not even a whole day yet, or just a day, and they're saying already, they're saying, He had his finger on the button, and he pressed it like we said he would, but they're so clueless. They have no idea—it's not a button. It's a code, or a series of codes, and a process. And you don't need to send them all at once, and we haven't sent them all. In terms of what we could do on a nuclear level, we have been very restrained, actually. But these beautiful towns and cities and highways below, we're going to do what we have to do to keep them safe.

Just for today we're going without the passengers, I said let's have the passengers, the Secret Service said not today. They said to be safe—frankly the safest place in the world right now is probably right here on Trump Sky Alpha, this tremendous flying machine. I think we could have had passengers, but I said, Fine, we're going to have a phenomenal flight, and all across the globe there are Trump Sky aircraft lifting off, and there are passengers out there I can see in the monitors from all over the globe, in absolutely the most beautiful style, and they're so happy to be on the finest aircraft anywhere, all my passengers, really, they're all doing great, all of these people across the globe who are so proud to be in these beautiful aircraft.

You wouldn't know it from the press, just how beautifully it's going, the media has been really terrible, there are a couple people—and I'm not going to name names—but there are a couple people who are just so disgusting, CNN and the failing *New York Times*. No administration in the history of the world who has dealt so beautifully with such a huge botnet in the cyber, and everyone on YouTube, the fact that you can see me shows how very beautifully it's truly going. People have called me up crying. Millions of people have tried to call the White Hose to thank me for saving their families. We are talking about billions I've saved, literally billions.

The press should be ashamed.

Europe, the stuff we're seeing from there—there's another one where I was proved right. Everyone said, How dare he say these things about NATO? And now you look at what's happening, people are saying, You know, Trump was right, NATO didn't save them from all these terrorists and all these refugees they let in.

I really think the press, you know, the media, I think the press, my opinion of the media is that in many cases, not in all cases, are not good people. They're stupid—I'm sorry, it's true, I'm not sure if it's that they're stupid or they're lying—both I think, quite a lot of the time, unfortunately—that's why I do these livestreams, because all they do is lie, because I have never received such bad publicity for doing such a good job.

It's such disrespect to our country, our flag, the things they've been reporting. I've heard that I was preoccupied, that I was too much time with the press and all their disrespect. Not at all, not at all. I have plenty of time on my hands. All I do is work. And to be honest with you that's an important function of working. It's called respect for our country and our soldiers. Many people have died, many, many people—not now, but in our history. Some now, sure. Many people are so horribly injured. Some from now, but from all our history and to be frank some not smart things from the past. I was at Walter Reed hospital and I saw so many great young people and they're missing legs and they're missing arms and they've been so badly injured. And they were fighting for our country. They were fighting for our flag. And then the fake news comes, they spit on the flag and they all line up to spit on all these great people and they spit on all those arms and legs, when it's the flag they should be wrapping all those arms and legs up in.

So we're here, up here in Trump Sky Alpha, such a gorgeous view. It's too cold, though. Cold doesn't bother me, but I can feel it—I can feel the temperature of the air. That's the bureaucrats, you know, they didn't want me to leave, to take off, and it's too bad, the heat's not set right. We don't have the usual passengers today, they said,

No way, no, Mr. President, like little babies, I'm up here and it looks just fine to me, just cold. That sort of thing doesn't bother me, but it needs to be fixed, this is absolutely top of the line, a crystal palace, and I can see, I can see right here in the video screens the other aircrafts in the fleet, they don't seem to be having problems. All around the world, China, Russia, Thailand, they're so tough, that's why they're winning. Looks like we may have just lost Brazil. Oh yeah, that looked bad. But that's their thing, they're absolutely in charge of their own security, that has nothing to do with us. The point is, there is no safer place, really, right now, than right here on Trump Sky Alpha, we've got truly beautiful security.

You know that there are cultures where they bury the subjects right there in the ground with pharaohs, with emperors, they bury living people right there in with them. And somehow everyone loses it when I suggest taking people out in this perfectly safe absolutely top-of-the-line luxury aircraft. Well, it's not the fault of my fans, my fans would be here with me, the American people are such big fans, such great supporters, and I really appreciate how they would all be here if they could, if the generals and the Secret Service, if they didn't want me to do this at all.

It may be cold but what about all those crybabies in the situation room? We have some wonderful generals, but also some crybabies. I have the best generals, the best information, and we don't need a situation room. What's that even mean, situation room? *Oh, here's the room where we handle situations?* So stupid. So stupid. We are going to move into a place soon that is much tougher and much smarter. It is time for everyone in this country who is talking all this garbage to get tough and smart.

You don't have to sit in the cold if you don't like it. There's a thermostat, you know. You can reach out and just change it. One way or another.

The people who are protesting, they show disrespect for our soldiers, our first responders, it's just disgusting and they have to watch what they say. I look out and see the fighter jets and helicopters around Trump Sky Alpha, our beautiful military escort, and I think: Are they serious? Disrespecting our troops?

How do you think my old opponent would have done up here? *OOOooWWooah WWOOOaaahh*, she would have been flopping all around, you think she could fly this thing? She'd be choking, choking to death, she couldn't take this, her lungs, her brain, those were things there that weren't good. Coughing, just coughing nonstop. No-good lungs and brains. You talk about a finger on the button, how do you do it with a finger that's coughing? It would be a total mess, just a disaster, and if you think about how she would have handled the thugs, it would be absolutely corrupt and it would have been just pure chaos.

You have these thugs that are rioting and she would have been so weak and fainting and coughing, and our great African American former president hasn't come out of retirement to tell them to knock it off and stop destroying our country—you have these animals wrecking our cities and killing our law enforcement like dogs in the street, and believe me, I have sent the military to so many places and they are going to do a fabulous job keeping all this contained even in the face of those who are saying let's destroy the whole country.

Did I see Ivanka? I saw Ivanka on TV, sure. Saying *no no no*. Does she even understand the records we've broken? It is very hard to understand how she could have turned on me if she had seen the records. And even if some family is gone now—and I'm very skeptical of those reports, we're talking about people with agendas saying, Oh this one's dead, that one's dead—even if some family is gone, even if some of her family is gone, I've still got my Ivanka, she doesn't know what she's saying. Maybe someone made her say it.

I'd say just you wait. Just wait until you see what we're cooking up. And I turn to CNN and I see her saying *no no no*, and I think . . . really?

She's in shock, she's basically what I call hysterical, and they stick a microphone in her face?

A lady who's in hysterics and who pukes right down the front of her blouse?

Not an attractive moment, I admit. But then they play it over and over? Her *no no no* was that she was going to puke! It wasn't about me.

She's the biggest, really the biggest supporter, my beautiful daughter, Ivanka.

You know ever since she was a child we dressed her in gold—golden hair, and our home, you know our home, gold walls, little gold tables everywhere, lovely gold-leaf sconces, very nice, gold candlesticks and clocks, the most karats and the highest purity you can get into gold leaf, even in all the gears of all the clocks and in the gears of all the golden clockwork toys, we made it all extra gold after she came into our lives. They call this the Crystal Palace, Ivanka, honey, I'll redo it for you, we're going to get some flags and bunting in here, some gold leaf, some of those nice gold-leaf cherubs.

All that gold leaf, all those years, that was money well spent. The most elegant, the most deluxe, you've got to spend it to make it.

You know how much money we spent on nukes over the years? Five trillion dollars. And they said we can't use them. *Oh no, don't use them.* We had eight years of the last guy who wouldn't even say ISIS.

The press is so dishonest and so unfair.

So the seats are empty today on Trump Sky Alpha—well, that was their call, not mine. These seats should be full and people wanted them to be full but there's considerations. So Trump Sky Alpha, it has a few dings and scratches. She is flying like a dream, and we are going to get her fixed back up, better than ever.

We're going to rebuild anything in this beautiful country that needs it, rebuild it much better than anything that was lost to these animals, and that has been greatly, greatly exaggerated. We're doing very, very well. You hear that, Ivanka? I know how to build and if it was lost it is not really lost, it is going back better, just fabulous.

Ooh! There goes Poland, looks like, ooh, that looks like a bad one, looks like we lost Kazakhstan, I'm going to turn off these video screens, it's really distracting, the incompetence, the sheer incompetence of these people and their security precautions.

Maybe we won't rebuild the Capitol building, not for a few years. Wouldn't that be nice? Some of these people, they need to be in prison, not a beautiful fabulous piece of real estate. Unbelievable what some of them are saying. Just unbelievable.

They say some things, and then they repeat it overseas, this dishonest, completely fabricated stuff, and it's criminal, it really is, it's to the point where you even have a dishonest prime minister saying that what I'm doing is going to end civilization as we know it.

I wish I had that power.

As for the Pentagon, they can just stay in Trump Tower for now, we've got all the room we need there, wouldn't that be great, me and all my generals there in Trump Tower.

They're really happy with what's going on. It's something that's been very well received. By the generals and even by the press, it's been very well received.

But why is it so cold? When what I'm talking about is getting a handle on radical Islamic terrorists and refugees that are all over the place. The last guy let them come in by the thousands and thousands—they're in our farms and cities. We have radical Islamic terrorists and they have to be killed. And in this same prime minister's country, it's really funny to me, you have people in his country there blowing up whole cities, families blown to bits, children, little crying children, you see arms and legs, disgusting, people blown up, hacked up, people running absolutely wild around all these people who are blown up, and these problems started with people he let in, the refugees he let in by the thousands and thousands.

And somehow I get the blame.

I honor all people military or otherwise that were killed and I think it's very important to do so. I honor the people that were killed in Benghazi, needlessly killed in Benghazi, under Crooked Hillary.

Cough, cough.

But when you have parts of the military that are not obeying orders that are not doing what they need to do, then those people will be dealt with, and it's being handled.

My understanding is that some elected officials are among those being talked to, some military, but this is a military operation, so I don't have all the details. Whatever our response is, it's all vetted by generals. It's all been very carefully vetted, and if something goes wrong, people are going to try to blame me, but it's not me. I don't mind protesters, but you have to be honest. I don't want the credit but I shouldn't get these attacks. Not when it's not true.

The generals give me the codes, and they're very beautiful. Some other generals, they need to be dealt with, but it's all been vetted.

I was viciously attacked, so I just have to sit there?

With the White House, when it comes to the White House, we are going to start over and it is going to be much, much better, really fantastic, that place was falling apart, Ivanka said to me, when we first moved in, she said to me, she looked at the first lady quarters, she said, *What a dump.* I mean they almost did us a favor, I think Ivanka would have said that . . .

So let's see what happens, hopefully the White House will be fine, but the Southern, I mean the Winter White House, or the Southern White House, that's what some people have begun calling it, Mar-a-Lago, the Summer White House, that's what they call it. Maybe that's where we'll go, my people, my family that are still my family, my Ivanka, we'll live there. Mar-a-Lago, she can go there with me, the old White House, you don't have to sit in a place like that, do you, Ivanka, it's still a free country.

It doesn't matter what Ivanka would have said.

Doesn't everyone's family come and go? You tell me.

I've known girls and boys, women, adult sons. Weren't there so many, so many that were something to me?

Isn't there a new life? Someone, someone talked about it, the evil, how we wouldn't take it, and some mercy that was really the best.

There's planes swooping in, look at our boys go, swooping in and out and all around. But it's cold. If you're listening, open your mouth, take out a mirror, look inside your mouth. If you've got gold in your teeth, open wide, let me see it when I land, we need some gold in here.

They'll go around, they'll collect the jewelry and the watches, so if you could just open your mouths.

They'll knock on your door and ask for the gold you've got, it's fine, it's just something they have to do now, just go along with it.

Does it get cold or hot when you're way up in the air? I thought it was hot way up by the sun, but it's setting, that's true, and it's so cold. The sun is setting, but there's lights at the horizon from all directions, ringing us around, just beautiful.

The number of people that have died in this country, now that has been greatly, greatly exaggerated.

I mean that's what people do for ratings. You see all these people who are dead, the mounds of people where no one can figure out who they are, and let me tell you, when it's even people, when it's not just decoys that some terrorists shoestringed together, when the mounds are actually people, what it is, is it's the people the last guy let in here and we have no idea who they were, no documentation, no idea where they came from, people coming in by the tens of thousands having some sort of civil war with each other, and that's why they're all scattered across the streets and stacked up in mounds. If they want to make it easy on us by just killing each other, be my guest.

It's easy to think, Hey, let's let it happen, why should I help all the fake news media who are trying to destroy me? The *New York Times*, if I made certain decisions, would not be the failing *New York Times*, but the smoldering *New York Times*.

I love the media, and I know you love me, but you've got to have balance.

Maybe there's some people that should be smoldering.

Maybe there's lots of things that would be better off as smoldering wrecks, and that would clean them up.

There's a map, on Twitter, here's a map of how it is now, with me, and how much worse it would be if it was Hillary. Look at that. Almost total devastation. That's what people don't understand.

They dislike me, the liberal media dislikes me. I mean I watch people—I was always the best at what I did, I was the—I was, you know, I went to the—I went to the Wharton School of Finance, did well. I went out, I—I started in Brooklyn, in a Brooklyn office with my father, I became one of the most successful real estate developers, one of the most successful businesspeople. I created maybe the greatest brand, and the greatest presidency. I was successful, successful, successful. I was always the best athlete, people don't know that. But I was successful at everything I ever did and then I run for president, first time—first time, not three times, not six times. I run for president first time and lo and behold, I win. And then people say, Oh, is he a smart person? I'm smarter than all of them put together, but they can't admit it. They had a bad year.

So a few things are blowing up? Things are always blowing up. Maybe it's a good thing.

You have a corrupt media and they're saying I'm responsible for this.

I've done nothing wrong, and that's been proven over and over, but the fake news won't understand.

Something isn't right.

It's cold in here. I'm in my beautiful Trump Sky Alpha, and there's gold spokes on the wheel and I know there's gold all over, but it's all smudged. I need more gold—I need to see it. If you're listening at home, it's time for the gold. Open up those jewelry boxes—hold what gold you've got out the windows. Who's got gold fillings? Let me see those chompers. Look up in the sky and open your mouths and let me see those chompers with the gold.

I'll send some guys around. Hand in your gold jewelry, your watches and jewelry, and then let's talk about the teeth. I need what's in your teeth.

I used to live in golden rooms above the city. You've seen them, all those pictures, me and my family in golden rooms.

My daughter, she says to me, she says, Daddy, no, and then she goes on TV and she says it. She's disgusting. It's just disgusting. She says *no no no*, the fake news take that to mean that she thinks what I'm doing is wrong, that we have a choice, that this isn't what we want. Really? We have a choice?

Such a lie. And they know it's a lie! And spread the word, folks, but they know it's a lie. She's a baby, she's being a baby. And I don't throw babies out, believe me. I love babies! I love my children, I love babies. I don't throw babies out, believe me.

We just need some gold.

Wherever you are, if you're watching this, if we can open up some of the computers, there's gold in some of those, gold in the wires.

Gold chips, gold pins and lids, all those computer chips from all those fantastic companies.

I mean, my own daughter, I thought she was smart, she says *no no no*? What a baby.

And she thinks just because we've lost some family that we're lost somehow? Let me tell you, we have lost some family, they've lost a lot of families out there, and that's why we have to do it, we don't have to be babies about it.

We just do it.

We do what we have to do.

I don't lose often. I almost never lose. I have worked hard. It has not been easy for me, it has not been easy for me. And you know I started off in Queens, my father gave me a small loan, and I made so much more. So much money.

Those tenants complained. They complained so much. Families, poor families, rooms that are dirty, rooms that were wrong, babies that were screaming, little babies who didn't get it at all. I'd do a walk-through, I'd say, You don't have to sit here in the cold.

You can reach right up and fix it.

Don't ask me to fix it, you do it.

The years with your children are gold, they say that's the golden age. My kids, they're not kids anymore, but they're kids as far as I'm concerned. They'll always be my kids. Even the kids that aren't anymore, these are my kids, kids come and go.

I have made a great deal of money and success by getting into certain businesses and getting out of others, and it's been really fantastic for me. And internationally speaking, yes, we have to get out of certain businesses and get into others, and it can all be very, very profitable, for us as a country, right now. The things and events that have happened—terrible, terrible things—the terrible things all around the world that are happening are things from the weakness and the rot that the last guy put in it, but there is still profit there to be made if you get out right.

I would say, Ivanka, read the polls, this is all so popular, and we can get out, too, get out of things that are failing, I am very good with getting out. Ivanka, look at yourself, your mouth and your hair, look at how beautiful you are. And I would say, What did I do? What did I do? Look at *my* mouth and *my* hair. Aren't we the same? I loved you, you know?

And the other. Wasn't there one? How many are there? How many children do I have?

On TV someone cut my head off, and they all cried. I had to tell them, it's not me. I'm still right here. Hey, kids, your daddy, he's still alive and he's going to be alive a very, very long time.

Maybe forever.

They're saying now you can live forever, and maybe it's really true. Maybe it's true. It could be true.

So if I'm going to live forever, how is it that I'm expected to apologize?

How am I supposed to live forever with an apology when it's not even fair?

You're puking, and I should apologize?

Look, Ivanka puked on TV and that's not nice to look at.

Should I apologize? I think apologizing's a great thing, but you have to be wrong. I will absolutely apologize, sometime in the hopefully distant future, if I'm ever wrong.

She has said all of these terrible things, *no no no*. And I have a terrific relationship with the generals, and we've got all these generals saying I'm right, so I should listen to her? If we could just get some of you with the gold teeth to just wrench them out, if people near them would help them wrench them out, and collect the jewelry, all of it, whatever you got, and I'll send some guys to pick it all up. All these generals who will pass me the code and I have to say I'm wrong somehow?

People say I have sacrificed no one and lost no one and I have lost people. I have lost, I have lost—the people I lost are some of the best people you could ever lose, and the people doing the saying are garbage.

Ivanka, honey.

She is so beautiful, I mean what a girl.

If she wasn't my own daughter?

She's gold.

Her beauty that's gold came through me, and anyone can see that. Anyone can see it. But there is another beauty, inside and out, you could cut her open and see a whole new way of being beautiful.

A father could cut open his daughter or really just open like a door in her side and find the beauty inside, and find that everything is gold in there, like clockwork.

They say a king touches his food and it becomes gold, and he can't eat it, but I can.

I can eat gold.

I can eat all kinds of gold.

And I know that she has lost people, and that she feels lost, but she hasn't lost me.

Together with the gold that's in us, together we'd be in a golden room, all our gold animals, the tigers and singing birds, it would be so fabulous.

If she wants to lose me then that's fine.

You hear that, honey? It's just fine.

Your call.

Be a baby.

I really could care less.

So they're blowing up everyone all around us, so they're attacking all that, all of us.

Whoa.

Whoa! That was a big one, but folks, I'm fine, this beautiful aircraft, they call it the Crystal Palace of the Sky, but look at us, we're still flying, more beautiful than ever.

It's the kind of thinking you need, it's phenomenal, that we're still flying, it's all excellent, the best deal. It's complicated, but it will be, it will be one of the great deals.

Mar-a-Lago, it's not so far off now, it's right on schedule, maybe there'll be some extra lights there, maybe a few flames, but it's the Winter White House, fabulous.

I hope everyone listening is okay. I wish I could see you all, I know you all look great, you really do. I think people haven't been sleeping well, it's affecting their brains.

Not me. I sleep like a baby, it's true.

Where do you think my old opponent is? Old and sick and dead, I guarantee.

If they knock at your door and ask for some gold, don't make a fuss.

Maybe just leave it outside your front door. But keep an eye on it— don't let anyone take it until my guys are there.

We're all sharing now, if I could offer the generals one piece of advice, I'd say, Let's wrap up the things in gold. If we're going to use these things no one has ever used, shouldn't they be gold? I mean no one has used them before so let's wrap them in gold leaf, gold filigree, more karats than you've ever seen, a world record, beautiful, fabulous, it's better than anyone's ever done, in gold.

They said it couldn't be done, we've done it.

Some people may be knocking, do what they say, no fuss, no problem. If they say go with them, go with them. If they say open your mouth, you open wide.

Last night I dreamed of El Dorado, of the seven cities of gold.

I dreamed of Heron of Alexandria, who boiled his daughter's body and chopped up the corpse into little bits, and he made a fabulous new family of clockwork and bone and gold, and set it free in the world, and that family, that family has been making their way ever since, it's true, through all those centuries.

I dreamed of all the presidents, and they were all, this is true, they were dead meat, it turned out you know that they were just dead meat in their graves, and then I saw the emperors of old who were still living, black robes with gold brocade, these huge black robes with gleaming golden fringe, nodding and welcoming me in.

Why shouldn't the last guy have gone out there and done something about the thugs, come out of retirement, before he died?

You've got to wonder about that guy, you really do.

There's computer chips in the walls, all around our great country, there's chips in the walls, little trilobites running around in the walls plated gold, it's true.

You can break into the walls and grab them, grab one and pop it in my mouth, when I land.

Bring me a bite.

Bring me back a bite for when I land.

Open up your mouth.

With all the people whose doors we've knocked on and whose gold we're getting, or whose bones we're getting down there on the ground, or will get when all this is wrapped up, when I'm not way up here in Trump Sky Alpha.

We've got gold leaf right here on the ship's wheel, on the spokes and handles, and I can eat it off anytime I want.

It feels like it's finally getting warm.

Is it just me or is it finally getting warm in here?

Part of me feels hot and part of me doesn't.

Part of me feels really, really hot and part is ice.

Are we getting some gold?

We've got gold at Mar-a-Lago, I can't wait to see all that gold.

I'm going to wrap it up in even more, even more gold than we've had, and we've had so much, so much.

The biggest mansion in Florida, who knows, it may be the biggest in the country by now, depending on what's happening.

Would that be such a bad thing?

Get me a trilobite, and set one aside for Ivanka, I'm sure she's on her way.

If I have to die, shouldn't everyone? They buried them in the tombs with the kings and emperors of old, but they didn't bury everyone.

We're going to bury everyone, the gold, all of that and everyone.

But who says I even have to die.

Me and death, me and dying, I'm really not sure, it doesn't sound right.

Ronny Jackson is a doctor, he is actually the doctor that gave me my physical. And he said that I am in great shape. And the Democrats, liberals, deep state, they were very upset to hear that.

They were thinking—maybe—that I'll die. I know some were hoping that.

But why should I die? I created maybe the greatest brand. I was successful at everything I ever did and then I run for president, first time—first time, not three times, not six times. I ran for president first time and lo and behold, I win. And then people say oh, is he a smart person? I'm smarter than all of them put together, but they can't admit it. They think I'm not smart? And they think he's someone who's going to die someday? They had a bad year.

You've all been so incredible in this. In the beautiful statements you've made about the job we're doing. Everyone, all across this country, united, making beautiful statements about the job we're doing. I'm here, aren't I? You put me here. What a beautiful thing, what a very beautiful thing, and everything I've given you to see.

So let's do it.

Let's just do it.

I have talked to the generals and the generals who are with us have given me some really, really wonderful codes to work with, and the codes are beautiful, just beautiful. Reach through the sheetrock to the gold. I am not going to let anything happen here. We'll find our families and we'll save our families if our families can be saved. So, the first events were small little events, and with some of the others, they're still gathering the data, and we'll know soon, but now's the time to act. I'm landing now, and here are the codes. Ivanka, I'd like you here when we do the next response. It is contained but we need more response, and then we'll go up to the Mar-a-Lago living room with its thousand-wing gold-leaf ceiling. These are the codes. I can see Mar-a-Lago now, how it's all gold. Everything they are saying is that it is contained, and they are saying they really love our response, they're all saying it's gold, but the gloves are coming off. I've been nice, but I don't have to be so nice anymore, we can't listen to the babies anymore, all the little crying babies, waah waaaaah. I'm taking the gloves off, right? Yes? Take the gloves off. Taking the gloves off. The generals are saying, the ones who are any smart at all, they look around and say, Look at all this gold, all this gold you've made, let's take the gloves off. They're saying we won't be able to survive up there in the living room, but they don't know us, do they? The thousand-wing ceiling, and my fingers, they're gold. Yes? Here are the codes. Can you see those on camera? Here's all of the codes. Guys, let's go all in. We're doing the big one. The response we did this afternoon, I'm a real estate guy, I build things, I built real estate and I built a family and built so many terrific buildings, some of the very best buildings, and I want to tell you, the response we did was the most beautiful thing I think I've ever built, bones flecked in gold and wrapped up in all kinds of slashing golden light. But this will be ten times bigger. I had boys and girls, I lose track sometimes. It will be ten hundred times bigger. Sending everything we've got, everything, every last thing. They'll all be here. Sure they will be. All my boys and girls. And what a phenomenal thing to see. And believe me, we've got much, much more like that, now that the gloves are coming off, the gold that's coming is so much more than all the gold that's been in all the worlds that have been. So I think in terms of my response what you'll see is we're doing very, very well, that that one was one of the best, did you even see that, the response we did? We'll build things in gold and we'll build things in bones. The codes, you've all seen the codes? And the next one, it's going to fill us up, Ivanka, honey, fuck the babies, run the codes, it'll be gold all up through everything, the best ever.

trump_sky_alpha/3_resolver_daemon

3_3_keyname:secret

After the events at the Birdcrash compound, the relaunch of the *New York Times* was halted, and Galloway was moved from Modesto to a military base in Northern California.

The general in charge of the Office of Communication Oversight told Galloway not to worry, the magazine launch would still happen, most likely on the eighteen-month anniversary.

Galloway said that the pieces were keyed to the first anniversary—they wouldn't work later.

The general said, Now Tom, that's not true. The pieces are mostly evergreen.

Two years, the general said, could even be fine, though he didn't think that sort of delay would be necessary. But the thing was, Rachel, for the moment, she had to be their priority. Her health, her recovery. She was in a coma, yes, but there was hope, unquestionably. And her investigation had unearthed a lot—wonderfully, but also . . . there is a shadow on it, he told Galloway. A shadow on the whole launch of the magazine, to those watching from above. Given the whole business with Birdcrash et cetera. Some very fruitful, very interesting things. But complications of this magnitude, they call for a period of reassessment. And, the general added, though he couldn't go into details here—there's trouble in the provinces.

Galloway said, I don't need to know anything about that.

Tom! You make this sound like some kind of trap. I'm telling you, I think we could partner on this stuff, I've grown to like you quite a bit, and telling this story the right way, that's going to be key. That will be the anchor piece in the magazine. Keep the other light pieces, of course, but we're at a critical time. There's, ah, unrest out there, and we've been . . . a little scanty with the details and I understand why people are getting tired of that. If we get this story right—and it has to be done in the right way—it's a story about a certain incompetence in the past, but things now are different. Things are in hand, experts are hard at work. Obviously, we've been going with the foreign powers thing, that they were the ones who did the internet attack, and I think we stick with that story. The evidence supports it, in all honesty. Sebastian, you know, he was from the Philippines. And there's a China link, and I'm sure Korea once we sort it all out. The Aviary might have been a handful of people, it might have been a hundred. It was decentralized, but they certainly got it together and delivered in the clutch. So foreign powers is still the thing, but also, the domestic enemy. We can't just have a whole new story, we need to add on to the one we already have. The enemy without and the traitor within—that's our story.

That's a good story, Galloway said.

Yes, I think so. We've found all kinds of really wonderful piquant details. There are notebooks, Birdcrash had these notebooks. He was involved in a massive cryptocurrency heist, he had a crazy idea about an internet made out of birds. Do you know where his name came from?

Galloway said that he didn't.

There was a cassette—it was released by a little record label in Oregon. It was called *Birdcrash*, and apparently he was quite obsessed with it: it had resisted the internet, that was his idea, you see, the music wasn't on any streaming site, it was this analog artifact from the late '80s. Only a few hundred copies ever made, a sort of amateur basement music, and it was this great music, he thought, that had somehow resisted the totalizing power of the internet. Sort of a fun peg, isn't it? You use it if you want to. Your call, of course. I'm also going to get you some pages from de Rosales's novel. I'll admit I can see why it wasn't a bestseller. There's so little actual *story*. That's what I like about you, Tom. You can tell a story. I'll have the lyrics transcribed.

Galloway's job was to spend the day at Rachel's side, reading to her, making a familiar voice heard. His phone and network access were suspended. The general gave him access to a small library beside his office.

Galloway pulled detective novels, a humor book by David Sedaris, a volume of Chekhov plays.

One afternoon, the general called Galloway into the office. He maneuvered Galloway onto a couch, unzipped his pants, and began to suck him. It was unpleasant, seeing the general's head attaching itself to his own body this way, a head jerking in rhythmic little lunges as though it were dead flesh wired up and stimulated by a series of electrical pulses. Galloway tried to push the head away, but the general's hands were on his own, lowering them back to his side. Galloway had shot before he could really process what was happening. The general told him to zip up and then handed him a few pages from *The Subversive*, "Notes for a Philosophy of Time," along with screenshots from a subtitle site for *Vanya on 42nd Street*. Try reading her these, the general said, holding the door open. Little blasts from her past. Maybe something will spark her brain, get the engine humming again. Off you go now, Tom. We all have our jobs.

The general closed the door. Galloway rolled the pages into a tight tube. He thought of the thousands of blowjobs he'd received throughout his life—not the individual acts, but the notion of it, that he had received thousands of blowjobs in that other world, that other lifetime. That this unpleasant thing was quite possibly the last one . . . he felt a scream of rage and indignation catch in this throat.

On This Day.
  Today in History.
  List of historical anniversaries.

Even before the internet, the greeting card industry liked it, the news liked it, less the acquisition of knowledge than the acquisition of a feeling, perennial information parceled out day to day, each day like unwrapping a new gift, little nuggets of the past, some abstracted but utilitarian sense that one had learned, that one had done one's part for history.

As Galloway read to Rachel he would feel himself enter something near a trance. He would rather have been back in Modesto putting together the magazine, but he was here, and that life in Modesto felt distant, off in the fog, and also something terrible, something he didn't like thinking about, now that it was past.

November 8, January 27, January 29, December 13, October 29, February 28, November 8, June 12.

Moctezuma welcomes Cortés to the island city of Tenochtitlan; three astronauts burn up on a Cape Kennedy launchpad; Anton Chekhov is born; Ella Baker is born and dies; ARPANET is deployed; Oscar Wilde is called a posing Somdomite; Donald Trump is elected president; the first Tupperware party.

June 24, June 24, June 24.

Miguel López de Legazpi founds Manila, the capital of the Republic of the Philippines; Samuel de Champlain discovers the mouth of the Saint John River, site of Reversing Falls; Lonesome George, the last Pinta Island tortoise, kicks the bucket, and a subspecies that had numbered more than a million individuals throughout its time on the planet (but less than ten million, according to estimates) is at last released to extinction.

She was small, hardly more than five feet, and she seemed insubstantial under the blanket, tubes strapped to her mouth, smaller ones on her hand, her hair damp and stringy on the pillow, a network of blue veins visible at her forehead beneath her thin pale skin. It was cruel to try to bring her back into whatever the world was now. He stared at the machines, the IV, from time to time, and thought about it: an air bubble in the IV. Or turn off the respirator.

He would take a break from reading and think, holding her hand, concentrating as hard as he could, *Die now, you can die*. A sense of how ridiculous the idea was would soon overtake him—the idea that he could somehow beam it into her brain by thinking hard enough—and he would sit back, ashamed and tired.

The news about what was happening outside of the territory controlled by the government, to the extent that it reached him—conversations in passing, alerts through the PA system, elliptical words from the general after their encounters—was increasingly bleak. Several containment zones had been captured. On both sides, massacres, wholesale slaughter.

Galloway increasingly had the feeling that he was part of some terrible machine, and yet in another part of himself he felt that none of it mattered, that they were all just ghosts going through certain motions of a strange life long extinct. But yet another part of him would think that no, this moment would open out to a new future, that his work on the magazine would resume and give his life meaning, and offer meaning and hope to other survivors, even as so many parts of him wanted to die.

Galloway's meals were brought on a plastic tray, sometimes in a bag, or on a paper plate—there was no constancy there. He tried not to think too much about the food. On a good day lunch might be saltine crackers and sardines and a candy bar. On other days, it was a nutriment mush. A good dinner—one with the general in his office—was some sort of pork in a brown sauce, something like Chinese. Or breakfast for dinner, pancakes with corn syrup and powdered eggs. Every day he read to Rachel, though her condition didn't change, the blue veins in her temple seemed to get bluer and more prominent—when he asked a nurse if that was a good sign, she gave him a look that was annoyed and pitying. Weeks went by.

On This Day.

List of historical anniversaries.

To the roughly 20 million whose birthday fell on any given day of the year, the information might be of interest.

To the historically inclined, to the bored, to the superstitious, to those with a mind for conspiracy, or at least for patterns, it might be of interest.

Go back to the liturgical calendar, the saints' days, for instance go back to Saints Crispin and Crispinian, possibly brothers, possibly twins, beheaded October 25, in either 285 or 286. Then a thousand-year-plus jump to October 25, 1415, the battle of Agincourt.

> And Crispin Crispian shall ne'er go by,
> From this day to the ending of the world,
> But we in it shall be remembered—
> We few, we happy few, we band of brothers.

It was double now. The beheadings, the battle of Agincourt, they were noted and bound together.

From this day to the ending of the world.

This day not in fact the day of the battle, but the one on which Shakespeare wrote it down, the speech—over decades and centuries— reproduced, passed on, producing variants, errata, moving into and out of hundreds of languages, thousands of these translations, a global efflorescence that would make it one of the few relatively ineradicable texts from its century.

We few, we happy few.

Many things would thenceforth be noted and bound together, who was born, who died, what popes and treaties, what Hollywood prizes and nuclear tests, the centuries after Shakespeare were a time of noting and binding together.

First she blinked, then she was moving her hand.

They took her in for a surgery, a tracheotomy, she was having a persistent infection in her upper throat.

They brought her back groggy, barely responsive, but out of the coma. She did not speak, or seem to register his presence. He was to hold a cup to her lips and give her little sips of apple juice. He read to her from Sedaris and the lyrics and Chekhov and de Rosales.

Sedaris: *I think about death all the time, but only in a romantic, self-serving way, beginning, most often, with my tragic illness and ending with my funeral.*

Birdcrash cassette: *This town will follow you around / up and down the side streets alleyways and back around / front stairs back stairs it'll be there / and when you've finally forgotten someone tells you they care where you are / and it's not just your name it's your heart you surrender in this town . . .*

De Rosales: *It is hard for us, as human animals, to imagine the death of Lonesome George, to think that the species only ever had a million or even ten million and then went extinct.*

Chekhov: *Not "till we meet again," but goodbye. We won't see each other ever again.*

Birdcrash cassette: *You know I hate you I love you this town.*

De Rosales: *Lonesome George was found in the Galápagos National Park by Fausto Llerena, his forty-year caretaker, who later told the environmental news website Mongabay, I feel like I've lost a best friend, there is a void and there is sorrow, especially when I see the photos, in my heart I'm not convinced he's dead.*

Galloway added, improvising, It is hard for us to imagine the hundred billion–plus humans who have lived on this planet. The seven billion–plus humans alive on 1/28, and the one billion left a week later, with their stupid gold eyes.

Galloway thought about the general. He thought about the juice moving through Rachel, all the way through and out into the bag under the bed. He thought that was good, if the juice would do that, it was good, it meant her system was coming back online. And she did take a sip every now and then when he put straw to lips. After a while, he went to the general's office.

Three hundred sixty-six days of the year, and for each thousands of pages, a branching, evolving set, cut and pasted, intercut, reposted, some dormant for a decade or more, some lost (404 error) in the proliferation and flow.

No real center to the calendar, to the days: all 366 in a sense the same. A steady distribution of oddities and epoch makers.

Slap up some ads, farm the content. Like song lyrics, easy to steal. But here there were no rights holders sending out takedown notices. The facts, the dates, they were there, they were out there. What would it mean to sue a site that had reposted your content verbatim, when you had lifted the same yourself?

That the pages for February 29 looked more or less the same as the rest says something about the fractal or bottomless nature of history.

Each day casts its net, draws forth its haul.

Today in history.

No center, no bottom.

Not until time itself seems to be ending.

When he wasn't reading to her, Galloway told her about his plans for the magazine—the number of pages in the first issue, how long until they got back to the old size. When they could start selling ads again. Nutriment mush, that's what they needed, to get the nutriment mush people on the phone, sell them on the inner front page, the back page, a spread in the middle, for nutriment mush.

The transpacific cable from San Francisco to Manila is completed on July 4, 1903. From his home near Oyster Bay on Long Island, President Theodore Roosevelt initiates a telegram to Governor Taft in Manila at 10:50 p.m. EST.

Governor Taft's reply is received by Roosevelt at 11:19 p.m.

At 11:23 p.m., Roosevelt initiates the world's first around-the-world telegram. The message leaves Oyster Bay and goes from New York to San Francisco, and on to Honolulu, Midway, Guam, Manila, Hong Kong, Saigon, Singapore, Penang, Madras, Bombay, Aden, Suez, Alexandria, Malta, Gibraltar, Lisbon, the Azores, and back to Oyster Bay, where it is read by Clarence Mackay, head of the Commercial Pacific Cable Company, at 11:35.

Clarence Mackay's reply makes the same stops in the opposite direction, going eastward across the Atlantic and Europe and on to Asia. It beats Roosevelt's, taking nine and a half minutes to make the trip, to Roosevelt's twelve.

As the message circles the globe it is passing not only through space but through time: night and day shimmer and lost some part of their hold on the world. Information has made an excursion from today into yesterday and arrived back at New York within an hour of the time it started.

Newspapers take pains to explain this—the strange new quality of time—but their explanations are not quite up to the task.

We have connected the world, and in so doing, time has been broken, somehow.

On November 22, 1977, a delivery van sent packets that went from San Francisco to Menlo Park to Boston, then Norway and then London, into space, and then to West Virginia and back to California. Three separate networks—wireless packet radio, a satellite hookup bridging the Atlantic, and the ARPANET, all bridged with TCP/IP. And the internet, the network of networks, is born.

All those smart men working on something, knowing not to what end. They had their tasks, connect this to that. Connect all you can, multiply the connections, increase the bandwidth, if you build it they will come. Licklider and Baran and Kahn and Cerf. Andreessen and Wales and dear Jon Postel. They made it. All of them together, somehow. They made it, and we did, we all did, to the end of the world.

Then one day her eyes went wide and she made little gasping squeaks. It sounded like a mouse was caught in her throat. *Squeak squeak squeak.* Galloway pressed the button to call for the nurse. She drew in quick panicked breaths. Her eyes locked on him, and she said a word he could barely understand.

She said it again: *Resist!*

He could not fully credit his impression, but he thought that her lips curled into a palsied sneer, and that the word, even in her semiconscious state, was thick with irony and venom.

And she vomited a thin liquid, and choked and squeaked.

Her eyes locked on his, and for a second or two, before the next choking fit, she watched with an enraged and bitter irony, eyes like talons.

For the next days, Galloway is kept in his room. The general has forgotten him, it seems, then at last Galloway is brought back to his office.

She's doing better, the general says, but still faces a considerable amount of rehab.

The general says, The thing is, Tom, it's been decided that we should keep you two apart—keep the information streams separate, you know. Her memories are very fragile, and we don't want her access to those memories to be contaminated. She was told the password—or at least she says she was—but she can't remember it, and says the recorders didn't pick it up. So we're having her write up almost everything in the hope that that will bring the password to the surface.

So what do I do? Just wait here and do nothing?

No, I'm afraid that won't work. You understand there's a security issue—not that we worry about you, but it's a policy, we just can't have a civilian wandering around a military base. And I'm afraid that the powers that be, with what you know about so many things, they don't want you mixing back into a civilian group either. Which is just as well. Things are getting dicey, and we don't want anything to happen to you. So, I'm quite embarrassed to say this, but, ah, until we get this Rachel business squared away, we're going to have to confine you. Basically, put you in prison. In solitary. I'm afraid you'll have to have a bit of a sense of humor. Listen, this *is* temporary.

What about the story you were pitching me, Galloway says coldly—foreign powers, but also the traitor within?

Tom, I am still in love with that idea, and I think that it still could happen, but I have to tell you, there have been some shifts. Some destabilizations, it feels like the magazine needs to be pushed back a bit. It's hard to get the messaging figured out when things outside are so . . . in flux. I think what we do is hold on to the stories we've locked in, the evergreen ones, and pretty soon we'll figure out the Birdcrash thing and if and how we tell it. And whenever we do, I would love for you to be a part of it.

His time in solitary in a gray prison uniform was a maddening blur. He was there, he was distressed, he wished he'd killed himself while he could have.

He thought obsessively about *The Subversive*, whole pages appeared before his eyes in the dark.

On 1/28, the first commercial telephone exchange is established in New Haven, Connecticut, and a locomotive passing through Panamanian jungle links the Atlantic and Pacific Oceans.

On 1/28, a fifteen-inch snowflake falls on Fort Keogh, Montana.

On 1/28, Charlemagne, King of the Franks and Holy Roman Emperor, curses the known and unknown worlds he's left unconquered, and his dumb ass croaks and becomes a ghost.

On 1/28, Canuplin is born.

On 1/28, Jon Postel will reset the system.

One day the general came to visit.

Tom, listen, you'll be out of here soon. Rachel is up, and she's been writing, writing, writing! We've made a little deal with her. She's writing a full report on everything—everything pertaining to Birdcrash and Sebastian de Rosales but she says she's withholding the last piece of information until we actually take her to Prospect Park. Birdcrash's password for the last Pastebin post. And we thought that if you were there it might be a bit of extra inducement. I have to say, I don't 100 percent trust that she knows this password, and I don't trust that even if she does, she'll give it to us.

I trust Rachel. I don't think you need to involve me. My sense is, she just really, really wants to get to Prospect Park. Then she'll tell you anything you need to know.

That's good of you to say, Tom. But we can't escape the feeling that we *don't* know that we'll know everything we need to know.

We are under great pressure to present as full a report as possible. Birdcrash is dead by Rachel's hand. Poor Sebastian is dead—just after her visit. Not her fault, but still, you see what I'm saying. The optics. But you are a resource. Rachel is a resource.

I just want to get back to my work. Whatever you need to clear things and satisfy any doubts so that I can get back to that.

Tom, I believe you, the general said. There are others who may feel differently, but I do believe you. I think you're a team player. As a journalist you're independent, but on the team. Let us be clear. Rachel may have information of extreme importance. She's had holes drilled into her head. She's had acid poured into the holes. There's a lot of trauma. It's lucky for her, in a sense, because thirty-seven soldiers died in there, saving her. The powers that be don't like that kind of loss. They want to blame someone. And Rachel was under suspicion. So I think you and I are on the same page. You're our Rachel-whisperer. Do this, and I'll get you set back up with your magazine. And all this will be behind you.

Their lights were crashing through so much snow coming down. *Headlights.* Galloway wondered if they were called headlights on a helicopter. The pilot and a soldier sat up front, and back here, facing Rachel and Galloway, there was the general, expression blank, and a soldier beside him with a rifle in his lap. Rachel breathed heaving little breaths, bent over her knees, little shocks of breath cascading through her, and the vibrations of the helicopter, the lights slicing through the snowfall in the dark, picking out a chaos of snowflakes outside.

The general raised his voice over the din of the helicopter, Rachel, the way that this will work is that we will put the helicopter down near the gravesite. You will give us the password, and then you will be permitted to leave the helicopter and spend five minutes out there. We believe that the area is clear from enemies, but it won't be for long.

Galloway says, Rachel.

He thinks: If she is dead, then I am too. He watches her breathe, doubled over and the two men with rifles and the helicopter passing over land. They brought her back from a coma, and what was the point? To visit a grave? They should have left her in it, they should have let her die, it was all empty and terrible and too much work.

They are over Prospect Park, the copter is setting down in the thick snow.

This is it, the soldier says.

He remembers Jack. He remembers Jack for himself: he will not share it with Rachel, no matter what. He can keep it alive if he keeps it just for himself: that boat, the smile, the beach towel, opening up the motor in the bay as that Mariah Carey song blasted on Christmas morning, the way the wheel felt, the spray in their faces, and the smile, Jack standing beside him, cold and leaning in and pulling the beach towel around himself, pulling away from Galloway and opening the huge pink and white beach towel and wrapping them both up.

Rachel says to Galloway, Do you think this is the place?

She has to shout. The snow is coming down heavily, and the helicopter is idling.

Open the door, Rachel says.

The general nods.

Galloway looks out. A great field in Prospect Park, fires somewhere off in the distance lending a glow to the field and the ruins of Prospect Park West, the ruined mansions and apartments of Prospect Park like jagged teeth in the distance. He looks around, and even though he can't see much, and she's not looking at him, he finds himself glancing at the white and the glow and the cutting lights of the helicopter in a few directions, quickly, appraising. Yes, I think it is. I think this is the place.

The general repeats himself: Now for that password.

Rachel says, Our deal is, I get out, pay my respects, then the password.

The general says, I hope I'm not being made a fool of, Rachel! Then he turns to Galloway. He says, Go with her.

Galloway is trying to feel out the moment. He sees nothing in the general's eyes, nothing he can hold on to.

Rachel steps out. She tells Galloway to stay in the helicopter, but the general is waving him out and smiling.

So he goes out after her, she is walking ahead into the snow.

Two soldiers step out behind them. Not too far, one shouts.

And Galloway is thinking, Do we stay with them, or do we run? What is the big picture here? Do we get killed no matter what we do?

Galloway doesn't think Rachel has any password. He wants to ask her, but also, he doesn't.

If this is a question of life and death, Galloway thinks, how ridiculous am I allowed to make myself look? How much a coward?

This, here, she says. They're buried here somewhere.

Yes, Galloway says.

The snow is cutting down in sheets that shock up solid and swirl away like nothing—but then a bulk of snow again, a whole wagon of it, so the helicopter is mostly gone beyond the white.

Uncle, we shall rest.

And he doesn't know if he's going with her, or letting her go. He waits to see what she'll do.

She takes his hand and says, Do you remember this meme, it was a dog, it would say *so scare* . . .

It's a Shiba Inu, she says, I don't know how to pronounce it—it's *doge*, and she says it first as *dog*, then with a long *o*, then a long *o* and soft *g*, then a long *o* and French soft *g*.

And she laughs, but she doesn't move, she doesn't let go of his hand, her hand sits there in his own hand, clutching, disconnected from the laughter.

And he wants to tell her something, but he can't think of what it is.

This world was beautiful, she says. Good but . . . it was really dumb.

The snow is striking her face. He feels the snow cutting against his eyes, the sharp wind hitting where the snowflakes melt on his face, and a shiver that grips his whole torso and squeezes.

She says, I think I was supposed to do something else. I think *we* were. I shouldn't have brought us here.

He wants to say, *Rachel, why don't you just run, it's okay with me, you should just go ahead and run.*

She smiles at him—is it a smile? His eyes are stung and the snow is turning between them, and there's something in her eyes and mouth that he admires, and he would like to match—something that seems to *resist*, and what has he done, Galloway, except yield? And he tries to match her smile—he can't quite see it in the snow, but he thinks it's an ambiguous smile, a model's smile, and the turning of the snow over it is a part of the effect, and he tries to match it and think of what to say, something with some wit, about how she's getting them killed, some little stinger that is warm and witty and sums it up, puts a button on it, something about fate and the password and all the swirling white, but a wind is clutching his voice. The shiver hits his torso again, and he feels he's about to double over with it, lose his footing, when a voice tears out through his throat and says, *Run!*

Then he's holding her hand—he's flung their hands out in front of them—and he's waiting for what the soldiers will do in the snow—the noise of guns if there are going to be guns, and how it would feel, to die that way.

But there's nothing, not yet. He's waiting—they both are, in that instant—hand in hand—and he's shouting it again, *Run!* and the word is tearing through him, it's being torn out of his body like it's everything inside of him, all the parts, all coming out at once, and finally it's really true, he's running—they both are—into the white.

Acknowledgments

Thanks to Fiona McCrae and Steve Woodward for their extraordinary and transformative editorial work; to Paul Nadal for his love and support and for his many insights into the history and literature of the Philippines; to Bill Clegg and Marion Duvert for finding beautiful homes for *Trump Sky Alpha*; and to Kimberly King Parsons and Binnie Kirshenbaum for their early reads. I owe a great debt to my brother, Chris Doten, for his many hours of consultation and brainstorming on online security issues, and I am likewise grateful to Josh Archambault for his ideas and expertise. Thanks to the entire Graywolf team, including Marisa Atkinson, Katie Dublinski, Casey O'Neil, Ethan Nosowsky, Caroline Nitz, Yana Makuwa, and Karen Gu. Thanks to Ben Marcus, Sam Lipsyte, Dennis Cooper, Stephanie Burt, Rivka Galchen, and Virginia Seewaldt; and to my parents and sister.

Alexander R. Galloway's *Protocol* helped set me on the path of *Trump Sky Alpha*. Other important books include *Inventing the Internet* by Janet Abbate; *Under Three Flags* by Benedict Anderson; *Tubes* by Andrew Blum; *Who Controls the Internet?* by Jack Goldsmith and Tim Wu; *The Geopolitical Aesthetic* by Fredric Jameson; *Ruling the Root* by Milton Mueller; *Kill All Normies* by Angela Nagle; *Protocol Politics* and *The Global War for Internet Governance* by Laura DeNardis; and *From Counterculture to Cyberculture* by Fred Turner.

"Town" by Oklahoma Scramble appeared on the *Birdcrash* compilation cassette (K Records, 1988). Oklahoma Scramble were

Jennifer Seymore (Jenny Montgomery), Argon Steel, and Marianne Kawaguchi; all lyrics by Jennifer Seymore (Jenny Montgomery).

The screenplay to *Vanya on 42nd Street* was written by Andre Gregory, based on *Uncle Vanya* by Anton Chekhov, adapted by David Mamet.

Mark Doten is the author of the novel *The Infernal*. In 2017 he was named one of *Granta*'s Best of Young American Novelists. He wrote the libretto for the oratorio *The Source*, which had its world premiere at BAM's Next Wave Festival in October 2014 and was called a "21st-century masterpiece" by the *New York Times*. He is the literary fiction editor at Soho Press and teaches at Princeton University and Columbia University. He lives in Princeton, New Jersey.

The text of *Trump Sky Alpha* is set in Chaparral Pro. Book design by Ann Sudmeier. Composition by Bookmobile Design and Digital Publisher Services, Minneapolis, Minnesota. Manufactured by Versa Press on acid-free, 30 percent postconsumer wastepaper.